A Marquess for Christmas

Violet Sinclair

Copyright © 2024 by Violet Sinclair

All rights reserved.

No portion of this book may be reproduced in any form without written permission from the publisher or author, except as permitted by U.S. copyright law.

Contents

	Prologue	1
1.	Chapter One	7
2.	Chapter Two	13
3.	Chapter Three	23
4.	Chapter Four	33
5.	Chapter Five	45
6.	Chapter Six	53
7.	Chapter Seven	65
8.	Chapter Eight	79
9.	Chapter Nine	89
10.	Chapter Ten	99
11.	Chapter Eleven	105
12.	Chapter Twelve	115
13.	Chapter Thirteen	127

14.	Chapter Fourteen	135
15.	Chapter Fifteen	145
16.	Chapter Sixteen	157
17.	Chapter Seventeen	167
18.	Chapter Eighteen	177
19.	Chapter Nineteen	187
20.	Chapter Twenty	199
21.	Chapter Twenty-One	215
22.	Chapter Twenty-Two	229
23.	Chapter Twenty-Three	237
24.	Chapter Twenty-Four	245
Epilogue		255
About Violet Sinclair		262
Also by Violet Sinclair		263

Prologue

The frostbitten December air clung to the countryside like an unwelcome shroud. The rattling of wheels and the rhythmic clatter of hooves on the frozen dirt road broke the morning stillness as the coach trundled forward, its occupants bundled against the cold. Inside, three guards sat stiffly, their weapons within easy reach. Across from them, Christopher Langford's wrists chafed against iron shackles, his weary eyes staring through the small window at the gray, endless horizon.

A gust of wind rattled the coach, and one guard shifted uneasily. "Road's too quiet," he muttered, his fingers brushing the hilt of his pistol.

"Quiet's a blessing," the driver called down from the box, his breath forming clouds in the frosty air. "Means no highwaymen or restless rabble."

Langford said nothing, his expression unreadable, though his shoulders were tight with tension.

It came first as a distant sound, faint and rhythmic, barely discernible over the creak of the wheels—a whip cracking through the air.

"What was that?" one guard asked, straightening in his seat.

The driver leaned forward, squinting down the road. "Rider," he grunted. "Fast one. Real fast."

The whip cracked again, sharper this time, and moments later, the vehicle came into view: a sleek black-and-red curricle pulled by a pair of powerful grays. The horses moved like liquid muscle, their coats glistening despite the chill.

"Bloody hell," another guard muttered, gripping his musket tighter. "Who the devil drives like that?"

The curricle barreled closer, the figure on the box standing tall despite the reckless speed. A black beaver hat sat jauntily atop his head, and his five-caped greatcoat billowed like a banner in the wind.

"Stop the coach!" came the shouted command, the voice rich with authority.

"Not bloody likely," the driver muttered, snapping the reins to urge the horses faster.

But the curricle was faster. With a crack of his whip, the driver closed the distance in moments, his matched pair surging ahead. Hawthorne's voice rang out again, this time sharper, colder.

"I said, stop the coach."

"Damn fool," the driver spat. "You'll get yourself killed!"

The guards shifted uneasily, but before they could react, the curricle veered sharply, cutting in front of the coach in a daring maneuver. The lead horses reared, their harnesses jangling, and the coach lurched violently as the driver hauled on the reins to avoid a collision.

A MARQUESS FOR CHRISTMAS

The curricle skidded to a stop, blocking the narrow road, and its driver leapt down with fluid grace. Lord Hawthorne stood tall, a pistol gleaming in one gloved hand.

"Out," he commanded, his voice a blade of ice.

The guards hesitated, exchanging glances.

"Now," Hawthorne snapped, raising the pistol until it pointed directly at the coachman's temple.

One of the guards sneered. "You think one pistol scares the three of us?"

Hawthorne's smirk was wolfish. "I don't think. I know."

The guard hesitated, his bravado faltering. Slowly, he raised his hands and stepped down, the others following suit.

"Unchain him," Hawthorne ordered, gesturing toward Langford.

"You've got a death wish," one guard muttered as he fumbled with the keys.

"Not today," Hawthorne replied, his gaze fixed and unyielding.

The chains fell away with a heavy clink, and Langford stepped free, rubbing his wrists and glaring at the guards.

"Chris," Hawthorne said, his tone softening just slightly. "Get in."

Langford nodded, climbing into the curricle.

"You're mad." A guard pat, glaring at Hawthorne. "You'll never make it past the roadblocks."

Hawthorne's smile widened. "Watch me."

With that, he backed toward the curricle, his pistols still trained on the guards. Then, with one smooth motion, he leapt onto the box and took up the reins.

"Hold on, Langford," he said, the corner of his mouth twitching in a grin.

The curricle sped down the Dover Road, the rhythmic pounding of the horses' hooves a relentless drumbeat. Behind them, shouts grew fainter, punctuated by the distant crack of a gunshot. Hawthorne's gloved hands gripped the reins tightly, his injured arm trembling with the effort of keeping the team under control.

"Damn it, Hawthorne, you're bleeding all over the rig!" Christopher Langford's voice was taut with concern. He clutched the side of the curricle for balance as they careened around a bend in the road.

"It's nothing," Hawthorne replied through gritted teeth, his voice as sharp as the wind biting at their faces. "Just a scratch."

"Scratch, my arse!" Langford shot back. He reached for Hawthorne's arm, but his friend jerked away, his expression a mixture of determination and irritation.

"Focus on staying alive, not my arm," Hawthorne growled. "We've got a long way to go yet."

A burst of movement behind them caught Langford's eye. He twisted in his seat, his breath fogging the air as he peered back. The guards had mounted horses and were in pursuit, their forms dim shadows in the mist but unmistakably gaining ground.

"They're catching up," Langford muttered, his voice low but urgent.

Hawthorne cracked the whip, urging the horses to pick up their already grueling pace. The team surged forward; the curricle jolting violently as it hit a patch of uneven road.

"Steady, old boy," Hawthorne murmured to the lead horse, his voice soft yet commanding. He leaned forward slightly, as though sheer force of will could drive the team faster.

Langford glanced at his friend, his expression torn between gratitude and guilt. "You didn't have to do this, you know. I'm not worth this risk."

Hawthorne's jaw tightened. "You're my oldest friend, Christopher. I couldn't very well let them cart you off to rot in Botany Bay, now could I?"

"You wouldn't have had to if I'd kept my damned mouth shut," Langford shot back. "This is my own doing."

"Nonsense," Hawthorne said sharply. His eyes flicked briefly to Langford before returning to the road. "I encouraged you to write those articles, to stand by your convictions. If anything, this is on me."

Langford shook his head. "I still say you're a bloody fool for getting involved. If they catch us—"

"They won't," Hawthorne interrupted, his voice hard as steel. "I've got this under control."

As if to test that claim, another gunshot rang out. The horses shied, their ears flicking back nervously. Hawthorne snapped the reins with his good hand, his injured arm hanging stiffly at his side.

"Keep it together!" he barked at the team, his voice rising above the cacophony.

The curricle careened down a hill, the wheels skidding dangerously close to the edge of a shallow embankment. Langford's knuckles turned white as he gripped the side of the rig, his breath hitching with every jolt and lurch.

"You always did have a flair for the dramatic," Langford said through clenched teeth, his attempt at humor falling flat in the face of their peril.

"Dramatic?" Hawthorne shot him a sidelong glance, his lips quirking into a wry smile despite the sweat beading on his brow. "I prefer to think of it as memorable."

Langford let out a bark of incredulous laughter, the sound mingling with the thundering hooves and creaking wheels. "Well, you've certainly achieved that."

Ahead, the road straightened, offering a brief reprieve from the treacherous turns that had plagued their flight. Hawthorne's shoulders relaxed fractionally, though his eyes remained fixed on the horizon.

"They're falling behind," Langford observed, twisting to look back again. The guards were little more than dark smudges in the distance now, their shouts drowned out by the wind.

"For now," Hawthorne replied. He slowed the team slightly, allowing the horses a chance to recover. The rhythmic pounding of their hooves softened, though the tension in the air remained thick.

Langford leaned back in his seat, his expression thoughtful. "You've got a plan, don't you?"

Hawthorne's lips curved into a faint smile. "Always."

"And you're not going to tell me what it is."

"Not a chance."

Langford shook his head, a reluctant smile tugging at his lips. "You're an infuriating bastard, you know that?"

"So I've been told," Hawthorne replied lightly. He glanced at Langford, his gaze briefly softening. "But I'll see you safe, Christopher. You have my word."

Chapter One

"The matter is not open to discussion, Emmeline," Mrs. St. Clair declared, her scissors snapping like the beak of an ill-tempered bird. Seated in her well-worn chair by the hearth, she cut another strip of fabric with all the determination of a general marshaling the troops.

Emmeline set aside the fraying petticoat she'd been mending and met her mother's sharp gaze. "I haven't even been invited, Mama," she protested, flicking a stray thread from her fingers as if dismissing the absurdity of it all. "It's Rosalind Aunt Arabelle wants, not me."

Mrs. St. Clair gave an exasperated sigh, though the noise was drowned by the clatter of scissors. "Your aunt's exact words were that she felt a duty to her widowed sister's family. High time, too, if you ask me." She brandished the scissors with enough force to make Emmeline lean back.

"I've no doubt she'll regret the sentiment when I arrive in Rosalind's place."

"Not if you mind your tongue," her mother snapped. "And for heaven's sake, sit up straight. You'll crease that gown."

"Mama, this gown was creased before I was born. I doubt even my best posture will fix it," Emmeline quipped, her lips twitching at her mother's scandalized expression.

Mrs. St. Clair pressed a hand to her forehead, as if asking for divine providence for patience.

"Aunt Arabella's guests are certain to include gentlemen of standing," her mother added softly. "Perhaps one might take a liking to you."

"And what a thrill that would be," Emmeline replied dryly. "I'll make sure to practice my angelic sighs."

Emmeline, perched on a battered chair with a mending basket at her feet, stilled. She glanced out the small window, where the distant outline of the grand St. Clair manor loomed against the wintery horizon. It had once been their home, before her father's death and the entailment of the estate went to a distant cousin. The memory still stung—a house filled with laughter and light now belonged to strangers, while she and her sisters had been relegated to this cramped cottage.

The faint scent of mothballs lingered in the air, a reminder of the salvaged furniture crammed into every corner. Her mother's prized mahogany chest now bore scratches from its ignominious journey from manor to cottage. Even the fire seemed to sputter apologetically in its narrow hearth.

"So, you mean to send me in her place even though my name wasn't mentioned?"

Her mother sighed, cutting through another length of fabric with a sound like distant thunder. "Your aunt wrote to extend her duty toward this family, not just Rosalind. With five daughters to settle, I shall take any opportunity that might benefit. She'll understand."

"Will she? Aunt Arabelle has never struck me as the understanding sort. And what of Sir Edmund and his plans? Shall I inform him I am the substitute sister, delivered like a poorly wrapped gift?"

Mrs. St. Clair clicked her scissors again. "Emmeline, you exaggerate. Your aunt is too polite to object to such a minor change in her plans. And she is more concerned with filling her house and keeping Sir Edmund's good graces than making a fuss."

Emmeline snorted. "I should think that a two-and-twenty-year-old spinster wouldn't be much of a prize for her efforts."

"Nonsense," Mrs. St. Clair said briskly. "You are still young, no matter what you've convinced yourself to believe. Society is far too quick to cast judgment. And I'll not have you brooding over imaginary faults when there's a real chance to meet respectable gentlemen."

It wasn't that she wanted to be a debutante again, traipsing through ballrooms and curtsying to eligible gentlemen. No, Emmeline wanted something else entirely—what, she wasn't sure. But she knew it wasn't this: mending petticoats, enduring her mother's scissors, and being shipped off like a surplus parcel to fulfill some familial duty.

Emmeline folded her arms. She had no intention of tossing herself at any gentleman, no matter how respectable. The very thought of playing the docile debutante at her age made her stomach turn. "Respectable, perhaps. But I doubt he'll be pleased with the bait-and-switch."

Mrs. St. Clair dismissed the concern with a flick of her hand. "Young men are rarely particular when it comes to beauty. You are every bit as handsome as Rosalind, though I do wish you'd cultivate a softer demeanor. Besides, dark hair and eyes are quite the fashion these days, or so I've heard."

Rosalind's admirers always praised her dreamy glances and angelic sighs. Emmeline could only hope her biting wit wouldn't send Aunt Arabella's guests fleeing for the door.

"Then you shall suppress it."

Suppress her personality? Emmeline's mouth twitched with unbidden laughter. Her mother might as well have asked her to grow wings.

"Suppose I should add 'dreamy' to my repertoire," Emmeline said, her tone drier than the scorched winter fields outside. "What's next, Mama? Do I perfect Rosalind's sigh or her angelic glances?"

Mrs. St. Clair exhaled a long-suffering sigh. "I expect you to try, Emmeline. Try, at the very least, to appear docile."

Emmeline groaned, turning her gaze to the window. Bare hedges and frost-coated fields framed the small cottage beyond, the last remnants of the old St. Clair estate lurking on the horizon. "I shall endeavor to manage it."

"Good. It's not as though Rosalind can travel in her condition."

"Her condition," Emmeline laughed. "You mean her wildly inconvenient case of the measles? At her age! Who catches a childhood illness at four-and-twenty?"

"You shouldn't laugh at your sister's malady, but be sympathetic. Not everyone had the good fortune to suffer through them all at once in the nursery, as you did," her mother replied primly. "She was spared then, only to succumb now, thanks to poor little Charlotte bringing them home from the vicarage."

"Poor little Charlotte," Emmeline muttered, flicking a loose thread from her mending. "I am sympathetic. I've read every insipid word of Rosalind's poems to her until my voice gave out. Twice over that horrid one about the pining shepherd."

Her mother frowned, a faint blush creeping up her still-pretty face. "I've said before—it's unseemly for a lady to write for money. And under her own name, no less! Thank heavens the editor obscured it in print. But... it was a thoughtful poem."

"It's also dreadful. Whoever edited that paper had no consideration for the public when he published it."

Her mother fixed her with a glare that might have cowered a lesser opponenent. "That is quite enough, Emmeline.

"And Cousin Gabrielle? Surely he'll be insufferable, as usual." Emmeline rolled her eyes. "He'll tell his tiresome tales, and I'll be expected to smile and nod while he recounts how he single-handedly subdued a fox hunt gone awry."

Mrs. St. Clair's lips pressed into a thin line. "Gabrielle is your cousin, Emmeline. And a gentleman. You will treat him with respect."

"A gentleman?" Emmeline huffed. "Gabrielle wouldn't lift a finger to help you carry a footstool when we left the manor, Mama. And you expect me to tolerate him for an entire Christmas season?"

Mrs. St. Clair didn't rise to the bait. "Now, we must see to your wardrobe. Thank goodness you and Rosalind are of a size. You shall take her new sprigged muslin. And her traveling cloak you will need it on the coach."

"The coach?" Emmeline asked, her brow lifting. "Is Aunt Arabelle not sending a carriage?"

"Unfortunately, no."

"How charming. Perhaps I'll find other impoverished relatives below stairs to huddle with," Emmeline quipped. "We can commiserate over scraps and admire the finery from a safe distance."

How fitting that she would leave this place by mail coach—her aunt, unsurprisingly, having declined to send a carriage.

The old pinch-penny.

For a moment, Emmeline studied her mother's face, softened by the glow of the firelight. It was a lovely face, still proud and strong despite the years of sacrifice and the burden of raising five daughters without the security of a son to inherit.

"You'll do just fine, Emmy," her mother said, softening as she turned back to her daughter. "As long as you remember to mind yourself."

Emmeline lifted her chin, a spark of mischief lighting her eyes. "And if I don't?"

"Then heaven help us both," Mrs. St. Clair replied with a sigh, though a flicker of a smile betrayed her affection.

Chapter Two

Miss Emmeline St. Clair was decidedly unwell. Riding backward had never suited her constitution, and the erratic lurches of the mail coach were proving catastrophic to her stomach. She pressed a hand to her middle and swallowed hard. Across from her, a farmer's wife shifted, her basket of dubious-smelling wares jostling against her lap. Mincemeat pies, Emmeline guessed, or possibly their sad, overripe cousins. The addition of damp wool and wet straw to the bouquet was a cruel assault.

It was a perfect encapsulation of her current lot: a stand-in, an afterthought, sent in place of her prettier, more polished sister to endure an interminable journey and make an impression her aunt likely wouldn't notice. She pressed her lips together, the sting of resentment sharp enough to momentarily distract her from her nausea.

She glanced at the frost-etched window, briefly tempted to lower it for a breath of fresh air. But the sight of the coach's other passengers, huddled and miserable in their cramped corners, made her abandon the idea. Fresh air might cost her life—either from the cold or the ire of the basket lady.

The coach hit a pothole, jolting her so violently she bit her tongue. From the corner came a loud oath.

"Confounded coachman! Thinks he's driving a cartload of pigs, not passengers!" declared a young sailor on his way to rejoin his ship.

"Are you all right, Polly?" Emmeline asked, turning to her maid, whose complexion had taken on an alarming shade of green. Polly groaned in response, her plump hands clutching her middle like a child caught in a storm.

"I hope it's only the journey," Emmeline murmured, though her voice lacked conviction. She suspected Polly's misery was headed toward a far worse conclusion.

This entire journey had been a mistake. She'd argued against bringing Polly—argued with all the passion of someone who'd known her maid's propensity for motion sickness at the slightest jolt of a cart on cobblestones. "You need Polly here, Mama," she had said. "Besides, I can manage my own hair far better than she can." But her mother had been immovable. No daughter of hers would travel unaccompanied, even if the coach passed directly by the gates of Hollybrook Manor.

It wasn't propriety alone that had driven her mother's insistence, Emmeline suspected. No, Mama hadn't wanted her only daughter on public transportation to arrive looking anything less than respectable at her wealthy sister's estate. Appearances mattered. They mattered to Aunt Arabelle and, therefore, they must matter to her.

And now, here she was, rumbling along like a parcel hastily wrapped in brown paper and tied with twine, sent to stand in for Rosalind.

Rosalind, who had been specifically invited. Rosalind, whose dreamy demeanor and perfect curls would have suited a festive gathering like Hollybrook. But no—Rosalind was safely at home, ill with measles, while Emmeline sat here, fretting over what reception awaited her as the substitute sister.

"It shouldn't be much farther now," Emmeline said, patting Polly's hand. She had already swapped Polly's seat with the farmer's wife to give her maid the benefit of forward motion—and to remove the offensive basket from her immediate vicinity.

The coach creaked and groaned as it plodded along the muddy track. The farmer's wife muttered something about holiday delays, but Emmeline wasn't listening. Her thoughts had turned dark and resentful. What would it have cost Aunt Arabelle to send her carriage to fetch them? Or even a pony cart? Surely the extravagance of avoiding this misery wouldn't have bankrupted her.

From his perch atop the curricle, Lord Benjamin Durham, the Marquess of Hawthorne, tightened his grip on the reins. The gray pair responded with a surge of speed, their hooves pounding the muddy road. The mail coach ahead jostled its passengers like dice in a cup, and he smirked at its ungainly bulk.

"Can't they move that blasted thing off the road?" he muttered to himself, his irritation sharp. He'd spent far too long navigating winding lanes already, and the thought of delays turned his mood darker. His purpose—his only purpose—was to ensure Christopher Langford's safety, but the wretched coach was an unwelcome obstacle.

As he passed, his sharp eyes caught a figure glaring at him through the streaked glass. A young woman, her dark eyes flashing like storm clouds. The intensity of her scowl almost made him laugh, and for a fleeting moment, he wondered at the fire in her expression. But the thought was gone as quickly as it came, replaced by the unrelenting focus on the road ahead. He had no time for distractions, however intriguing they might be.

The clatter of hooves behind them interrupted the grumble of Emmeline's thoughts. She turned to look just as a flash of gray horseflesh and scarlet harness streaked past, the curricle's wheels brushing far too close to the coach.

"Oh, my heavens!" Emmeline cried as the mail coach swerved dangerously, tilting precariously toward the ditch. The interior erupted in shouts and cries, and she clutched the seat with all her strength, breath held in terror until the vehicle finally stilled.

It was nothing short of miraculous that no one inside was injured. The passengers on top—schoolboys returning home for the holidays—had jumped clear with only a few sprains and bruises. The coach itself, however, had not fared as well. The broken axle rendered it useless.

The coachman, red-faced and swearing, was unhitching a horse to send for help when Emmeline approached. "Pardon me," she said, cutting through his blustering tirade. "How far is it to Hollybrook Manor?"

He turned, his fumes of brandy nearly knocking her backward, and squinted as if gauging her importance. "Not far, miss. Within walkin' distance. We'll have yer baggage sent along once repairs are done."

The wind howled its agreement with her ire, tugging at the sodden edges of her cloak. The road stretched before her like a bleak, unending purgatory, and for a moment, she wondered if the wilds of the countryside would conspire to swallow her whole.

Behind her, Polly groaned faintly from the box where Emmeline had seated her, her face pale and pinched. Despite her clear misery, she struggled to sit up, clutching at the edge of the wooden plank.

"You're not thinking of coming with me, are you?" Emmeline asked, her brows lifting in incredulity.

Polly nodded weakly, but determinedly. "I—I can't let you go alone, miss. It wouldn't be proper."

"Proper?" Emmeline planted her hands on her hips. "Polly, you're as green as the vicar's garden after a storm, and you look like you might faint if a breeze so much as glances your way. You'd be more hindrance than help, and we'd both end up in a ditch."

"But, miss—"

"No buts." Emmeline placed a firm hand on her shoulder, pressing her gently but decisively back down. "You'll stay here and rest. I'll send someone to fetch you the moment I reach the manor."

Polly clutched at Emmeline's cloak, her grip feeble but determined. "If your mother finds out you went ahead alone, she'll have my head. And yours too."

"Then we'll both have to trust that Mama won't hear of it." Emmeline smiled faintly, though her voice softened with affection. "Besides, I have no intention of letting the wilds of Surrey devour me. It's only a short walk."

Polly's eyes narrowed despite her obvious discomfort. "The coachman said it was a short walk. Do you really trust his judgment?"

Emmeline faltered, glancing down the long, muddy road. "Well, no," she admitted, "but I trust mine. Stay put, Polly. I'll be fine."

As she turned away, a pang of guilt struck her. What if Polly grew worse while she trudged along the road? What if no one noticed her maid, slumped and ill, left by the wrecked coach? Emmeline paused and turned back. "I'll send someone back straight away, Polly. I promise."

Polly's weak nod did little to reassure her, but the maid's muttered, "Don't dawdle," was enough to coax a small smile from Emmeline as she pulled her cloak tightly around her and stepped into the wind.

With that, she wrapped Rosalind's traveling cloak tightly around her and set off down the road. The biting wind whipped the edges of her cloak into chaotic flutters, each gust a stinging reminder of how ill-prepared she was for this journey. The muddy road seemed to stretch endlessly. Mud sucked at her boots, and the biting chill stung her cheeks. What the coachman had deemed an "easy walk" seemed an eternity of trudging misery. She was contemplating whether collapsing onto a log would be more humiliating than continuing when the clatter of hooves reached her ears. A cart approached, its plodding cob kicking up muddy splashes.

The driver, startled to see a lone young woman on the road, pulled to a stop. "Oh, I say, miss," he called, raising his battered beaver hat. "Are you all right?"

She had expected a farmer, but the man was clearly a gentleman. His voice, his bearing—even his threadbare greatcoat—spoke of a man fallen on harder times but no less refined for it. His gray eyes, though faintly bloodshot, held genuine concern.

"I am perfectly, well, sir, thank you for your concern," she said without slowing her pace.

"Where are going? And might I ask why you are walking along the road unaccompanied?"

Emmeline hesitated. A sensible woman might have lied about her identity to a stranger on an empty road. Unfortunately, she was too cold and too tired to muster even a shred of pretense. "I am Miss Emmeline St. Clair," she said with a faint smile. "I was traveling by mail coach from Middlesex to my uncle's estate, Hollybrook Manor, where I am to spend the holidays."

Mr. Hollingsworth frowned, his expression clouding with concern. "You came by mail coach?" He glanced toward the muddy road, his brows knitting together. "And your uncle didn't send a carriage for you?"

"No, he did not," Emmeline replied, sharply with barely restrained exasperation. She waved in the direction she'd come. "The mail coach broke a wheel some distance back. The coachman assured me Hollybrook Manor was within walking distance." She sighed, looking down the seemingly endless road ahead of her. "I suppose his definition of walking distance and mine do not quite align."

"That's... shocking," Mr. Hollingsworth said after a beat, his voice tinged with indignation. "Your uncle sent no one to collect you? Not even a cart?"

Emmeline gave a tight smile and mumbled under her breath, "My uncle is not one to loosen his purse strings unnecessarily."

"What was that?" he asked, though his grin suggested he'd heard her perfectly well.

"Nothing at all," she replied, though the upward quirk of her lips betrayed her. "Let's just say my uncle is a man of... practical sensibilities."

At that, Mr. Hollingsworth threw back his head and laughed, the warm sound cutting through the chill in the air. "Practical sensibilities! That is a delicate way to phrase it, Miss St. Clair. You've been very diplomatic indeed."

"Well, one must preserve family harmony," she said dryly, though her smirk suggested otherwise.

"Hollybrook Manor is still a good two miles away," he said. "You look positively frozen. Please, allow me to take you."

She opened her mouth to protest, imagining what Mama would say about accepting rides from strangers, when the sound of racing hooves cut her off.

A streak of gray horses and a gleaming curricle thundered past, sending a wave of muddy water splashing over her.

"Oh, blast you!" she shouted, her fury only slightly dampened by the cold muck dripping from her cloak.

The gentleman suppressed a smile as he handed her a handkerchief. "Let it dry first," he advised. "Easier to brush off once it's set."

She took the handkerchief with a tight-lipped thanks, glaring in the direction of the curricle. "That man should be locked away. He nearly killed us back at the coach."

"Really?" The gentleman raised a brow as he helped her into his cart. "That explains the reckless speed. Still, I wonder what brings him to these parts?"

"He must have stopped nearby," she mused. "Perhaps to see someone at a neighboring estate?"

"Unlikely," he said with a wry smile. "Forgive me." He tipped his hat with a self-deprecating smile. "I'm Mr. Graham Hollingsworth. My estate," he grimaced, "or what remains of it, marches next to your uncle's."

Emmeline nodded politely, her mind still churning over the curricle and its insufferable driver. "I could swear it was the same fools who ran us off the road earlier," she muttered. "Surely there can't be two such blockheads in the area."

"Possible," Mr. Hollingsworth said lightly. "More likely, he's part of some ridiculous driving club. They take wagers, you know."

"Wagers," she muttered. "I'd wager he needs a lesson in manners."

Mr. Hollingsworth chuckled. "A safe wager, indeed. Here, let me help you." He extended a hand, gloved but well-worn, and steadied her as she climbed into the cart. The wooden seat creaked beneath her weight, but she was too relieved to care. The warmth of the cob's steady breath and the rhythmic crunch of hooves on the frost-covered road were small comforts in the bitter cold.

As the cart lurched forward, Emmeline pulled Rosalind's cloak more tightly around her. "You said you're familiar with Hollybrook Manor?" she ventured, glancing sideways at her companion.

"I am," he replied lightly. "Your uncle's estate is rather well-known in the area—though mostly for its size, I suppose, rather than its hospitality." His smile was wry but not unkind.

"That does sound like Uncle Edmund," Emmeline admitted with a sigh. "My aunt does her best to remedy the deficit, of course."

"Ah, yes, Lady Hollybrook," he said. "A gracious woman. Though I must confess, I've not had the pleasure of attending her gatherings in recent years."

Emmeline raised a brow, curiosity sparking. "Why ever not? Have you been dreadfully naughty, Mr. Hollingsworth?"

His laugh was rich and warm. "Not naughty, Miss St. Clair. Merely... out of step with the times, I think. My invitations must have been misplaced." He glanced at her, the twinkle in his eye belying any bitterness.

"Misplaced, indeed," she said, her tone teasing, but her curiosity piqued. "What a shame. It seems Hollybrook has been deprived of excellent company."

"You're too kind," he replied with a slight bow of his head. "But perhaps the fates thought I might be better suited to rescuing."

The outline of Hollybrook Manor's gates loomed into view. Iron bars rose against the winter sky, their scrolls and flourishes softened by a dusting of frost. Mr. Hollingsworth pulled the cart to a stop with practiced ease.

Emmeline blinked, startled. Before she could ask what he meant, he tipped his hat again. "Happy Christmas, Miss St. Clair. May the rest of your visit improve."

Chapter Three

The bell clanged loudly, its metallic echo piercing the crisp winter air. In the distance, the baying of hounds rose in response, their chorus carrying an air of wild, untamed energy. Before the sound had entirely faded, an elderly woman emerged from the gatehouse, her gray curls peeking out from beneath a lace cap. Clad in an outdated neckerchief and a stomacher, she bustled forward to swing open the well-oiled gate, her movements brisk despite her years.

"Apologies for the lad's absence," the woman said, gesturing toward the shadowed woods beyond. "You'll want to take the path there. It's a shortcut to the manor—cuts off all the winding twists of the carriage road."

"Thank you," Emmeline replied, a polite smile fixed firmly on her face, despite the fatigue creeping into her limbs.

She followed the indicated path, the hounds' cries growing louder as she went. Hollybrook Manor soon came into view, emerging grandly from the forested backdrop like a lord surveying his domain. The house was sprawling, its architecture a chaotic blend of eras. A weathered wing with thick stone-shafted bow windows, each composed of tiny diamond-shaped panes, hinted at medieval origins. The central structure, elegant and symmetrical, bore a distinct French influence that could have been plucked from the court of Charles II. And, in a nod to more recent English fashions, a Georgian wing completed the puzzle, its red brick a stark contrast to the manor's older stone.

For a moment, Emmeline allowed herself to marvel at the scale and grandeur of the place. The half-mile walk ahead seemed almost pleasant in the shadow of such history—until the hounds descended.

They were a rambunctious pack, their enthusiasm deafening as they surrounded her in a chaotic flurry of fur and mud. While their intentions seemed friendly enough, her sister's pristine traveling cloak was not so fortunate. Each new paw print splashed across its fabric was a fresh insult, and by the time the last dog bounded away, Emmeline's temper had surged anew.

By the time she reached the door and knocked, her frustration was a storm barely contained behind her wind-chapped cheeks. When the towering butler who answered fixed her with a look of disapproval so cutting, it could have etched glass, she very nearly gave him a piece of her mind.

Things did not improve upon entering.

Lady Hollybrook reclined upon a rosewood chaise, the very picture of languid luxury in a room so pink it might have been dipped in sugared icing. From cabbage roses climbing silk wall coverings to the sugared icing tones of the damask curtains, the space seemed to suffocate under its own femininity. Emmeline felt like a lone weed choking in a garden of cloying sweetness. Eyes closed, her aunt appeared serene—until they snapped open, widened, and filled with unmistakable horror.

"What on earth!" she exclaimed, pushing herself upright with some difficulty. Her curls—an improbable shade of gold—framed her face in chaotic ringlets, her cap perched askew like a tiara in rebellion. "You cannot be Rosalind."

"No, Aunt. I'm Emmeline," she replied, stepping further into the room. "Rosalind took ill and could not travel. Mama thought you would prefer to have some member of our family in attendance, so she sent me instead."

This preposterous statement had precisely the effect Emmeline anticipated.

"Well, it's hardly the same now, is it?" Lady Hollybrook huffed, her cheeks puffing with indignation. "How inconsiderate of Catherine! To send... well, you... instead of the young lady I specifically invited. I have enough children underfoot as it is, and now of all times. What was Sir Edmund thinking?" She waved a hand in exasperation, then fixed her gaze on Emmeline's muddied cloak and wind-tangled hair. "And what does it show you arriving looking like this? Like some rag-tag gypsy?"

"What it shows, Aunt," Emmeline said sharply, her patience worn thin, "is that I was in a coach accident. I've walked miles down a muddy highway, been splattered by some lunatic driving a curricle, and endured the indignities of a pack of hounds. And," she added with a pointed look, "I am two and twenty."

Lady Hollybrook did not appear remotely impressed. "You still look the same hoyden I remember," she sniffed. "I recall telling your mother you had enough mischief for a dozen boys. It seems nothing has changed."

Emmeline drew a deep breath. "I was hardly responsible for the coach breaking an axle—"

"No, I daresay you weren't," Lady Hollybrook interrupted, waving her hand as though to brush away the irrelevant details. "But let me make something very clear, Emmeline. Your conduct here must reflect well on this family. For I doubt you have the faintest idea of who our guest of honor is."

Emmeline stared at her blankly, biting back a retort about mind-reading. Instead, she said, "I was under the impression this was a family gathering."

Her aunt's face brightened with self-satisfied glee. "For the most part, it is. Which makes it all the more extraordinary that his lordship has chosen to grace us with his presence. Sir Edmund was astonished to hear of the connection, though it's distant, of course. Still, it shows how important blood ties remain to certain individuals."

"Who is it?"

Lady Hollybrook drew herself up, her expression triumphant. "Lord Hawthorne!"

Emmeline blinked. "I've never heard of him."

The horrified silence that followed could have swallowed the room whole.

"Well, that certainly speaks volumes," Lady Hollybrook huffed, her chest puffing with pride. "Everyone who is anyone has heard of the Marquess of Hawthorne. He's simply the most sought-after bachelor in London. Belongs to the most exclusive clubs, commands the largest fortune, possesses the looks of Adonis, and—according to Gabriel—is an unrivaled nonpareil when it comes to all the sporting activities gentlemen hold in such absurdly high regard."

"Indeed?" Emmeline replied, her brow arching with disinterest she didn't bother to mask. "And is he the one you invited for Rosalind?"

Lady Hollybrook's snort was as ungenteel as it was emphatic. "Pray do not be absurd. Lord Hawthorne is so far above Rosalind's touch as to make the very notion ludicrous. I wouldn't dream of appearing to promote such an unequal match. And," she added sharply, narrowing her gaze, "I will not allow you to entertain such ideas either, Emmeline."

Emmeline opened her mouth, a tart reply poised on the tip of her tongue, but her aunt pressed on, words tumbling out with the fervor of someone enjoying the sound of their own voice far too much.

"No, I intend to see that his lordship receives the deference he is due. Gabriel and I have gone to great lengths to ensure all of Sir Edmund's rustic relations understand the singular privilege of being under the same roof as Lord Hawthorne. Not that I expect *you* to comprehend the gravity of the situation. This is no village fête, Emmeline, with pickled eggs and currant cakes passed around like gossip. The *ton* is an entirely different world, and Hawthorne is its brightest star. You, my dear, would do well to orbit at a safe distance—quietly."

Emmeline's eyebrows arched in defiance, but her aunt had not yet exhausted her enthusiasm.

"Gabriel has idolized him for years. Idolized! As have all the young gentlemen in his set—or so I'm told. Why, Lord Hawthorne has only to tie his cravat in a certain fashion, and every gentleman in London is suddenly incapable of dressing otherwise. Gabriel has pestered Sir Edmund for weeks, begging for a curricle with red leather seats simply because—"

"A black curricle with red leather seats?" Emmeline interrupted, her tone slicing cleanly through Lady Hollybrook's monologue, sharp enough to halt her mid-sentence.

"Why, yes. And why Sir Edmund insists on being so tightfisted, I'll never understand. I should think he'd want to—"

"The owner of a black curricle with red leather upholstery is staying here?" Emmeline demanded, her pulse quickening.

Lady Hollybrook's eyes narrowed. "You really must not keep interrupting in such a graceless fashion, Emmeline. I had hoped Catherine taught you better manners. I've gone to great lengths to impress upon you that we have a gentleman of the highest station staying here, and yet all you seem concerned about is his equipage. It's quite beyond me." She waved her hand as if dismissing the entire subject. "But we've no time for this. Dinner will be served in an hour, and it will take you at least that long to become remotely presentable."

"Unless my maid and luggage are fetched from the side of the highway," Emmeline replied tightly, "there is no prospect of me being presentable at all."

Lady Hollybrook sighed heavily, as though Emmeline had personally conspired to ruin her evening. "Oh, very well. Though it is highly inconvenient to be saddled with a sick servant when the household is already at sixes and sevens. I cannot imagine what possessed Catherine."

"Mama had no idea Polly was unwell, I assure you," Emmeline replied, her jaw clenching with restraint as her aunt continued to grumble.

"Humph. Riggs," Lady Hollybrook snapped to the butler who hovered nearby, "see to it that the maid and luggage are retrieved. And take Miss St. Clair to the blue room. Though," she added with a pointed glance at Emmeline's travel-worn gown, "you'll have to come to dinner as you are. Unless," her expression brightened momentarily, "you'd prefer to dine in your room?"

Emmeline opened her mouth to reply, but her aunt quickly overruled herself. "No, the servants are quite busy enough without added burdens. Just try to remain inconspicuous."

"And if his High-and-Mightiness has the misfortune to clap eyes on me," Emmeline muttered under her breath as she followed Riggs, "am I expected to bow, scrape, and tug my forelock?"

For the merest moment, Riggs's shoulders trembled, a faint but unmistakable sign of stifled laughter. The august butler recovered quickly and resumed his stately pace toward the tiny guest room assigned to Emmeline. He seemed unaware, however, that his charge had stopped following.

Emmeline had frozen, rooted to the spot in front of an open doorway.

The faint scent of soap and something she couldn't identify—lingered in the corridor as a manservant exited with a basin balanced carefully in his hands. The red-tinged water made her pause, but she quickly dismissed the thought. Surely it was nothing.

Her gaze was fixed once again on the gentleman inside.

The figure in the looking glass was unmistakable. Emmeline had only caught fleeting glimpses of him before—an arrogant profile through the mail coach window, that hawkish nose turned up ever so slightly as though the very air beneath it carried a stench. But now, with silver-blond hair gleaming in the candlelight and sharp black eyes cutting her way, there was no doubt.

It was him.

Her pulse quickened—not with fear, but fury. Her mother had often remarked that Emmeline lacked the good sense to temper her indignation in the face of rank or power. It seemed that defect would serve her well now. Straightening her spine, she stepped boldly into the room, disregarding the fact that this was very much his territory.

"Do you, by chance, drive a black racing curricle with red leather seats?" she demanded, her voice steady despite the heat rising to her cheeks.

The man's gaze flicked over her mud-streaked attire, lingering just long enough to make her feel like an inconvenience. There was no rush to his movements, no urgency to acknowledge her presence. Yet, beneath that deliberate nonchalance, Emmeline detected something—an exhaustion or weariness that tugged at the edges of his composure. She dismissed it immediately.

"I do," he replied, the corners of his mouth twitching upward in a hint of amusement before his attention returned to his cravat in the mirror.

Emmeline's eyes narrowed. "And what, pray, makes you believe you own the highway?"

"I labor under no such impression," he replied smoothly, tilting his head to inspect the angle of his starched neckcloth. "But it seems I've stumbled into a rather one-sided trial. Tell me, Miss...?" His voice lilted upward, inviting her to fill the silence.

"St. Clair," she snapped, her temper flaring. "Miss Emmeline St. Clair. And you, sir, are insufferable."

A fleeting flicker of amusement crossed his features before vanishing, like a shadow chased by the sun. He seemed to study her more closely then, as though weighing her indignation for its sincerity rather than its volume.

Her temper flared. "Then I must assume you're simply heartless. You forced a coach to capsize into a ditch and rode on as though nothing had happened! Did it not occur to you that someone might have been killed?"

At that, his dark eyes met hers again, this time with a faint glimmer of curiosity. "Was someone killed?"

"No," she admitted through gritted teeth, "but there were bruises and sprains enough, and my maid—who was already ill—became quite hysterical. She's likely to catch her death, waiting in the cold for a rescue."

If she'd hoped for guilt or even mild regret, she was doomed to disappointment. His expression remained a portrait of boredom, as though she were reciting a particularly tedious sermon.

"Nothing to say for yourself?" she pressed. "Even a heathen would have turned back to check on the damage they caused."

The man sighed, abandoning his reflection to regard her fully. "Miss—whoever you are—I did not turn back because, first, it was not convenient, and second, as you've just admitted, the accident was not serious."

"Not serious?" Her voice rose a pitch. "Perhaps not from the comfort of your red leather seat, but I assure you, to those of us being tossed about like—like—"

"Ninepins?" he offered dryly.

"No, certainly not ninepins! Ninepins roll over neatly onto their sides. We were thrown, rattled, and crammed into a pile of screaming humanity!"

"Charming imagery," he remarked. "Though I'm afraid your indignation is misplaced. I was in no way responsible for your coach's mishap. Your driver had ample room to pass, but instead handled his team like a drunkard. And judging by the stench of brandy on his breath, I'd say that assessment is generous."

Emmeline opened her mouth, closed it again, and then snapped, "Even if there's truth in that, it doesn't excuse your callousness."

"I suggest," he said, retrieving his black coat from the bedpost with practiced ease, "you direct your outrage toward the coachman. And now, if you'll excuse me, I must dress for dinner. I suggest you do the same."

He slid into the coat, its tailored fit accentuating broad shoulders and a lean frame, and Emmeline hated herself just a little for noticing.

Her voice hardened as her anger reignited. "As if wrecking the coach weren't enough, you later had the audacity to splash me with muddy water!"

This time, his composure faltered—just slightly. His brow creased, and his lips parted as if to respond, but she didn't allow him the chance.

"You may be the darling of London society, sir, but in my estimation, you're precisely the sort of spoiled aristocrat that inspired the French Revolution."

It was, she thought with satisfaction, the perfect exit line. Without waiting for a reply, she swept from the room, her chin held high.

As she stormed down the corridor, she nearly collided with a returning manservant carrying a basin.

Two thoughts struck her simultaneously: first, that the valet had likely been within earshot of her entire tirade; and second, the basin—now half-empty—bore a faint tinge of red. Blood. Her first instinct was to scoff at the idea of him suffering any inconvenience, let alone an injury. Yet, the possibility lingered, unwelcome and stubborn. Could this man—so effortlessly smug, so infuriatingly composed—have been hurt? And if so, why conceal it? Her anger flickered with unease, but she quickly snuffed it out. Whatever secrets he held, they were of no interest to her.

She shook the thought away. "Good day, Lord Hawthorne," she muttered sarcastically under her breath as she rounded the corner.

Chapter Four

Emmeline stood by the tiny window of her cramped bedchamber, vigorously brushing Rosalind's cloak. As Mr. Hollingsworth had predicted, the mud stains were showing signs of surrender. The faint scent of lavender clung to the fabric, a comforting relic of home that briefly softened the edges of her frustration. Just as she imagined the cloak's salvation, a furious pounding rattled the door.

"Come in—" she began, but the words were barely out before the door burst open and an overwrought young man stormed in.

Gabriel. Of course.

He was attired in evening clothes so precise they seemed almost aggressive. His shirt points threatened his earlobes, his shoulders were padded to near caricature, and his satin waistcoat cinched his middle to alarming proportions. Diamonds gleamed at his throat and fob, and his mouse-colored hair had been curled and swept forward into a style so severe it looked as though it might strike back. Yet none of this elegance could redeem his face: pale blue eyes bulged slightly over a receding chin that, despite its best efforts, seemed to hide from confrontation.

The scent of pomade hung in the air as Gabriel stormed forward, his boots thudding heavily against the floorboards. Emmeline had to fight the urge to cover her nose; the overpowering aroma of rosewater and cloves might have been bearable in moderation, but in Gabriel's case, it clung like a fog.

At the moment, however, his complexion burned with indignation, and his bulging eyes threatened to pop entirely.

"You—you—you—how dare you!" Gabriel spluttered, storming across the room like a toddler on the verge of a tantrum. "It's not as though you were even invited! Mama specifically asked for Rosalind!"

"Good evening to you too, Gabriel," Emmeline replied sweetly, her lips curling into a smile designed purely to irritate him further. "It's nice to see you've grown a bit. When we were last together—what, nine years ago?—I thought you were destined to remain a midget. Now I'd say you're almost as tall as me. Quite average, for a woman."

"I'm two inches taller than you!" he snapped, his voice cracking indignantly.

"Are you? I can't believe it. Shall we stand back to back in front of the mirror to be certain?"

"Absolutely not! And stop trying to change the subject!"

"Change the subject? Why, I didn't even know we had one."

Gabriel's face turned an even deeper shade of crimson. "We damn well do! How dare you waltz into this house—uninvited, I remind you—and tear into the most important guest we've ever hosted! If Lord Hawthorne packs up and leaves tonight, it will be entirely your fault!" His voice wavered, and to Emmeline's disbelief, his eyes glistened suspiciously. "He'd just given me leave to call him Benjamin."

"Benjamin?" Emmeline repeated, raising an eyebrow. "How cozy. Personally, I can think of several other names I'd like to call him."

Her words were light, but a pang of unease rippled beneath her composure. Lord Hawthorne's presence carried a weight she couldn't quite decipher, and the thought of being tied to his departure unsettled her more than she cared to admit.

"You calling him anything is precisely the problem!" Gabriel screeched. "You clearly don't understand just how condescending it was of him to come here in the first place. I'm warning you: from now on, stay as far away from Hawthorne as possible."

"Well, then I can ease your mind entirely," Emmeline said, her smile sharpening. "For once, we're in perfect agreement. I can think of nothing I'd like better than to keep my distance from that odious Lord Hawthorne. May I suggest, cousin, that you do the same? Your groveling does your dignity no favors."

"Groveling?!" Gabriel's voice cracked again. "I'll have you know that aligning oneself with Lord Hawthorne is nothing short of genius. Clearly, you're too provincial to understand, but the Hawthorne set is the pinnacle of society. Hostesses would kill for his presence. And once I'm established in his circle—well, the invitations will flow like champagne. I wouldn't be surprised if I were invited to join the Four-in-Hand Club. The first stare! That's what I'll be."

"Unless," Emmeline interjected smoothly, "your horror of a country cousin has already ruined your grand ambitions."

Gabriel froze mid-rant as a distant sound echoed up through the floorboards—three hollow, resounding thuds. His face turned ashen.

"Oh, my God!" he whispered, aghast. "He's doing it. He's actually doing it! I explicitly told him not to!"

Emmeline frowned. "Who's doing what? And what is that dreadful noise?"

"It's Cook!" Gabriel wailed. "Papa thought it would be 'festive' to have Cook beat his rolling pin on the dresser to announce dinner. Like some deranged gong!" He turned toward the door in a flurry of satin and indignation. "This is bedlam—absolute bedlam! I have to find Benjamin and explain!"

"Do hurry, Gabriel," Emmeline called after him, a wicked smile playing on her lips. "Wouldn't want to lose favor with your 'Benjamin.'"

He whirled back, eyes blazing. "Vixen!"

"Toadeater," she replied sweetly, watching with satisfaction as he stormed out.

When the door finally slammed shut, Emmeline chuckled softly to herself. "Well, at least Gabriel and I are still on the same terms." Turning back to Rosalind's cloak, her fingers brushing idly against the cloak's soft fabric. Gabriel's outburst had rattled something in her, though she couldn't name it. It wasn't guilt—of that she was certain—but a faint unease lingered, as though she'd just glimpsed a crack in the polished veneer of this household.

The dull thuds of the rolling pin's summons had not produced immediate results, Emmeline realized as she hurried into the great hall.

The sharp chill of the drafty corridors was a rude reminder of Hollybrook Manor's age, and she tugged her thin shawl more tightly around her shoulders. Her cheeks, still pink from her earlier exchange with Gabriel, tingled from the cold as she descended the final staircase.

Breathless from settling Polly in the servants' quarters and unpacking her own things, she had assumed the rest of the household would already be at dinner. But the sight before her revealed that the peculiar signal had likely baffled the guests as much as it had amused her.

The hall clung to its antiquity with a stubborn charm. Pine mingled with the earthy aroma of burning wood, and the polished oak floor gleamed like a dark mirror beneath the firelight. Every creak of the heavy furniture seemed to echo with memories of generations past. Above the projecting mantel, a portrait of a knight in full armor gazed solemnly into the room, his frame adorned with fresh holly berries that gleamed crimson in the firelight. Pine mingled with the earthy aroma of burning wood, creating a cozy yet heavy atmosphere that clung to the skin.

Other festive touches—a pair of burnished suits of armor, an enormous set of antlers, and several ancient, cumbersome pieces of furniture—hinted at the manor's storied history.

At first, Emmeline thought the gathered company looked incongruous in such a medieval setting. But after surveying them, she amended her opinion: this group would have looked incongruous anywhere.

It was a mishmash of relatives, ranging from ancient aunts and uncles to blooming debutantes, comfortable matrons with their portly spouses, somber spinsters, and a gaggle of exuberant schoolchildren. Their evening clothes ranged from cutting-edge fashion to genteel shabbiness, a clear testament to the uneven distribution of the family's fortunes. Emmeline felt a flicker of relief that her own white crepe gown, though wrinkled and plain, would not put her to shame among such variety.

The laughter of a boisterous uncle rang out over the room, followed by the high-pitched squeal of a young cousin dodging an elder's attempt to adjust his cravat. Emmeline smiled faintly; despite her weariness, the scene was not entirely unpleasant.

Her eyes sought out a focal point, and it didn't take long to spot him. All she had to do was follow the collective gaze of the room—females and males alike—to Lord Hawthorne.

He stood near the fireplace, a picture of effortless composure, flanked by Aunt Arabella and Gabriel. One gushed while the other fawned, and Hawthorne endured their attentions with an air of polite detachment. The firelight played tricks with his features, softening the sharp lines of his jaw and casting his black eyes in shadow. Emmeline had to remind herself that the man was no benevolent hearthside hero but the very same insufferable aristocrat who had splashed her with mud.

Emmeline couldn't help but feel a mean-spirited pleasure that his understated elegance thoroughly outshone Gabriel's overdone finery. Perhaps if Gabriel dared ask, he might secure the name of the marquess's tailor.

Her gaze lingered a moment longer than intended, her irritation flaring as she recalled her cousin's breathless admiration. "Benjamin," indeed, she thought sourly. For all his supposed charms, the man carried himself with a haughtiness that grated on her nerves. Was it too much to expect that a nobleman might also possess a modicum of humility?

She studied Hawthorne's face again, this time with a critical detachment. Aunt Hollybrook had called him an Adonis, but Emmeline found him entirely too rigid, his features sharp as if chiseled from granite. His black eyes betrayed nothing, though she'd wager a monkey that he wasn't listening to a word her relatives were saying.

As if sensing her scrutiny, those dark eyes turned her way. Startled, she averted her gaze and looked determinedly at the floor. Her heart gave an unwelcome lurch—annoyance, surely.

"Can this truly be little Emmy?" a warm voice spoke at her elbow.

Emmeline turned and found herself face-to-face with a stately gentleman whose gray hair gleamed in the firelight. "Uncle Edmund?" she ventured hesitantly.

His smile widened, and he beamed down at her with a kind, paternal air. "Indeed, my dear! What a beautiful young lady you've grown into."

Emmeline suppressed a laugh. Her memories of Uncle Edmund were hazy at best—he had rarely joined his wife and son on their visits to Middlesex Cottage, being far too preoccupied with governmental duties.

"It means so much to have family around me during Yuletide," he continued warmly. "I only wish your mother and sisters could have joined us as well."

Emmeline wondered if he genuinely believed they had been invited but kept her thoughts to herself, smiling politely.

The warmth of his welcome stirred a faint ache in her chest. The hollowness of her mother's words came rushing back: "They'll never truly see us as family, Emmeline. We're a reminder of what they prefer to forget."

"For the rest of the year, I'm buried under ministry affairs and trapped in town by society's modern ways," he said with a touch of wistfulness. "But at Christmastide, I am bound and determined to keep the old traditions alive. Arabella has her way with the townhouse, but here at the Manor, I insist on preserving our heritage." His smile turned indulgent. "Gabriel calls it one of my 'freaks,' but I think it does the soul good to honor the past, don't you agree?"

"Absolutely, Uncle," Emmeline replied, biting back a smile at his enthusiasm.

As the hum of conversation swirled around her, Emmeline resolved to play her part for the evening. She would endure the company, avoid Hawthorne's infuriating gaze, and—if nothing else—make it through without biting anyone's head off. For once, she thought, she might even try to blend in.

"Ah, but I see it's time to lead our guests to dinner." He straightened, then gestured to a lady disengaging from a chattering group. "But first, allow me to introduce my sister. Clara has been most eager to make your acquaintance. Clara, my dear!"

Emmeline turned to greet the approaching lady, her initial reaction tinged with sympathy. Miss Clara Hollybrook moved with an awkward, halting gait, her pronounced limp forcing her body into a laborious twist with every step. The effort seemed painful, and Emmeline's heart instinctively went out to her.

But as Clara drew closer, Emmeline's perception shifted. The limp might have been awkward, but Clara's presence was anything but. There was a quiet dignity in the way she carried herself, her head held high despite the obvious strain. Her gray eyes, calm and steady, met Emmeline's with a warmth that felt genuine and unassuming, erasing any trace of pity.

Clara's serene expression and composed manner only deepened Emmeline's admiration. Handsome features framed by soft, light brown curls peeked from beneath her modest cap—a cap that made Emmeline wonder if Clara truly needed such a concession to age. Whatever the answer, Clara's bearing made it clear: she was a woman defined not by her physical limitations but by an inner strength that was impossible to overlook.

As if reading her thoughts, Uncle Edmund chuckled. "Clara is my youngest sister—the baby of the family. We're twenty years apart, though you'd hardly know it by the way she runs this household."

Miss Clara smiled modestly as Edmund excused himself to tend to Aunt Arabella. During their slow progress toward the dining room, Emmeline learned Clara was the acting mistress of the manor.

"I've lived here all my life," Clara explained. "I know the servants and their families, their histories... everything. Your aunt visits so rarely that it only seems fair to allow her a holiday from household cares when she does."

The tactful response only increased Emmeline's respect for Miss Clara. Her tone was gentle, her words measured, and her presence exuded a quiet strength that felt entirely out of step with the frivolity swirling around them.

As they entered the dining room, Emmeline glanced back toward the great hall. The fire's glow flickered on Lord Hawthorne's impassive face. Her gaze lingered for a moment longer than she intended before she forced herself to look away.

Like the great hall, the vast dining chamber exuded an air of antiquated grandeur. Heavy oak paneling lined the walls, gleaming with the patina of centuries of care. Portraits of stern-faced Hollybrook ancestors gazed down, their austere expressions softened somewhat by the festive garlands of holly and ivy draped around their frames. A massive buffet stretched along one wall, its polished surface reflecting the warm glow of the candlelight. Among the gleaming silver and family heirloom plates stood two tall Christmas candles surrounded by vibrant greenery, their flickering flames adding a touch of warmth to the somber atmosphere.

Despite the honor bestowed upon Lord Hawthorne, seated at the head of the table beside Lady Hollybrook, the rest of the seating arrangement was informal. Emmeline sighed in relief when Miss Clara Hollybrook directed her to a spot near the middle of the long, heavily laden oak table. It was comfortably removed from both her aunt and Gabriel, sparing her any immediate scrutiny or theatrics.

As the first course was served, Emmeline marveled at the abundance spread before them. Platters of roasted meats, tureens of steaming soup, and an array of delicate pastries adorned the table, filling the air with rich, tantalizing aromas. "My goodness," she murmured, her eyes widening at the display. "What on earth will Christmas itself be like?"

"Traditional, I assure you," chuckled a round-faced, middle-aged gentleman seated beside her. His chubby cheeks and genial smile gave him the appearance of a well-fed cherub.

Across the table, Miss Clara smiled warmly and introduced the man. "This is Dr. Wickham. He keeps us all in good health."

"Ah, Miss Hollybrook flatters me," the doctor protested, though his twinkling eyes suggested he welcomed the praise. "The truth is, Miss St. Clair, that your cousin here is my greatest rival. She brews potions and tinctures from the herbs she grows, prescribes remedies, and even administers doses herself. I dare say she'll put me out of business yet, for most of my patients only come to me on her insistence! If she ever charged for her services, I'd be ruined." He grinned. "My only recourse would be to accuse her of witchcraft."

"Pay no heed to him, Miss St. Clair," Clara said with a laugh. "Dr. Wickham is a shameless jester, as you'll soon discover."

"Not at all, young lady," the doctor replied, turning serious. "Miss Hollybrook is far too modest. She is a truly gifted healer. With her, medicine is an art. I, on the other hand, am merely a man of science."

Clara waved away the compliment with a soft smile. "He does exaggerate. But before I insist we change the subject, Miss St. Clair, I must tell you—your maid, Polly, has just broken out in spots."

Emmeline's stomach dropped. "Spots? Oh, no… The measles." Her brow furrowed in concern. "Two of my sisters have had it, but Polly insisted she'd already endured them, as I have. If I had known—"

Her words trailed off as her eyes drifted down the length of the table to where her aunt sat, her gaze riveted on Lord Hawthorne. Lady Hollybrook's fork hovered midway between her plate and her mouth, her attention utterly absorbed in monitoring every movement of their illustrious guest. Emmeline shuddered to think how the formidable woman would react to the news that her unwelcome niece had brought measles into her household.

Miss Clara seemed to sense her thoughts. "I see no reason to trouble my sister-in-law with a minor domestic matter," she whispered. "Most of the servants have already had it, and Polly does not appear to be gravely ill. Still," she added, turning to Dr. Wickham, "you will take a look at her, won't you, Doctor?"

"Very well," he agreed with a good-natured sigh. "Though I'd stake my life that Miss Hollybrook has already done everything necessary for the patient."

With that, Dr. Wickham turned to converse with the lady at his other side, leaving Emmeline free to survey the forty or so guests gathered at the table. Her gaze wandered across the varied assembly, noting the Oxonian youths who were too fresh-faced and the portly married gentlemen who were clearly there with their wives.

Her eyes eventually returned to Lord Hawthorne, and a realization dawned: in terms of age and eligibility, there was no one else present who could possibly fit the description of the gentleman invited for Rosalind. A pang of annoyance struck her. Her heart sank, though she wasn't quite sure why. Was it disappointment that he hadn't been invited for her? Or merely irritation that such a man might be considered worthy of her sister? The question left an unsettling sting.

And even if it were, she told herself, she wouldn't care. Rank and fortune did not impress her, and Lord Hawthorne's cold demeanor only solidified her disinterest. She sighed, her thoughts heavy with frustration, and let her eyes drift toward the table's end.

She hadn't expected to meet his gaze.

Lord Hawthorne's black eyes locked on hers with unsettling precision. There was no hint of warmth, no flicker of amusement—only an intense, level stare that seemed to see straight through her. To Emmeline's horror, heat crept up her neck and into her cheeks. She averted her eyes hastily, focusing intently on her plate as if it held the secrets of the universe.

Her irritation flared anew. How utterly infuriating that a man so completely insufferable could reduce her to blushing like a schoolgirl. She stabbed at her roast beef with more force than necessary, willing herself not to look his way again.

As the dining hall buzzed with conversation and clinking silverware, Emmeline resolved to avoid Lord Hawthorne entirely for the remainder of the evening. That is, if fate—and her aunt's scheming—would allow it.

Chapter Five

Emmeline stayed close to Miss Clara's side as the ladies left the dining chamber, grateful for her new acquaintance's steady, unpretentious presence. Though she suspected she would find few truly congenial souls at the manor, Clara was proving to be an unexpected exception. The way Clara leaned in during their conversation, her voice dropping to a conspiratorial whisper when she made an observation about their hostess, gave Emmeline a sense of camaraderie she hadn't realized she craved. Clara's sharp but good-natured humor felt like a balm after the barbed comments she'd endured from others in the household.

Their conversation in the withdrawing room confirmed Emmeline's impression. Clara possessed a dry wit, intelligent and sharp but free of malice, a quality that stood out in stark contrast to the biting remarks of others in the household.

When the gentlemen joined the ladies after dinner, Clara tried to dissuade Emmeline from accompanying her to the card table. "They'll be dancing, you know," Clara said gently. Her eyes flickered briefly toward the dance floor where the guests were already gathering. "You really should join the younger set."

"I'm quite content here, thank you," Emmeline replied, a polite smile softening her refusal. Pleading fatigue after the trials of her journey, she did not argue. She suspected Clara's suggestion was more strategic than kind; no doubt Clara understood that Lady Hollybrook would be best pleased if her country niece remained as inconspicuous as possible.

But Lady Hollybrook's wishes were soon thwarted in spectacular fashion when Lord Hawthorne approached the west table and asked to join them.

Lady Hollybrook's reaction was one of thinly veiled horror. All her attempts to redirect him toward the dance floor—insisting the young ladies would be utterly devastated if he did not join—were met with a polite coolness that left her speechless. Her aunt's mouth tightened into a thin line as she watched him pull out a chair, her fingers clutching her lace handkerchief so tightly Emmeline feared it might tear.

Emmeline, meanwhile, was astonished when his lordship took a seat at their table. Relief washed over her when she realized she wouldn't be partnered with him; seconds earlier, an elderly gentleman with a distinct wheeze had taken the seat opposite her.

Her relief was short-lived. A competitive fire ignited in her, a sudden, burning desire to humiliate Lord Hawthorne by besting him at cards. If only his insufferable arrogance could be toppled as easily as a house of cards, she thought with a spark of vindictive glee. But her hopes for even this minor triumph were soon dashed. If he'd partnered with anyone other than Clara, Emmeline might have accused him of outright cheating. Together, they played with flawless precision, trick after trick falling effortlessly into their hands. Clara's quiet signals—a slight tilt of her head or a subtle tap of her finger—combined with Hawthorne's infuriating ability to anticipate the game, made them an unbeatable duo.

As for Emmeline, she had the misfortune of being paired with the elderly gentleman, whose attention constantly wandered, leading him to play cards almost at random. At one point, he placed a card with such a triumphant flourish that Emmeline was momentarily hopeful—until she saw it was the wrong suit entirely.

Every misstep on his part required Emmeline to stifle her growing frustration. Her fingernails bit into her palms beneath the table, and the satisfying snap of her cards landing was her only solace, though it did little to mask her partner's mounting blunders.

The amused glances Lord Hawthorne cast her way, did not improve her disposition, particularly when her partner inadvertently topped what would have been a winning card. The faintest quirk of his brow as he surveyed the table suggested he was enjoying himself far more than he let on, a fact that only stoked Emmeline's irritation.

Lord Hawthorne himself seemed to delight in drawing out his turns. He would stare at his cards, select one, then change his mind at the last possible moment, snatching it back into the safety of his hand. The deliberate slowness of his movements, paired with the faint tap-tap of his fingers against the table as he contemplated his next play, was maddening. As he placed his card, his gaze lifted briefly to meet Emmeline's, a flicker of amusement in his eyes that only stoked her irritation. She had the maddening sense that he knew exactly how much he was getting under her skin—and enjoyed it.

As he deliberated over yet another play, Emmeline studied him covertly from beneath lowered lashes.

Why on earth had he chosen the card table over the dance floor? His boredom with the entire gathering was evident, but surely there were more entertaining ways to endure the evening than lingering here. No. Reason told her his decision was deliberate. She examined him more closely. His pallor, the deepened lines around his mouth... Could he be ill?

Then she remembered the servant carrying the bloodstained basin from his room. That couldn't have been from shaving. Could it? Her gaze narrowed on his hand, where he held his cards awkwardly, as though avoiding unnecessary movement.

His voice interrupted her thoughts. "Do I perhaps have gravy on my chin, Miss St. Clair?"

She startled, mortified to be caught staring. "Er—why, no. I was simply wondering if you're quite well."

His dark eyebrows rose. The corners of his mouth tilted ever so slightly upward, though the amusement in his eyes was far more pronounced. "Should I not be? Or is this concern merely an attempt to unnerve me, a continuation of your earlier tongue-lashing?"

"I hardly think I made much of an impression," she retorted, rallying quickly. "I was simply wondering if you'd hurt yourself. Your arm, perhaps?"

His lips quirked in the faintest suggestion of a smile. "While I should be grateful for your concern, I admit to being puzzled by it. After all, we have only just met. I'd have no basis to judge whether you are yourself looking more haggard than usual."

Clara glanced between them, her expression unreadable. A flicker of surprise crossed her face before she quickly masked it, though her gaze lingered on Hawthorne's arm as if considering Emmeline's observation. Thankfully, the elderly gentleman finally made his play, and the game resumed.

Emmeline's relief was palpable when tea was announced, signaling an end to the evening's activities. She realized then that her temples were throbbing—a headache, she decided. That must be what prompted his lordship's "haggard" remark. Still, the memory of his amused smile lingered in her mind far longer than she would have liked.

Sir Edmund insisted on gathering everyone near the great fireplace for tea, declaring that shared fellowship was the true spirit of Christmastide. The group assembled in a semicircle of chairs and footstools, the fire's glow casting flickering shadows across the faces of the gathered company.

Emmeline adjusted her skirts, acutely aware of Lord Hawthorne's gaze across the room. She resolutely avoided meeting his eyes, though the weight of his attention was impossible to ignore.

The group shifted uncomfortably as the fire cast dancing shadows across the room. Emmeline adjusted her skirts, acutely aware of the weight of Lord Hawthorne's gaze. She had made a point to sit far from him, but the arrangement of chairs had still left them facing one another.

"An unseasonably mild December, wouldn't you say?" ventured a squire with a loud clearing of his throat. His observation hung in the air like a damp coat, eliciting only murmurs of agreement.

Emmeline hid a smile behind her teacup. *How perfectly droll*, she thought. The fire cracked loudly, as though in agreement.

Across the room, Hawthorne leaned back in his chair, his fingers drumming softly on the armrest. Emmeline's eyes flicked to his hand, noting its stiffness. Was it discomfort—or distraction? She couldn't say.

It was her former card partner who broke the uneasy silence, leaning forward with a conspiratorial air. "Oh, I say, Sir Edmund," he began, his voice raised to compensate for years of diminished hearing, "is it true that Hollingsworth Hall has a new occupant?"

Emmeline's gaze, despite her efforts to avoid it, locked on Lord Hawthorne. His fingers, drumming idly on the arm of his chair, stilled. The flicker of firelight caught the faintest tightening of his jaw—a fleeting reaction, so subtle it might have gone unnoticed by anyone else.

Beside her, Clara stiffened, her teacup trembling slightly as she set it on the saucer. Sir Edmund's genial expression faltered, his hands tightening on the arms of his chair.

"I believe I did hear something of the sort," Sir Edmund said. "Now, shall we—"

"Well, when you stop to think on it," the old man interrupted, oblivious to the discomfort his question had caused, "it's a wonder. An estate that old—been in one family since the Conqueror, wouldn't surprise me—suddenly getting passed around like a hot potato! Shocking, I call it."

Emmeline's curiosity prickled. She glanced at Clara, who was staring resolutely at her lap, her lips pressed into a thin line.

"Actually," another gentleman chimed in, "it's not being passed around, so I understand. It's reverting. By hook or crook, Graham Hollingsworth managed to buy it back."

The words landed like a blow. Clara's hand slipped, and her teacup fell to the floor, shattering with a loud crack. The noise startled everyone, and for a moment, the only sound was the fire's steady crackle.

"Clara, my dear, are you all right?" Sir Edmund asked, his brow furrowed.

Clara forced a smile, her cheeks pale. "Yes, of course. I... I suppose I'm clumsier than usual this evening."

Emmeline bent to help her retrieve the shards, but her focus kept straying to Lord Hawthorne. His expression was unreadable, but something in his stillness betrayed him. He was holding something back.

What, Emmeline wondered, was his connection to Hollingsworth Hall? And why, for the first time, did it feel as though the Marquess wasn't quite as unshakable as he seemed?

Chapter Six

The delicate chime of shattered china was met with a collective gasp, but Sir Edmund's hearty laugh cut through the tension like a bell at dawn. "No harm done!" he declared, clapping his hands together as a footman darted forward to retrieve the broken fragments of Miss Clara's teacup. Miss Clara, her face pale but composed, murmured apologies, her usual calm shaken.

Meanwhile, Emmeline's attention was drawn to the well-informed cousin who was now on the receiving end of a hushed but ferocious scolding from his wife. The woman's whispers might have been muted, but her rigid posture and furious gestures conveyed volumes. For a fleeting moment, Emmeline almost felt sorry for him. Almost.

Sir Edmund, eager to restore the festive atmosphere, raised his voice. "Well now, how about some ghost stories? Nothing like a good spine-tingler to keep the cold at bay!"

The suggestion was met with a wave of polite but awkward protests. His wife looked horrified, her fingers twisting nervously in her lap, while Gabriel muttered something about "such morbid nonsense" being unfit for such an occasion. Sir Edmund opened his mouth to press the matter further, but he was interrupted by the sound of the butler clearing his throat at the doorway.

"Mr. Alistair Moorefield has just arrived," the butler announced.

All eyes turned toward the entranceway, where a young man in a riding coat and buckskins stood, framed by the flickering light of the hallway sconces. He appeared to be in his late twenties, his light brown hair slightly tousled from the ride, and his keen blue eyes swept the room with quick efficiency, his polished boots tracking faint smudges of frost onto the worn carpet.

And then, for just a moment, those eyes lingered on Emmeline. A flicker of something—amusement, curiosity?—danced there before he turned his gaze to Sir Edmund.

Oh, now this is interesting, Emmeline thought, the corner of her lips quirking into an involuntary smile. *So this is Rosalind's young man. Christmas has just become infinitely more promising.*

Sir Edmund crossed the room in a few quick strides, clasping the new arrival warmly by the hand and ushering him toward the fire. "Alistair, my boy! We were beginning to worry. Thought you'd have been here hours ago. I trust your journey was uneventful?"

"Uneventful enough, sir," Alistair replied, his voice deep and even, though his eyes held a glint of humor. "Though I must admit, the frost made the roads rather less friendly than one might hope."

"Ah, well, no matter! You're here now, and that's what counts," Sir Edmund said, clapping a hand on his shoulder before turning back to the assembled company. "Pray allow me to introduce my invaluable secretary, Mr. Alistair Moorefield." He swelled with pride, and his next words were delivered with a flourish. "I'll not trouble you with presenting the entire company just yet, Alistair, but I must make you known to our most honored guest—Lord Hawthorne."

"Actually, we're acquainted," Mr. Moorefield supply. The lack of warmth in his voice raised the newcomers standing in Emmeline's eyes.

The room seemed to hold its breath as Alistair turned toward Hawthorne, who had yet to rise from his seat. The marquess's dark gaze met Alistair's unflinchingly, and for a brief moment, the air between them felt charged with an unspoken challenge. Then, with the same cool composure that seemed to define him, Lord Hawthorne inclined his head in greeting.

Hawthorne's thoughts remained carefully guarded, though the appearance of Alistair Moorefield was an unwelcome complication. Whatever the man suspected—or thought he knew—could not be addressed here, not in a room full of curious onlookers. Hawthorne's jaw tightened imperceptibly as he returned the other man's gaze.

"Mr. Moorefield," Hawthorne said, cooly, "it seems you've arrived just in time to rescue us from Sir Edmund's rather... enthusiastic suggestion of ghost stories."

A ripple of polite laughter eased the tension, and Alistair's mouth curved into a charming grin. "A narrow escape, indeed, my lord," he replied with practiced ease. "Though I admit, I'd be sorry to miss such tales. From what I've heard, Sir Edmund has quite a flair for the dramatic."

Emmeline watched the exchange with growing intrigue. Alistair Moorefield was, without doubt, charming—and far too clever by half. She had the distinct feeling he saw more in a moment than most people saw in an hour. And yet, as his eyes flicked briefly back to her, she found herself unaccountably pleased by the attention.

"And did you just arrive as well, Hawthorne?" Mr. Moorefield asked.

"Good God, no. I've been here a donkey's year," Hawthorne drawled. "Why do you ask?"

"Simple curiosity."

Mr. Moorefield turned to his focus toward Sir Edmund once more. His smile was warm and disarming as he replied, "I do apologize for being late. I made excellent time, though I must confess my arrival was delayed by some pressing matters in London. I'll share the details shortly, but may I first partake of your tea board? The journey was too swift to allow for supper, and I fear I am famished."

With a genial laugh, Sir Edmund led his secretary toward the fire, offering him a plate of plum cake and a steaming cup of tea. Most of the company, clearly weary from the day's events, had begun to drift off to bed, but Emmeline found herself wide awake. She poured herself another cup of tea and settled into a chair within earshot of Moorefield.

Moorefield, it seemed, enjoyed building suspense, for he said little as he ate with deliberate leisure, savoring every crumb of the plum cake. "Now, then, Alistair," Sir Edmund prompted with both amusement and impatience, "out with it! Tell us what's happened. I trust the Regent is well, or else you'd have spoken sooner."

"No harm has come to his person," Moorefield said, pausing for effect, "if that is what you mean. But his state of mind, I fear, leaves much to be desired." His significant pause drew the room's full attention.

"For heaven's sake, lad, get on with it," Sir Edmund pressed, though the slight arch of his brow betrayed his curiosity.

Emmeline silently echoed the sentiment. She was finding Moorefield's penchant for theatrics tiresome.

"Well, sir, the matter is this," Moorefield began at last, setting down his empty teacup with a decisive clink. "The Regent is unlikely to be pleased that Christopher Langford has been... rescued."

A collective gasp rippled through the room, punctuated by the clatter of Emmeline's saucer as it rattled against her teacup. "Christopher Langford!" she exclaimed, her voice breaking the sudden hush. All eyes turned to her, and she flushed under their scrutiny. "The journalist?"

"Yes," Moorefield replied, his expression faintly irritated to have been interrupted. "Do you know him?"

"Not personally," Emmeline admitted, her voice steadier now. "But I know of him. He edits *The Lyceum*, does he not?"

Gabriel snorted. "Well, that clears it up entirely."

Emmeline shot him a glare before turning her attention back to Moorefield. "Why on earth would Mr. Langford need rescuing? And from what?"

"Oh, for God's sake, Emmy," Gabriel groaned, slouching back in his chair. "Have you been living under a rock?"

Moorefield resumed, clearly savoring the attention. "As I was saying, Langford's rescue occurred during his transfer from Newgate to the prison ship bound for Botany Bay. His carriage was held up before dawn by a single man armed with pistols, who demanded the guards release their prisoner. Remarkably, the guards complied, and the pair disappeared into the labyrinth of the thieves' kitchens."

"An astounding tale," Sir Edmund said, though his eyes betrayed skepticism. "One man against three armed guards?"

Moorefield nodded. "The guards claim they were taken completely by surprise. The assailant had his pistol at the coachman's temple before they could react. It seems they valued their lives over their duty."

"I still don't understand," Emmeline pressed, leaning forward. "What exactly did Langford do to warrant deportation?"

"Langford's crime," Moorefield said with a smirk, "was forgetting the purpose of his publication. Rather than sticking to drivel—poetry and philosophical musings, he launched a vicious attack on the Regent. Seditious and treasonable, as the courts found."

"Drivel?" Emmeline's eyes flashed. "The Lyceum publishes some of the finest poetry in England! And Christopher Langford has championed writers who would otherwise go unheard."

"Ah, a defender of the arts," Moorefield said, his smirk broadening. "Perhaps some of your own verses have graced its pages?"

"Not mine," Emmeline replied, her chin lifting. "But my sister's. Rosalind's work is admired by all who read it. Including Mr. Langford."

Gabriel's jaw dropped. "Rosalind? A bluestocking? Well, that explains everything. Comes of a house full of women and no man to guide them."

"It comes of intelligence and talent," Emmeline snapped.

Moorefield raised a hand, clearly intent on reclaiming the floor. "Regardless of its literary merits, Langford's attack was deemed seditious—and treasonable, as the courts found. Hence his arrest and subsequent sentence."

"And yet," Sir Edmund interjected mildly, "Botany Bay feels extreme. A reprimand or fine would have sufficed, don't you think?"

"Perhaps," Moorefield conceded grudgingly. "But the Regent has grown weary of public ridicule. Respect for the monarchy must be upheld."

"Respect," Emmeline muttered, "is earned, not demanded."

"Careful, Miss St. Clair," Hawthorne interjected. "You'll have Mr. Moorefield adding your name to the list of traitors. Why, just this evening, you were ready to see me marched to the guillotine."

Emmeline's cheeks flamed. "Thank you so much, Lord Hawthorne," she muttered through clenched teeth. Whatever hope she'd had of making a favorable impression on Moorefield had surely just gone up in flames.

"I still contend," Sir Edmund replied mildly, "that the Regent—or rather, the courts—overreacted. While I agree that holding the acting monarch up to ridicule is in the poorest possible taste, this is still England. And even setting aside the issue of free speech, the whole matter would have been better ignored."

He glanced toward Emmeline with a faint smile. "*The Lyceum* has a rather small, though, I dare say, *select* circulation. Among those few readers, the piece would have been forgotten in a matter of weeks. But as it stands, the affair has been blown entirely out of proportion. Mr. Langford has become a martyr, and with the populace already divided over the royal marriage, the Regent's popularity now teeters at an all-time low."

Emmeline noted how deliberately her uncle avoided looking at Alistair Moorefield, whose jaw tightened at the word *martyr*.

"As I've said before," Sir Edmund continued, "it would have been far wiser to give Mr. Langford only a reprimand. Deportation to Botany Bay? That hardly fits the crime."

Miss Clara nodded in agreement. "I would have thought His Royal Highness might have learned something from the public outcry when the Hunts were jailed."

"Ah, but that is precisely the point, Miss Clara," Mr. Moorefield interjected, his voice sharp with zeal. "When the Hunts attacked the Regent in print, they received, as your brother so graphically put it, a mere reprimand."

"Oh, come now," Sir Edmund countered. "Two years in prison and a hefty fine is hardly a rap on the knuckles."

"Prison?" Moorefield scoffed. "Hunt was given accommodations that would shame some citizens' drawing rooms. He entertained his friends, continued publishing his rag, and emerged more influential than ever. It's no wonder the Regent sought firmer measures this time."

"Well, it's all a bad business," Sir Edmund sighed, steering the conversation away from the growing tension. "I only hope that with Langford's escape, this whole matter will soon be forgotten. I suspect His Highness might be just as relieved to see it end this way."

"Begging your pardon, sir, but I don't believe it has ended," Moorefield replied, his voice measured, but his expression tinged with smugness. "The authorities are conducting an intense manhunt as we speak. Langford and his accomplice will not get away. I'd stake my reputation on it."

"In fact," Moorefield continued, his voice swelling with pride, "one reason for my delay in arriving was that I was summoned to Bow Street to provide assistance. It was known I would travel this way, and as the fugitives are almost certainly aiming to board a ship in Dover—where the King's men are already assembling—the magistrates felt it prudent that I make certain inquiries en route."

"What inquiries?" Gabriel asked, his curiosity outweighing his usual disdain. "Surely they didn't expect you to single-handedly apprehend them?"

"Not quite," Moorefield replied, his lips curling into a faint smile. "But there was one particularly intriguing report. A witness described a rig fleeing the dock area at breakneck speed. A flashy contraption, they called it. Black and red, with polished trim."

He paused dramatically, his gaze sliding toward Lord Hawthorne.

"The description is quite distinctive, wouldn't you say, my lord?"

Hawthorne met his gaze evenly, though his pulse quickened. His mind raced through possibilities—who could have been seen, and how closely they were tied to him. Outwardly, he allowed a faint smile to curve his lips.

"Don't you own a curricle of that description, my lord?" Moorefield pressed.

Hawthorne shrugged lazily. "I do. Had it for over a year. Which means every dandy in London has copied it by now. Truth be told, I've been considering getting rid of it. Gabriel, you wouldn't want to take it off my hands, would you?"

Gabriel ignored him, his focus entirely on Moorefield. "Really, Alistair," he sputtered. "You're not suggesting that Hawthorne was involved in this escapade? That's absurd!"

"Absurd?" Moorefield repeated with mock surprise. "Lord Hawthorne and Langford attended school together. Are they not close friends?"

Hawthorne took his time responding, his dark gaze cool and unreadable. "No," he said at last. "We attended school together, yes. But I wouldn't say we were friends. Acquaintances, at best. We didn't exactly share the same interests."

"Such as?" Moorefield prompted.

"Poetry," Hawthorne replied dryly, his lips quirking faintly. "Or politics. I was far more interested in sport."

"I'll tell you what interests me," Gabriel snapped, rising to his feet. "Not insinuations against my guest. You've overstepped, Moorefield."

"Softly, Gabriel," Sir Edmund interjected. "There's no need to leap to conclusions. I'm sure Alistair meant no offense."

"And even if he did," Hawthorne added with a sardonic chuckle, "I admit I'm flattered. One man holding up a heavily guarded coach? It's almost flattering."

"I didn't say heavily guarded," Moorefield corrected. "There were three guards, in fact."

"Still," Hawthorne mused, leaning back in his chair, "it's impressive. But, alas, I'm afraid I couldn't have managed it. I haven't yet mastered the art of being in two places at once."

"Nor would I suggest otherwise," Moorefield replied smoothly. "For the simple reason that the man who rescued Langford was shot."

Emmeline's fingers tightened on her teacup as Moorefield spoke, her knuckles whitening with the effort to appear calm. But the moment he said the rescuer had been shot, her grip faltered. The delicate china tipped forward, sending a stream of hot tea cascading onto her lap.

She gasped, jerking back and staring down at the dark stain spreading across Rosalind's pristine muslin gown. A horrified curse escaped her lips before she could stop it. "Damnation!"

Every head turned toward her.

Emmeline's thoughts raced. Could it be true? Could Lord Hawthorne, of all people, have risked his life to save Christopher Langford? The very idea seemed preposterous, yet... the image of the bloodstained basin surfaced in her mind, refusing to be dismissed.

Miss Clara made a soft sound of alarm, half-rising from her seat. "Oh, Emmeline! Are you burned?"

But Emmeline was frozen, with her eyes fixed on Lord Hawthorne. And when she didn't answer, Mr. Moorefield asked in a deceptively light tone. "Is something the matter, Miss St. Clair?"

Emmeline swallowed hard, forcing a tight smile to her lips. "No, Mr. Moorefield. I simply dislike violence, as any civilized person would."

"Of course," he said, his voice laden with polite skepticism.

But he didn't look away.

Neither did Lord Hawthorne.

A MARQUESS FOR CHRISTMAS

Hawthorne watched Emmeline closely, noting the sudden stiffness in her posture, the way her gaze darted toward him and then away. Suspicion, yes—but something more. A flicker of unease stirred within him, though he forced it down, masking his thoughts behind a practiced indifference. He could not afford for Moorefield—or Miss St. Clair, for that matter—to uncover anything he didn't choose to reveal.

The two men exchanged a glance, something unspoken but unmistakable passing between them, and Emmeline felt the heat of suspicion settling uncomfortably in the pit of her stomach.

She wondered if she knew more about Christopher Langford's escape—and his mysterious rescuer—than she was meant to.

Chapter Seven

Emmeline tossed and turned through the night, her mind an unruly storm of doubts and half-formed convictions. She clutched her pillow tightly, as if it might anchor her thoughts, but the effort was futile. The darkness around her seemed alive, her imagination conjuring shadowy figures slipping through the trees or the sharp crack of gunfire on the Dover Road.

It was absurd—utterly ridiculous—to think Lord Hawthorne had anything to do with the crime in London. Simply because she disliked the man, it hardly made him a villain.

And yet.

She flipped onto her stomach, glaring into the darkness, seeking comfort and finding none. There was the small matter of his wild ride down the Dover Road—reckless, dangerous, and entirely unbecoming of a marquess. Add to that the peculiar timing of his arrival and the strange discrepancies in his story.

He had, without question, given Mr. Moorefield the impression he'd arrived much later than he actually had. And then there was the basin of water tinged with pink and his persistent favoring of his left arm.

She huffed out a frustrated breath. "Guilty as sin," she muttered into her pillow. The man could hardly deny it.

But guilty of what? Rescuing an old friend? A school acquaintance? A journalist who, if one were to believe the whispers, might well deserve admiration rather than censure? What some might even call heroism?

"Poppycock," she grumbled, rolling onto her back and staring at the ceiling. The word felt hollow, even to her. How was it possible that she, who had been so quick to condemn him, was now teetering on the edge of labeling him a hero? It was utterly preposterous. Yet the thought lingered, unwelcome and immovable, like a splinter buried too deeply to extract.

What truly concerned her, though—what gnawed at the edges of her composure—was Christopher Langford's fate. Or rather, Rosalind's reaction to it.

She had teased her sister once, accusing her of being in love with the infamous journalist. Rosalind had denied it, of course, her face flaming with indignant color. *"In love with him? Don't be absurd, Emmeline! I've never even met the man. I only said I admired his letters—his intellect."*

And yet, the way Rosalind spoke of him had been... telling. Emmeline's lips twisted into a wry smile. Rosalind was as timid as a mouse in most things, but in matters of the pen, she was a lioness. Their correspondence—if one could call it that—was likely the only romance Rosalind had ever known. What a tragedy it would be if it ended on a prison ship bound for Botany Bay.

She rolled over again, clutching the bedclothes tighter. Perhaps Langford could continue his correspondence from France—if he ever made it there. Judging by Mr. Moorefield's grim predictions, the man's chances were slim indeed. And as for Langford's seditious writings, Emmeline thought bitterly, surely *The Lyceum* could have filled his space with one of Rosalind's poems instead. The kingdom hardly needed more division, let alone another martyr.

At last, exhaustion claimed her, though not before her mind conjured an absurd dream: Rosalind herself, planted in the middle of the highway, pistol cocked, shouting, "Stand and deliver!" as Hawthorne's black and red curricle hurtled toward her.

The rustling of curtains yanked Emmeline from her restless sleep. She bolted upright, her heart thudding in confusion, and stared a maid, who bustled about the room, a steaming cup of tea in hand. "Good morning, miss."

Emmeline blinked at her and reached for the cup, the heat seeping into her chilled fingers as she sipped gratefully. The cobwebs in her mind refused to clear, lingering stubbornly as she moved through her morning routine.

A brisk walk before breakfast, she decided, might do the trick. Striding into the icy air, she inhaled deeply, the chill sharp and invigorating against her skin. She was determined to shake the night's fancies, to let the cold burn them away.

But even as she set out toward her uncle's cattle, considering if there'd be an opportunity to ride later, her thoughts wandered unbidden to Lord Hawthorne, to his sharp gaze and the infuriating smirk he wore so well. *Ridiculous*, she told herself, picking up her pace. *Completely ridiculous.*

Emmeline was halfway down the path when a pitiful sound stopped her in her tracks—a plaintive, heart-wrenching cry that pierced the cold morning air. She paused, tilting her head to locate the source, then veered off the path, pushing through the dense hedge with more determination than grace.

What she found on the other side stopped her short: Lord Hawthorne, standing at the base of a towering beech tree, arms crossed, his head tilted back as he stared up into the branches. The pale morning light outlined his tall frame, and despite herself, Emmeline felt a flicker of annoyance at how effortlessly he seemed to fit into the idyllic scene.

"What are you doing out so early?" she blurted before she could stop herself.

Hawthorne turned slightly, the barest hint of surprise crossing his face before he settled into his familiar smirk. "Should I not be? Are decadent noblemen required to remain abed until noon?"

"Perhaps you were too uncomfortable to sleep?"

"While I agree the manor's accommodations are rather rustic, my bed is adequate," he said smoothly, his dark eyes glinting. "I take it you fared worse?"

"That's not what I meant, and you know it," she snapped. "I thought perhaps you were in pain."

"Sorry to disappoint Miss St. Clair, but I am quite well," he said with mock solemnity. "A touch of dyspepsia, perhaps, from last night's shellfish, but otherwise..."

A long, pitiful mew interrupted him, drawing both their gazes upward.

"What on earth?" Emmeline moved closer, craning her neck. High in the tree, a small, gray ball of fluff clung to the trunk, its color blending so perfectly with the bark that it was nearly invisible. "The poor thing! It's afraid to come down."

"Brilliant deduction, St. Clair," he drawled.

She turned to glare at him. "Did you frighten the poor thing up there?"

"Well, naturally. I was feeling bored with no coaches to run off the road, so I said to myself, 'By Jove, Hawthorne, why not chase a kitten up a tree?'"

"Must you always be so insufferable? Have you even tried to coax it down?"

"As a matter of fact, I only just arrived," he said, gesturing to the tree. "But I doubt my powers of persuasion would have much effect."

"Here, kitty, kitty," Emmeline called softly, holding out her hand. "Come on, I'll catch you."

The kitten responded with a plaintive mew, followed by a low chuckle from Hawthorne that set her teeth on edge. She turned on him again, her patience worn thin.

"Well, it's obvious someone will have to climb up and rescue the poor thing."

"It's not obvious to me," he said, leaning lazily against the trunk. "Cats have been getting themselves out of trees without human intervention for centuries. This one will come down as soon as we leave, I'd wager."

"How can you be so unfeeling?" she snapped, her voice rising with the kitten's cries. "You should climb up after it—you know you should," she added, narrowing her eyes. "But, of course, you can't. You've hurt yourself."

"I have not," he shot back, his voice hardening. "And why this obsession with my health? For your information, Miss St. Clair, the reason I'm not scaling this particular tree is because I've no intention of ruining a perfectly good pair of biscuit pantaloons."

"Fine," she said, her chin lifting. "I'll simply have to do it myself."

"That," he said, his voice dripping with disdain, "is precisely what I find most objectionable about your sex. A man refuses to engage in blatant idiocy, and your immediate reaction is to attempt it yourself, as though martyrdom is the only alternative. By all means, Miss St. Clair," he added with a sweeping gesture toward the tree. "Prove your superiority."

She glared at him, then turned to size up the tree with more trepidation than she let on. She hadn't climbed a tree since she was twelve, and certainly not while wearing her best French gray dress with its cherry-colored spencer.

"Having second thoughts?" he inquired smugly.

"Not at all," she retorted. "I'm simply waiting for you to leave."

"To fetch the gardener, no doubt?" he said, his dark brow arching.

"Certainly not. I need neither a gardener nor an audience. If you aren't going to help, at least have the decency to take yourself off."

"Never. Who knows? I may wish to stage a feline rescue myself one day, and I'd hate to miss the chance to study proper technique."

Grinding her teeth, she turned back to the tree and reached for the lowest branch. It was just out of reach. With a determined leap, she managed to grab hold, dangling precariously. For a moment, she swayed back and forth, feeling utterly ridiculous. Hawthorne's muffled chuckle did nothing to help.

"Instead of laughing like a hyena, you might give me a boost," she snapped.

"Oh no, not I," he said smoothly. "If you insist on breaking your neck, you'll have to manage it without my assistance."

Emmeline's suspicions, momentarily forgotten, returned in full force. "You don't care whether I fall or not," she accused. "You simply can't lift me—you're too injured."

"Hurt, am I?" His eyes narrowed, his lips curling into a faint smile. "Shall we put that theory to the test?"

Before she could protest, his hands gripped her waist, lifting her with a strength that belied her suspicions. She landed unceremoniously on the branch, clinging to it for balance, her cheeks flaming.

"Thank you," she said stiffly, refusing to look down at him. "You may leave now."

"Not a chance," he replied, leaning casually against the trunk. "I'll just stand here and admire the limbs. Of the tree, naturally."

Climbing a tree in skirts was mortifying enough without the added spectacle of an audience. Emmeline gritted her teeth and pressed herself closer to the trunk, moving cautiously upward. At least the sturdy branches of the ancient beech provided solid footholds. Still, she could feel the fabric of her French gray dress catching on the rough bark, a painful reminder that this particular garment was among her few remaining intact wardrobe items.

She'd made it halfway up before glancing downward—and immediately regretted it. The ground seemed impossibly far, and her vision swam. She clung to the trunk, her breath coming in shallow bursts.

"Never look down, Miss St. Clair," Lord Hawthorne called, his lazy drawl infused with amusement. "That was the kitten's first mistake. I shudder to think of you both stranded up there."

Wiping the smirk off his insufferable face leapt to the forefront of her mind. She shut her eyes and focused on steadying herself, forcing the dizziness to pass. When she opened them again, the kitten's pitiful cries spurred her forward.

"Hang on, dear. Emmy's coming," she murmured, inching closer. The tiny creature peered at her with wide, frightened eyes, its gray fur blending seamlessly with the bark.

She was near enough to reach for it now. But as she stretched out her hand, one arm still wrapped tightly around the trunk, the kitten recoiled, scrambling higher and wailing louder.

"Blast it!" she hissed, clinging tighter to the branch.

"Did you say something, Miss St. Clair?" Hawthorne's voice floated up, thick with mockery.

"Oh, do be quiet," she snapped. "You're frightening it with your shouting."

"I'm frightening it? It seems to me it's you putting the poor creature in a quake. Give it up and come down. Cats are perfectly capable of descending trees. It's only a matter of time."

"Or perhaps you could stop standing there like a useless lump and offer some assistance," she retorted, her frustration flaring.

"And ruin my biscuit pantaloons? Certainly not. Besides, if I did, I might miss your gallant display of heroism—or is it heroine-ism? Does such a word even exist? Damn if I know," he mused.

Emmeline was about to unleash a scathing reply when movement beyond the hedge caught her attention. She froze, narrowing her eyes. At first, she thought it was the wind rustling the branches, but a closer look revealed a figure crouched behind the greenery. Mr. Moorefield. He was peering intently through the foliage, his posture unmistakably that of a man spying. And the object of his attention? None other than Lord Hawthorne.

Her breath hitched. What was Moorefield doing? And how long had he been there?

"Do hurry, Miss St. Clair," Hawthorne called, his voice laced with mock impatience. "If I'd known this rescue would take so long, I'd have brought a book."

Steeling herself, Emmeline began her descent with far less care than she'd exercised on the way up. Her mind raced, preoccupied by

Moorefield's unsettling presence. She didn't notice the branch beneath her foot until it gave way with a sickening crack.

The world tilted violently, and she plunged downward.

"Oof!" The breath left her lungs as she landed hard—on something far more solid than the ground. Lord Hawthorne.

She sprawled across his chest, momentarily stunned, her palms stinging fiercely where the rough tree bark and her hurried descent had grazed the skin. The sharp bite of the scrapes barely registered as her mind scrambled to process the fall—and the fact that she was, indeed, still alive. Gritting her teeth against the discomfort, she quickly pushed herself up, her knees sinking into the frosted grass as she hovered over him.

"Oh, heavens—are you all right?" she gasped, peering at his pale face.

"What a damned question," he muttered, his voice tight with pain. "Now, for God's sake, get off me."

She quickly obliged, kneeling beside him as he shifted with a groan. "Do you think anything is broken?" she asked, her voice tinged with worry.

"Not likely. You just knocked the wind out of me." He sat up slowly, leaning back against the tree trunk, his movements stiff and deliberate. "Give me a moment to catch my breath, and I'll be fit as a fiddle."

"You don't look it," she said bluntly. "While I was in the tree, I saw Mr. Moorefield on the path. Let me fetch him. He's bound to have seen—"

"No need," Hawthorne interrupted faintly. "He's been following me all morning. But I doubt he'll care to make an appearance."

Emmeline frowned. "How very peculiar. Oh, heavens!" Her eyes fell to his left arm, where blood seeped through his sleeve, staining the fabric a deep crimson. "You're bleeding!"

"It's nothing."

"Nothing?" She gaped at him. "You need a doctor. I'll fetch help—"

"No," he said sharply. Then, more softly, "Come closer, if you will. I seem to have less strength than that blasted kitten."

Against her better judgment, she leaned in, intending to inspect the wound. Instead, with surprising swiftness for a man who moments ago could scarcely move, he slipped an arm around her waist and pulled her close.

"What are you—" The words faltered, lost to the charged air between them.

His gaze locked onto hers, dark and intent, a silent warning that left her frozen. And then his head dipped, his mouth capturing hers with a boldness that stole every coherent thought. His lips were firm, commanding, moving over hers with a heat that left no room for resistance. A jolt of sensation coursed through her, shocking her with its intensity, as if her entire body had ignited at his touch.

He tasted of salt and something darker, richer—whiskey, perhaps?—and his scent enveloped her, a heady blend of cedarwood and the faint smokiness of the outdoors. Her fingers, which had instinctively risen to his chest, curled into his coat, not to push him away, but to ground herself against the delicious onslaught. The world around them blurred and faded, leaving only the searing connection of their lips and the wild hammering of her heart.

His hand rose to cradle her jaw, the rough pads of his fingers grazing her skin with a startling tenderness that contradicted the unyielding hunger of the kiss. And for one reckless moment, she let herself fall into it, into him.

When he finally pulled back, the loss of his warmth left her breathless, her lips tingling from the fervent pressure of his. Her chest heaved as she stared at him, her pulse racing, her cheeks hot with a fiery combination of fury, embarrassment, and something far more perilous.

"You—" she began, her voice shaky with outrage and bewilderment, but his expression, equal parts smug and inscrutable, silenced her. He leaned back against the tree, an infuriating smirk playing at the corners of his mouth.

That shameless, decadent, lecherous... that... that marquess! How dare he find amusement because she's so easily given into his improper advances? If he thought for one minute... But the glint of laughter in his eyes made her pause. She followed his gaze to the ground, where the kitten, now safely on the frost-dappled grass, licked its paws with serene indifference.

"Forgive me," Hawthorne said, his voice a maddening mixture of amusement and apology. "But I did tell you so."

"Perhaps," she replied tightly, "you might explain what that little display was about, Lord Hawthorne. Am I to assume I'm now so thoroughly beguiled that I'll keep Mr. Moorefield from learning the truth he already suspects?"

Hawthorne smirked, though his pallor made the expression seem almost a grimace. "No, St. Clair. My goal was far simpler: to avoid speaking to Moorefield altogether. And, if I'm honest, to justify us walking very closely back to the manor. For the truth is, I don't think I can make it there unaided."

He saw her hesitation. "Oh, come now Miss St. Clair. There are all sorts of explanations for my injury besides the one that Mr. Moorefield suggested. An irrate husband, for instance. Oh, very well then. Since I doubt I could convince Moorefield of that either, I just as soon avoid the confrontation. Surely you can wrestle with your conscience later? It's not as if I'm going anywhere, you know."

His wry tone rankled, but the sight of him swaying on his feet softened her irritation. Muttering something unladylike under her breath, she jumped up to steady him, then realize to any interested onlooker, it would appear like a second embrace. "Oh, blast!" Oh, well. Come on, then. I'll help you." His arm fell heavily around her shoulders, his weight almost overwhelming as they began the slow trek toward the house, pressed against each other like a pair of lovers. And she was relieved to see that the bleeding appeared to have stopped.

"For someone so thoroughly sound of body, you're awfully heavy," she muttered, adjusting her grip on his waist.

"And for someone so determined to prove me a villain, you're surprisingly accommodating," he returned, his voice strained but amused. "I'll try to faint more gracefully next time."

"Oh, please do," she shot back, ignoring the warmth of his breath against her temple.

As they reached the path, she glanced over her shoulder, scanning the hedges. "He's gone," she whispered.

"No," Hawthorne murmured, his voice low. "He's merely shifted position. He's watching us still, just from a better angle." We're still under surveillance, so hang on for just a little bit longer."

"Oh? You have eyes in the back of your head? Well, I'll wager you that Mr. Moorefield has been toasting by the fire for a good half hour."

"So you think I just made up an excuse for intimacy? Well, it pleases you to think so, then by all means, indulge the fantasy," Hawthorne said, his smirk returning. "I'm certain it's no less outlandish than the ones you've already entertained about me."

"It does nothing of the kind!" She snapped, and they proceeded on in silence.

As soon as they came in sight of Hollybrook Manor, though, Hawthorne stopped using her for a crutch. "I can manage on my own now," he said. "No need to ruin your character any further."

"I'd say you've done an admirable job of that already," she answered glumly.

"With Moorefield? You surely can't care what that self important chip might think. Oh, I forgot. According to Gabriel, the plan was to throw you at his head. Trust me, St. Clair—you're far better off without him."

"Oh, you think so?" she shot back, crossing her arms. "I'd prefer to make that determination myself, thank you very much. Here, where are you going to go?"

"The servants' entrance. It's the shortest route to my bedchamber. This is where we park company in St. Clair."

"as much as that state of affairs appeals to me, I doubt you can make it on your own."

"I'm sure. Good day Miss St. Clair."

"That's it? Good day?"

"Unless you're planning to carry me further." His gaze flicked to hers, teasing. "Surely you aren't suggesting another kiss to speed my recovery?"

Her cheeks flamed. "That remark was entirely uncalled for. What I thought, my Lord, was that a word of thanks might have been in order."

"For what? Falling on top of me? No, of course not. You mean for supporting me this far? Well, I am grateful, Miss St. Clair. It's just that I didn't wish to waste valuable time in chatter."

"Chatter? Well, I wouldn't call civility chatter. But don't let me detain you further. Good day Lord Hawthorn."

He offered a lazy smile before turning away. "Good day, Miss St. Clair."

"And good riddance," she muttered to herself as she watched his slow and slightly unsteady progression towards the house.

She turned to leave, but a faint sound behind her made her pause. The kitten had followed them, its tiny paws pattering against the frosty path. Emmeline sighed, scooping the creature into her arms. "You've caused enough trouble for one morning," she murmured, cradling it close.

As she adjusted its weight, a flicker of movement caught her eye. She froze, her breath hitching. Moorefield stood just beyond the hedge, half-shrouded in shadow, his arms crossed. A faint, knowing smile curved his lips before he turned and disappeared into the trees.

Emmeline's heart thudded painfully as she stared after him, dread coiling in her stomach. No matter her intentions, appearances were damning.

The kitten mewed softly, its green eyes round with curiosity. "You're not the only one in peril this morning," she whispered, clutching it tighter as she hurried back to her room.

Chapter Eight

The faint scent of cinnamon and cloves greeted Emmeline as she stepped into the breakfast room, where garlands of holly adorned the oak beams. Sir Edmund looked up from his coffee, his face creasing into a warm smile.

Oh, there you are, Emmeline," Sir Edmund called cheerfully as his niece entered the dining room. "Come and join me. I believe we're among the last at breakfast. His lordship has yet to appear as I understand it. And as for Gabriel—" His mouth turned down in distaste. "Well, he rarely rises before noon. Do help yourself from the sideboard, my dear. We breakfast quite informally here."

Emmeline made her way to the spread, her stomach rumbling despite her jumbled thoughts. A fire crackled in the hearth, its warm glow casting flickering shadows over the polished floorboards. She filled her plate with Sally Lunn buns, a boiled egg, and a slice of ham before taking a seat opposite her uncle. The long oak table, so lively the night before, now felt vast and empty.

"Have you been walking?" Sir Edmund asked, watching as she took her first bite.

"Yes," she replied, her mouth full of bread. "The air was wonderfully bracing."

Her uncle tilted his head, a flicker of concern crossing his face. "And yet, you seem to have injured yourself. Is that blood on your dress?"

Emmeline froze, her fork halfway to her mouth. Her gaze darted down to the faint crimson streak on her French gray gown. *Not again.* Her heart thudded painfully as she scrambled for a response.

"Oh, that," she said with a nervous laugh, raising her palm. "I scraped my hand on a beech tree during my walk. It does not signify, Uncle, no need for concern."

She managed a small smile, but inside, a groan echoed in her chest. *Of course it's this dress.* One of her few remaining options, and now it bore the damning evidence of her morning mishap. Her mind raced. Could Polly remove a bloodstain without raising suspicion? She doubted it. Polly would fuss, Clara might hear, and suddenly the whole household would be discussing her "injury."

No, better to handle it herself. *Cold water, maybe salt... isn't that what they recommend?* She'd figure it out later. For now, she prayed Sir Edmund would drop the matter.

Sir Edmund's brow furrowed, but he accepted her explanation with a nod. "I trust it's nothing serious, then?"

"Nothing at all," she assured him, though her pulse refused to settle. As she glanced down at her plate, her thoughts whirled. Hawthorne's injury had been far worse, yet she'd left him to fend for himself. Should she check on him? No, that would be madness. Someone might see her, and there was still Moorefield to contend with.

Moorefield. The memory of his shadowed figure beyond the hedge sent a shiver down her spine. What had he seen? What conclusions had he drawn? And, most pressing of all—what did he plan to do about it?

She barely heard Sir Edmund continue. "Clara was looking for you earlier. She's gone to deliver some baby garments to one of our tenants. I believe she hoped you might join her. She thought you might enjoy the outing and a chance to see the countryside."

"Oh," Emmeline said, shaking herself free of her thoughts. "I should have liked that."

"No matter. We shall ensure you get a proper tour another day," he promised, his eyes warming. "We are terribly proud of this part of England, you see. Exceptional, even in midwinter. My sister, in particular, takes great pleasure in showing it off. She's taken quite a liking to you, you know."

"And I to her," Emmeline said sincerely.

Her uncle's expression softened. "I'm glad to hear it. Clara leads a very lonely life, I fear. She hides it well, but her infirmity makes her self-conscious, and she keeps to herself."

"She shouldn't," Emmeline protested. "At first, one might notice it, but then it quickly becomes inconsequential. She is so kind and clever—her other qualities overshadow it entirely."

Sir Edmund gave her an approving smile. "You're very perceptive, my dear. But society isn't always so understanding. I don't think it's prejudice on my part to say that, save for her one flaw, Clara is among the finest examples of her sex. Yet that flaw has, sadly, placed her outside the realm of what most men consider marriageable."

"I don't see why not," Emmeline said hotly. "She's intelligent, witty, and thoughtful."

"Quite so," he agreed with a dry chuckle. "Unfortunately, intelligence and wit are rarely the first qualities men seek in a wife."

"Well, they should be," Emmeline said firmly.

Sir Edmund smiled again, though it was tinged with melancholy. "I agree wholeheartedly. But Clara possesses one asset that has attracted the wrong sort of man in the past—her fortune. Several years ago, I had to put a stop to a planned elopement with a fortune hunter. He'd run through his own inheritance at the gaming tables and cared for nothing but her money. I couldn't stand by and allow him to ruin her life."

He sighed heavily, taking a sip of his coffee. "It was the right decision, of course. I had no choice. But I sometimes wonder—might she have enjoyed a brief period of happiness before disillusionment set in? Still, I expect I'm merely indulging in sentimentality. The season seems to bring it out in me."

Emmeline's chest tightened with sympathy. "Does your sister blame you?"

"No," he said, shaking his head. "If anything, her reaction made it harder. She never uttered a word of reproach. Poor thing. I fear she saw the man for what he was in the end. Afterward, I tried to introduce her to young men of better character—those who could have appreciated her qualities. But she politely rebuffed their attentions."

Emmeline's indignation swelled. It infuriated a woman like Clara, who deserved admiration and love, should be confined by society's shallow judgments. It made her wonder, too, how much of her uncle's regret stemmed from his own unfulfilled hopes for his sister.

He took a reflective sip of coffee before brushing the mood away with a wave of his hand. "Enough of my musings. I didn't mean to darken the mood at this festive time. Let's talk about happier things. What are your plans for the day? Some ladies have retired to the morning room to work on needlepoint and, no doubt, indulge in a bit of gossip. You might enjoy their company?"

Emmeline barely suppressed a shudder. "I'm afraid I lack talent in either endeavor."

Sir Edmund chuckled. "Well then, the younger guests are organizing games in the nursery—Blindman's Buff, Queen and Archer, that sort of thing. Or if you'd prefer solitude, the library here is exceptional."

She hesitated before brightening. "Would you mind terribly if I rode instead?"

"Mind? Not in the least," he said with a hearty laugh. "I'll be delighted for you to freely make use of the stables. But I must say, I'm amazed at your energy. A walk and a ride in the same morning? Youth!"

After Emmeline had changed into her riding habit—a practical yet flattering ensemble of dark green wool that accentuated her figure while offering freedom of movement—she hesitated outside her room. Should she check on Lord Hawthorne? Her instincts screamed against it. He was arrogant, insufferable, and entirely too aware of his own charm.

But then her better nature whispered its rebuke. *Odious as he might be, the man is still human. And humans bleed.* What if his injuries were worse than he let on? What if she returned from her ride only to hear that the infamous marquess had succumbed to his wounds, all because she couldn't summon the courage—or the decency—to inquire after his wellbeing?

With a sigh, she resolved to check on him briefly. Very briefly. Just long enough to reassure herself he wasn't lying on his chamber floor, bleeding out. Surely no one could fault her for that.

Lord Hawthorne leaned against the window frame, the frosted panes offering no comfort against the persistent ache in his arm. He had peeled away his bloodied shirt earlier, noting with clinical detachment the angry red streaks spreading from the wound. Infection, likely. Perhaps worse.

His gaze drifted to the estate grounds, where a few early risers braved the cold for morning walks. He saw her immediately—Miss St. Clair, striding through the frost-dappled gardens with an energy that made his own weariness all the more pronounced. What an infuriating contradiction she was: all sharp wit and defiance one moment, then unexpected tenderness the next. Her presence lingered, unwanted but unshakable, like the persistent ache in his arm.

His lips twisted into a wry smile.

By the time Emmeline reached Lord Hawthorne's door, her resolve faltered. *What if he misinterprets my concerns?* She thought, her cheeks flushing at the memory of their kiss—the way his lips had moved over hers with maddening confidence. *No. Don't be ridiculous. This is about ensuring he's not dying, nothing more.*

Still, she hesitated, her hand hovering near the doorframe. *Knock or not?* The indecision irritated her. Emmeline St. Clair was not a woman prone to dithering. Yet here she was, wavering like a girl at her first ball.

Before she could summon the courage to knock, the door flew open, nearly colliding with her. She stumbled back, startled, and found herself face-to-face not with Lord Hawthorne but her cousin Gabriel, who glared at her as though she'd committed some grave offense.

"What are you doing here?" he demanded.

Emmeline lifted her chin. "I'm a guest here, in case you've forgotten."

"An uninvited guest," he snapped. "And how you could have the gall to come here under these circumstances is beyond me."

"For goodness' sake, Gabriel." She folded her arms, summoning her best imitation of their Aunt Lavinia's withering glare. "Must you harp on the same tiresome theme? I know you'd have preferred Rosalind, but there's no sense making a tragedy of it. We needn't even acknowledge each other's existence."

"I'm not talking about *you* and *me*," he growled. "I'm referring to your complete lack of consideration for others. Do you even comprehend the disaster you've brought upon this household?"

Emmeline blinked, genuinely puzzled. "A disaster? Oh, Gabriel, must you always be so dramatic?"

His scowl deepened. "Do you not realize the risk you've created by bringing *her* here?"

"Her?" Understanding dawned. "You mean Polly? Oh, really, Gabriel, you're overreacting. She's well away from the other guests, and most of the household staff has already had the measles. Surely you've had them as well?"

"That's beside the point!" he thundered, his jaw tightening.

Her lips twitched despite herself. "You haven't, have you?"

"I *have*," he snapped, though his voice carried a trace of defensiveness. "But I'd be far happier if it were me."

"Far happier than what?" Her gaze drifted to the slightly ajar door behind him, and realization struck. "Oh, no. Surely not."

"Yes, most likely," Gabriel said grimly, his expression sour. "And all thanks to you."

"The marquess?" she gasped, her hand flying to her mouth to stifle a laugh. "Lord Hawthorne has the measles?"

"He's certainly sickening for something," Gabriel said, his irritation mounting. "Do you have any idea what an *honor* it is to have him spend Christmas here at Hollybrook? Do you? He's one of the most sought-after guests in England, and thanks to *you*, he'll never darken our door again."

Emmeline's shoulders shook with suppressed mirth. The sheer absurdity of the situation overwhelming her. "The marquess," she choked, "with measles. All broken out in spots! Oh, Gabriel, what will that do to his reputation?"

"There's nothing funny about this!" Gabriel barked, but her laughter bubbled up, irrepressible now. *Lord Hawthorne. The arrogant, unflappable, impossibly vain marquess. Covered in spots.*

The situation might have been a calamity to Gabriel, but to Emmeline, it was a much-needed spark of hilarity in an otherwise complicated and confounding week. And though she tried valiantly to compose herself, the vision of Hawthorne's dismay was too much to bear.

Gabriel's glare intensified as he crossed his arms. "Do you even realize what you've done, Emmeline? Thanks to your thoughtless actions, this entire gathering is on the brink of disaster."

Emmeline blinked. "Disaster? Oh, really, Gabriel, you're overreacting."

"Overreacting?" His voice rose, his face turning red. "If word gets out that Hawthorne is unwell—or worse, that he's contracted something contagious—our guests will flee faster than rats from a sinking ship. The entire Christmas gathering, ruined. And all because you couldn't think beyond your own selfish whims."

Her jaw tightened, a hot flush creeping up her neck. "Selfish? Is that what you think?"

"It's not just what I think, Emmeline. It's the truth. Bringing Polly here was reckless enough, but now you've endangered everyone—"

"Polly is completely isolated," she interrupted, her voice sharpening. "No one is at risk, least of all your precious guests."

"Oh, don't be naïve," he snapped. "You might as well have invited the plague into the drawing room. And as for Hawthorne—"

"The plague? That's Absurd."

"Absurd?" His voice was a growl. "Do you think this is a joke? You may find it amusing now, but when guests begin leaving, let's see how funny you find it."

Her laughter faded as irritation flared. "Honestly, Gabriel, must you always turn every little thing into a catastrophe? Perhaps if you focused less on your imagined calamities and more on behaving like a civil host, you'd enjoy the gathering."

Gabriel's eyes narrowed, and his gaze dropped to where she stood. "Speaking of hosts," he said coldly, "why are you lurking outside Lord Hawthorne's door?"

She stiffened, caught off guard. "I—" she began, but her words faltered under the weight of his scrutiny.

His lips curled into a sneer. "Surely you aren't thinking of throwing yourself at him, Emmeline. Hoping to entrap a marquess into marriage, are you?"

The words struck like a slap, wiping the humor from her face. "How dare you?" she said, her voice low and trembling with fury.

Gabriel didn't relent. "It's exactly the sort of stunt you'd pull. And if you think for one moment that I'll stand by and let you—"

"That's enough." Her voice was sharp now, like the crack of a whip. "You can insult me all you like, Gabriel, but don't presume to know my intentions."

His sneer faltered for a moment, but his disapproval remained. "See that I don't have reason to doubt them," he said curtly, before pushing past her and disappearing down the hall.

Emmeline stood rooted to the spot, her chest heaving. The memory of Hawthorne's kiss flashed unbidden through her mind, and her cheeks burned anew. But more than anything, Gabriel's words left a bitter taste in her mouth.

But what if the guests start to talk about Hawthorne being ill...

What would Moorefield think?

Then even more indignation simmered and unease crept in. Gabriel's suspicion wasn't just insulting; it was dangerous. If he began spreading his assumptions, what then?

What would Hawthorne think?

Hawthorne?

Ugh, why should I care what Hawthorne thinks?

Chapter Nine

The crisp morning air stung Emmeline's cheeks as she urged her mare into a canter, a bright laugh escaping her lips. The image of a bespoted Lord Hawthorne kept flashing through her mind, each iteration more absurd than the last. Dignity, she mused, was the one thing the man seemed to prize above all else. The idea of him humbled by something as mundane as the measles was too delicious to resist.

The air hit her lungs like needles, invigorating in its sharpness, and the frost glistened like a million diamonds scattered across the fields. She could hardly wait for her first glimpse of the sea.

When she reached the cliffs, she reined in her horse, taking in the view. Below, the waves crashed against the shore with rhythmic ferocity, their foam glinting in the pale sunlight. The vast expanse of ocean stretched endlessly before her, its roar a soothing counterpoint to her racing thoughts. She gave her mare her head again, letting the animal's steady rhythm guide her as her mind wandered.

As Emmeline guided her mare toward the shoreline, the crisp winter air did little to clear the lingering fog in her thoughts. She had left Hawthorne's door without knocking, her fingers still poised mid-air when Gabriel's biting words had chased her away. Not that she was deterred by Gabriel's suspicions, she assured herself. Rather, it was the weight of propriety, of Moorefield's shadowy gaze, that stilled her hand. And if she were honest with herself, the memory of Hawthorne's smirk—arrogant, knowing—had lingered just long enough to make her second-guess her resolve. Let him nurse his wounds alone. She owed him nothing.

Or so she told herself.

But still the events of the past days refused to settle. A black and red curricle had been spotted at the site of Christopher Langford's daring escape. A black and red curricle had also come thundering down the Dover Road like a hellhound unleashed. And the man who held up the prisoner's coach had been shot. Lord Hawthorne's mysterious injury, his favoring of his left arm, fit the puzzle a little too neatly. The question loomed: What should she do about it?

Her smile faltered as she considered the marquess. The absurd thought of him enduring a child's malady like the measles resurfaced briefly, but it was quickly chased away by a more sobering notion: Hawthorne might be suffering from something far worse than a fever. A bullet wound, she was certain of it. And yet, she had done nothing but leave him to his own devices. Was that not as reprehensible as any crime he might have committed?

Her musings were interrupted by the sight of a man near a beached fishing boat. She almost galloped past him without a second glance, but felt compelled to look back. Recognition struck.

"Mr. Hollingsworth!" she called, reining in her horse and dismounting with practiced grace. "How nice to see you again."

He looked up from his work, his face lighting with a warm smile. "Miss St. Clair! I must say, I wasn't expecting such fine company this morning."

"I nearly didn't see you," she admitted, extending her hand.

His grip was firm, his calloused hand a contrast to the fine gloves she wore. "Well, I might have wondered if you were avoiding me," he teased.

"Of course not," she replied lightly. "I'm still very grateful for the ride you gave me."

To her surprise, she found herself genuinely glad to see him. So much had happened since their last meeting that he had entirely slipped her mind. Yet now, his easy manner was a welcome relief. He wasn't handsome in the conventional sense, but there was something about him—an air of quiet confidence, perhaps—that she found compelling.

"Is this your beach?" she asked, pushing the thought aside. "Am I trespassing?"

"Not at all," he said, glancing at her mare. "She's a beauty. Your uncle's, I presume?"

"Yes, part of his stable," Emmeline confirmed, brushing an affectionate hand over the horse's neck.

"Sir Edmund always did keep a fine stable," he remarked. "Are you enjoying your stay at Hollybrook Manor?"

"It's been... interesting."

He chuckled, recognizing her diplomatic choice of words. "I must confess, I've always found your cousin Gabriel tiresome. Though, to be fair, he was just a boy when I knew him. Has he improved with age?"

"Not noticeably," she said with a wry smile.

They both laughed, and he seemed emboldened by her candor. "And what of Miss Clara? Does she still live at the manor?"

"She does. She's marvelous—intelligent, capable, and kind. I like her immensely," Emmeline said earnestly.

She has not married then?" Hollingsworth's voice carried a note of hesitation that piqued Emmeline's curiosity.

"No," Emmeline replied. "Which does seem a pity. At least it's supposed to seem a pity, though just why that should be is beyond my understanding. No one ever seems to pity bachelors."

As she spoke, her thoughts drifted to her earlier conversation with Sir Edmund. Clara, with her quiet strength and keen mind, deserved so much more than society's narrow judgment. The idea of her being reduced to a cautionary tale rankled. Emmeline felt a growing indignation, not only at the man who'd tried to exploit Clara, but at the entire system that allowed wealth and appearances to outweigh character and kindness. If anything, Sir Edmund's interference had been a mercy, sparing Clara from heartbreak. Yet, a small part of Emmeline wondered if the price of that mercy—Clara's apparent retreat from the possibility of love—had been too high.

He chuckled. "True enough. But it is a shame. She'd be far better suited to managing her own household than her sister-in-law's."

Emmeline couldn't argue with that. "The bright side, of course, is that Aunt Arabella is rarely at Hollybrook Manor."

His laughter was quick and warm, but his next words carried a weight she hadn't anticipated. "I should tell you, Miss St. Clair, that you'd be wise to keep your distance from me."

"Whatever do you mean?" she asked, genuinely puzzled.

He hesitated, then sighed. "I suppose you've not yet heard the gossip. Or, more likely, you've heard it but haven't pieced it together.

I'm the black sheep of this neighborhood, Miss St. Clair. A former convict."

She blinked, momentarily at a loss. "Oh, well, I suppose that's... interesting?"

He laughed softly, seeming to pity her discomfort. "Not quite the scandal you were expecting, perhaps?"

"I can't say I've much experience with ex-convicts," she admitted. "But you seem perfectly respectable to me."

"Respectable or not, people around here have long memories," Hollingsworth said, his tone self-deprecating, yet edged with bitterness. "I was arrested for gambling debts, clapped into the Fleet, and branded a disgrace. I've served my time, bought back part of my estate with what little was left of an inheritance, and returned to what remains of my family's name. But forgiveness?" He shook his head with a wry smile. That's a luxury I don't expect—not here, anyway. Around these parts, a reputation once lost is gone forever."

He hesitated, his expression hardening for a fleeting moment. "And for some, it's not just the gambling. For some, it was personal—a betrayal that cut deeper than any scandal could. There's no repairing that kind of wound, Miss St. Clair, not even with time."

The gravity in his words left Emmeline momentarily speechless. Was this what Sir Edmund had alluded to earlier? A rift between Hollingsworth and the Hollybrooks? It seemed possible. Or perhaps this bitterness was directed at another, someone whose trust he had irrevocably shattered. She longed to ask, but sensed the question would be unwelcome.

"But still," she ventured, "gambling isn't murder. Surely they can look past it in time?"

He smiled, but it didn't reach his eyes. "It's not just the gambling. Let's leave it at that."

Her curiosity burned, but she respected his boundaries. Instead, they talked of lighter things—Christmas traditions, his plans to restore his family's dilapidated manor, and the strange rumors of ghosts haunting its halls. He had a knack for self-deprecating humor that kept her laughing, but when he boosted her back into the saddle, his parting words lingered.

"Give my regards to... no, never mind. That wouldn't be appropriate."

Emmeline rode off, her mind spinning. She was certain now: Hollingsworth was the man Sir Edmund had thwarted from eloping with Clara. And yet, something in his demeanor suggested he cared for Clara still. Her heart ached at the thought.

As she galloped back toward Hollybrook Manor, she couldn't help but reflect on her encounters. A marquess with secrets, a disgraced neighbor with a haunted past—Hollybrook was proving far more intriguing than any ballroom at Almack's.

As Emmeline rode along the shoreline, Hollingsworth's words echoed in her mind. *Respectable or not, people have long memories.* He had served his punishment, rebuilt what he could of his life, yet forgiveness remained out of reach. How much worse, then, for a man like Hawthorne? His crime—if she dared call it that—was one of action, of defiance against laws that might not serve justice. Hollingsworth had gambled away his inheritance and been branded a disgrace, but Hawthorne...

What had Hawthorne gambled? His reputation? His life? To rescue a man society deemed dangerous?

She thought of Rosalind, her quiet admiration for Langford. Had Hawthorne acted out of loyalty to a friend? Out of principle? Or was it something darker—what was worth risking his life?

Her hands tightened on the reins, her gaze fixed on the horizon. She had been so certain in her convictions only yesterday, but now... now she wasn't sure what justice even looked like. What right did she have to decide what another deserved? And yet, to stay silent felt equally damning.

Hollingsworth had spoken of freedom, his voice steady but lined with an edge of bitterness. "To me, freedom is the most beautiful word in the English language," he'd said, and she had nodded, agreeing in principle. But what did freedom mean to Hawthorne? And would she be the one to take it from him, just as society had stripped it from Hollingsworth?

She glanced down at her riding habit, its clean lines unmarred by the dust and salt of the shore. But beneath the fabric, her scraped palm throbbed faintly—a small, raw reminder of how easily wounds could fester.

She clucked at her mare, urging her into a faster trot. Whatever decision she made, it would have to wait until she spoke with Hawthorne. She needed answers before she could decide whether to condemn or forgive him—or herself.

The faint murmur of conversation filtered through the walls of Hawthorne's chamber, but he paid it no mind. He sat in the chair by the window, his left arm resting on a makeshift sling fashioned from one of his cravats. The wound throbbed dully, though it was nothing compared to the ache in his pride.

Emmeline St. Clair.

Her name surfaced unbidden, as it had with irritating frequency since their encounter at the tree. A vexing creature, to be sure—sharp-tongued and spirited, with a knack for inserting herself where she had no business being. And yet, there was something about her... something infuriatingly vivid. The memory of her fire-laden glare, the unguarded softness in her voice when she spoke to the kitten, even the sting of her barbed retorts—it all lingered like the aftermath of too much brandy. Unwanted, but impossible to ignore.

Hawthorne scowled, shifting in his seat. She had seen too much, of that he was certain. The girl had the tenacity of a bloodhound and the moral fortitude to match. It was a dangerous combination, one he would do well to avoid. Let her sniff about, if she must. He would not be the one to supply her answers.

His fingers flexed reflexively, and a sharp pain shot through his shoulder. He cursed under his breath, leaning back against the chair. It was a distraction, nothing more—a fleeting, irritating distraction. He had more pressing concerns. Langford was free, for now, but Moorefield's suspicions had only just begun to fester. And as for the incident on the Dover Road... well, even the best-planned rescues rarely went off without consequence. Hawthorne had made his choice—reckless though it might have been—and he would bear it, just as he always did.

But then there was *her*.

A soft curse escaped his lips as the memory of their kiss flickered to life, vivid and unbidden. He hadn't meant to kiss her. It had been impulsive, irrational, and entirely unwise. And yet, the feel of her lips against his, the startled gasp that had escaped her, the warmth of her pressed so tantalizingly close...

He clenched his jaw, cutting the thought short. Desire. That's all it was. Base, physical attraction—the sort that came easily and passed just as quickly. Emmeline St. Clair was nothing more than a slip of a girl with a sharp tongue and a sharper temper, hardly the sort to ensnare him. He had kissed dozens of women, many of them more practiced, more willing, more alluring. This was no different.

And yet, it was.

His hand tightened on the armrest as his mind betrayed him again, conjuring the way her cheeks had flushed, the flash of determination in her eyes as she faced him down, utterly fearless. No, not fearless—angry. Righteous. She had every intention of cutting him down to size, and for a moment, he'd wanted to let her try. What on earth had possessed him?

"Fool," he muttered, his voice low and hard. He'd been careless—letting the girl distract him, letting his own instincts take precedence over reason. He could not afford such indulgences, not now, not ever. He was who he was, and Emmeline St. Clair was precisely the sort of woman who would demand more than he could—or would—give.

It was best, then, to forget the matter entirely. The kiss had been a lapse, a mistake born of proximity and circumstance. Nothing more.

And yet, as he stared out at the frost-dappled landscape beyond the window, the ghost of her touch lingered—a maddening, inescapable reminder of just how quickly one slip could unravel everything.

Chapter Ten

Emmeline entered the manor through the side entrance, her mind swirling with unanswered questions about her ride along the beach. She intended to head straight to her room, but the weight of her thoughts made the idea of solitude unbearable. Instead, she turned toward the library. Perhaps losing herself in a novel would provide some distraction.

Her hope for quiet was immediately dashed.

"Oh, Miss St. Clair," called Mr. Moorefield, rising from a chair near the library table as she stepped inside. A newspaper was neatly folded beside him, though his attention was entirely fixed on her. "You're just the person I hoped to see. You've been riding, I presume?"

"Yes, Mr. Moorefield," she replied with forced politeness, smoothing her habit. Her first impulse was to be irritated by his obvious observation, but she pushed the thought aside. It wasn't Moorefield's fault that her nerves were raw. His earnestness, while grating at times, deserved a fair hearing.

"May I have a word with you?" he asked, gesturing toward the seat across from him.

Her instincts told her to decline, but curiosity won out. She moved to the chair and sat gracefully, folding her hands in her lap. "Of course."

Moorefield remained standing a moment longer, as if gathering his courage, then lowered himself into his chair. His face was slightly flushed, and his gaze didn't quite meet hers. "You will perhaps think me presumptuous, Miss St. Clair, but I feel I must speak to you on a matter of some importance. Your uncle has been extraordinarily generous to me, and I feel an obligation to act in his best interest."

Emmeline tilted her head, her curiosity piqued. "And what matter might that be, Mr. Moorefield?"

He cleared his throat, visibly uncomfortable. "This is not an easy subject to broach. I debated whether to speak to Sir Edmund himself, but as his secretary, I am privy to the many burdens already weighing on him. I thought it best to address the matter directly with you.

Her lips twitched into a faint smile. "I see. And what matter is so delicate that it cannot wait?"

Moorefield shifted in his seat. "It concerns Lord Hawthorne."

Her composure faltered for the briefest of moments, but she quickly masked it with a look of polite curiosity. "Lord Hawthorne?"

"Yes." His tone grew more serious. "You may not be aware of it, Miss St. Clair, but his lordship's reputation leaves much to be desired. In fact, when it comes to the fairer sex, the man is a notorious rakehell."

Emmeline arched a brow. "I must say, Mr. Moorefield, this revelation does not come as a shock."

He frowned, clearly nettled by her lack of alarm. "You don't seem particularly concerned."

"Why should I be?" she replied coolly. "I am not in the least bit inclined toward reforming Lord Hawthorne or any other gentleman of his ilk."

"Then what," he pressed, his eyes narrowing, "am I to make of your behavior? I observed you in his company this morning."

Her stomach clenched, but she kept her expression neutral. "And?"

"I saw you kiss him," Moorefield said bluntly, though his cheeks darkened with embarrassment. "And after that, you walked back to the house together in what could only be described as an intimate embrace."

Emmeline straightened her posture. "Since you were spying on us so closely, I presume you also saw me fall on top of him. That kiss was not sought out by me, I assure you. And as for the walk, Lord Hawthorne claimed to be injured. I was merely assisting him."

"Injured?" Moorefield leaned forward. "Did he describe the nature of this injury?"

"He implied I'd cracked one of his ribs," she said lightly. "He seemed in genuine pain, though I suppose it's possible he exaggerated."

Moorefield's gaze grew more intent. "You believe he might have been lying?"

"I'm saying it's possible. Though, as my cousin later suggested, it may have been something entirely different. Gabriel thinks Lord Hawthorne is coming down with the measles."

"The measles?" Moorefield was incredulous, though a laugh escaped him. "I admit, that is a far cry from what I suspected."

"And what did you suspect, Mr. Moorefield?"

He hesitated, then admitted, "I thought he'd been shot."

"Shot?" Emmeline feigned surprise. "Why on earth would you think that?"

"Because of his timing, his behavior, and certain other... circumstantial details," Moorefield said. "At first, I believed he might have been the one to rescue Christopher Langford. After all, Hawthorne is known for his reckless exploits."

"And now?"

"Now I'm less certain," he admitted, though his suspicion seemed to linger. "Lady Hollybrook assured me he arrived far too early to have been involved."

Emmeline blinked. *Far too early?* That conflicted with what her aunt had implied earlier. "Surely his invitation was extended weeks ago?" she asked cautiously.

Moorefield shook his head. "No, Miss St. Clair. That's the most curious part of all. Lord Hawthorne sought out the invitation himself."

Emmeline's heart skipped a beat. "He sought it out?"

"Yes. He pressed the connection to Gabriel, though the two are barely acquaintances, let alone close relations." His expression hardened. "I believe his arrival here is strategic. Hollybrook Manor is conveniently located near the site of the prison coach incident. If Hawthorne is not directly involved, then at the very least, he is here to facilitate Langford's escape."

She fought to maintain her composure as the weight of his words settled over her. The revelation sent her thoughts spiraling. Hawthorne had sought the invitation. He had a purpose for being here—one that had nothing to do with family obligations or seasonal festivities.

"And yet my aunt and uncle seem to think highly of him," Emmeline ventured cautiously.

Moorefield's expression darkened. "I believe your aunt and uncle were simply flattered by his attention. And, Miss St. Clair, they are most eager that you and I become better acquainted."

Emmeline blinked, taken aback. "Surely you mean my sister," she corrected. "I believe their intention was for you to meet Rosalind."

His lips curled into a faint smile. "Then I am fortunate indeed that you came instead."

Her cheeks burned at the unexpected remark, and she quickly averted her gaze. Was this a genuine compliment, or was he merely attempting to distract her? Either way, it left her unsettled. If Moorefield was watching Hawthorne, did that mean he would also be watching her? And what of her aunt and uncle's supposed oblivion? Were they complicit in some larger scheme, or were they as ignorant as they appeared?

"You think he lent his curricle," she said aloud, more to herself than to Moorefield.

"It's possible," Moorefield replied. "His is the fastest vehicle for miles, and it would match the description given by the guards."

"And yet, as you've just said, his arrival timing makes it impossible for him to have been at the rescue."

"True, but I still believe he's involved. If not as the principal actor, then as part of a larger plot. Hawthorne is not a man to act alone."

Emmeline rose abruptly, feeling as though the walls of the library were closing in around her. "Thank you for your insight, Mr. Moorefield. I'll take it under advisement."

"Miss St. Clair," he said, rising as well, his gaze softening. "I know this is not easy to hear. But I value your good opinion and felt it necessary to warn you."

"I appreciate your concern," she said briskly, offering a curt nod before turning to leave. Her thoughts churned with unease as she ascended the stairs to her room. Hawthorne's presence at Hollybrook Manor was no coincidence—and now, she had to decide what to do with that knowledge.

As she ascended the stairs, Emmeline's steps quickened, the earlier thought of fetching a novel forgotten entirely. She clutched the banister, her mind racing. *Why did I lie to him?* The question gnawed at her, sharp and insistent. She had been so certain she needed more answers, more clarity, before she could make any decision about Hawthorne. Yet, without hesitation, she had fabricated a tale about cracked ribs to shield him from Moorefield's suspicion.

The realization sent a fresh wave of unease coursing through her. *What am I doing?* She wondered, but even as the thought crossed her mind, her feet carried her toward Hawthorne's room. She needed to warn him about Moorefield's suspicions, about the revelation that his invitation to Hollybrook Manor had not been entirely innocent.

It was madness; she knew. Protecting Hawthorne was a dangerous instinct, one that could easily implicate her in whatever scheme he might be planning. And yet... *I need answers;* she reminded herself. But the truth that lingered, unspoken and undeniable, was that she wasn't entirely sure she wanted to see him condemned.

Chapter Eleven

Emmeline reached the landing outside Lord Hawthorne's bedchamber, her heart pounding as she glanced over her shoulder. She had taken care to ensure Mr. Moorefield hadn't followed her, even so, the unease lingered.

What am I doing here?

She questioned for the hundredth time, her hand poised just inches from the door. She couldn't shake the feeling that this was reckless, that seeking him out—again—was courting disaster. And yet, Moorefield's suspicions, his thinly veiled warnings, and the revelation about Hawthorne's invitation left her no choice.

She took a deep breath, raised her hand to knock—and stopped short as the door opened abruptly. Lord Hawthorne stepped out, his dark eyes widening briefly in surprise before narrowing in scrutiny. He was dressed in a riding coat and top boots, though the effort of dressing had clearly taken its toll. His complexion was pale, his jaw tense, and his usual air of infuriating confidence was dimmed by an unmistakable weariness.

"Good God," Emmeline said before she could stop herself. "You look ghastly."

"Thank you very much, Miss St. Clair, for those words of encouragement," Hawthorne glowered as they walked toward the stairs, his steps more unsteady with each passing moment.

Emmeline cast a wary glance at a nearby maid, who was watching them with undisguised curiosity as she dusted. Dropping her voice, she muttered, "Get back in bed, you idiot, before you drop."

"Mind your own business, Miss St. Clair," he retorted sharply. But even as he spoke, his pallor deepened alarmingly, and his hand shot out to the wall for support. "The whole place is spinning like a damned top."

The maid hesitated before reluctantly answering the bell's summons, leaving Emmeline to sigh in resignation. She shifted to let his arm rest heavily across her shoulders, the weight of him sending a jolt through her knees. "This is fast becoming a habit. Lean on me—unless you'd prefer I call someone else to drag you back to bed. And for the record, I'm not eager to be seen supporting you again."

With herculean effort, she managed to steer him back into his chamber. He collapsed onto the canopied bed with a groan, looking so pale and vulnerable that her earlier irritation was immediately tempered by a pang of concern.

"Where's your man?" she asked, her gaze darting to the beads of perspiration glistening on his brow. His eyes fluttered closed, but his breathing remained shallow and uneven.

"Gone back to London," he murmured hoarsely.

"You mean he's left you?"

"He got word that his father's seriously ill."

"Damnation," she muttered, crossing her arms and fixing him with a sharp look. "More likely, he didn't want to stick around for whatever trouble you've landed yourself in. And I can't say I blame him. Now, let's get this coat off."

Hawthorne's soft leather gloves came first, her hands brushing against his feverish skin. "Good heavens, you're burning up," she said, alarm coloring her voice. "Let's get a proper look at that wound of yours."

His hand weakly brushed hers away as she reached for the silver buttons of his riding coat. "See here, Miss St. Clair," he growled, "you're taking entirely too much upon yourself. I think perhaps you've exaggerated the importance of that kiss I gave you. Believe me, you shouldn't—"

She halted just long enough to deliver a withering glare, though it was wasted, as his eyes were firmly shut. "Lord Hawthorne, if you're under the impression that I've been swooning over that over-practiced kiss, you are sadly mistaken. To be honest, I found the incident rather... underwhelming."

His dark lashes fluttered open, and his lips curved into the faintest smirk. "Underwhelming, was it?"

"Yes," she snapped, the word laced with enough venom to scorch. "And let me make something perfectly clear: I'm no more interested in becoming entangled in your affairs than your valet was. But since you've left me no choice in the matter, try to sit up so I can get this confounded coat off."

His attempt to comply was pitiful, leaving him slumping forward and muttering through gritted teeth, "Gad, you're cow-handed."

"Don't blame me. Blame your tailor," she shot back, maneuvering his coat free with difficulty.

"That sap-skull is an artist," he rasped. "Probably the finest tailor in the world."

"Well, I doubt he envisioned his masterpiece being worn over a gunshot wound," she said, unbuttoning his fine cambric shirt with brisk efficiency.

"You know, you seem to lack any sense of modesty," he drawled, his voice weak but teasing.

Emmeline's hands faltered as her gaze unintentionally lingered on the expanse of his chest, a disconcerting blend of bronzed skin and dark, surprisingly thick hair. For someone who spent his days gambling and carousing, he was far more muscular than she'd imagined. But the momentary distraction evaporated when she saw the angry red streaks radiating from the bandaged wound. Her stomach turned.

"Oh, heavens," she whispered. "I think you have blood poisoning."

"Watch it—ouch!" he protested as she tore the soiled bandage free, revealing a gory mess of blood and pus. The sight made her turn an alarming shade of green, and she sat heavily on the edge of the bed.

"Well, that settles it," she declared shakily. "You need a doctor."

"No," he said weakly, catching her wrist with what little strength he had. His touch was light as a feather, which somehow unnerved her more. "It's not just my own hide I'm worried about. There's Chris to consider. He's depending on me."

Chris. *Christopher Langford.* Her heart gave an unexpected lurch at the familiarity in his voice. So Langford wasn't merely a name to Hawthorne—he was a friend. A friend worth risking his life for.

"Well, you'll be no help to him dead, now will you?" she retorted, rising to her feet. "I'm fetching Dr. Wickham."

"No, dammit," he rasped.

"Yes, dammit," she countered. "You can ask him to keep quiet, but I won't stand by while you waste away from infection."

"Dr. Wickham's loyalty to your uncle won't extend to covering up a crime," he argued. "You're clever, Miss St. Clair. Use your head."

Her fists clenched at her sides. "Fine. But if you're not better in a few hours, I'm sending for him."

"That's all I ask," he murmured, his eyes closing again. "And... thank you. I'm in your debt."

"No, you're not," she said brusquely, the tightness in her chest making it hard to maintain her usual biting tone. "I'm not doing this for you."

As she moved toward the door, she paused and glanced back at him, a storm of conflicting emotions swirling within her. "By the way, everyone thinks you're coming down with the measles."

His eyes flew open, incredulous. "Measles? My God, how lowering. Whatever gave them that mutton-headed notion?"

"Never mind," she said, unable to suppress a faint smile. "If you've any sense, you'll let them believe it." Then her resolve faulted, just a bit, her mind drifting to Moorefield's words. *Hawthorne pressed for the invitation himself... Hollybrook Manor is conveniently close to the prison coach incident... He's here for a reason.*

She glanced at his pale face, his eyes shut against the pain. How could she bring up Moorefield's suspicions now, when he looked as though a stiff breeze might carry him off?

Now rest. I'll be back to check if you're still alive."

Emmeline peered cautiously into the hallway, her heart drumming as she checked for onlookers. Satisfied that the coast was clear, she scurried to her bedchamber. Once inside, she paced the room, her thoughts spinning in an unrelenting storm of doubt and resolve. Her conscience warred with her reason, but despite its best efforts, she had made up her mind.

She needed help—but discreetly.

It took some time to locate Miss Clara Hollybrook. Emmeline finally found her in the kitchen, deeply engrossed in conversation with the cook over the day's menus. Clara's calm authority radiated as she offered suggestions and jotted notes in her ever-present ledger. Emmeline hesitated in the doorway before summoning her courage.

"Miss Clara," she whispered, stepping forward. "Might I borrow you for a moment?"

Clara turned, her eyes soft with curiosity. "Of course, my dear. Is something troubling you?"

"Yes, well..." Emmeline leaned in closer, lowering her voice. "I was wondering if you might know of a remedy... something to draw out poison, perhaps?"

Clara studied her for a long moment, her expression flickering between concern and suspicion. "Poison?" she echoed. "Are you feeling unwell, Emmeline?"

"Oh no, not unwell exactly," Emmeline stammered. "But I—well—I fear I've developed an awful boil."

"A boil," Clara repeated, the corner of her mouth twitching as though she were suppressing a smile. "How unfortunate. But yes, I believe I have just the thing."

Clara led her through a side door and down a narrow staircase into the cool, musty depths of the manor's cellar. Emmeline was taken aback by the sight that greeted her. Shelves lined every wall, filled with neatly labeled jars, tinctures, and dried herbs. It was like stepping into an apothecary's shop.

"Why, this is remarkable," Emmeline murmured, her gaze roving over the collection. "Dr. Wickham wasn't exaggerating when he said you rivaled his stores."

Clara chuckled, brushing off the compliment. "Oh, Dr. Wickham likes to exaggerate. Medicine is simply a personal interest of mine. My mother taught me to make remedies when we were still reliant on home treatments."

She began scanning the shelves with practiced ease, eventually plucking a small jar from among the rows. "Comfrey salve," she announced. "This should prove quite efficacious for... your boil."

"Thank you," Emmeline said, clutching the jar with feigned relief. She turned to go, eager to escape before Clara's astute eyes pried too deeply into her motives.

"Oh, just a moment," Clara called, reaching for another bottle. She blew the dust off its glass surface and handed it over. "Here, take this as well. It's laudanum. If your boil grows unbearably painful, this should help you sleep and allow Nature, the real healer, to work her magic."

Emmeline accepted the bottle with a gracious smile, though inwardly she felt a pang of guilt at her deception. As they ascended the stairs, she chattered incessantly about trivialities, hoping to divert Clara from asking any probing questions. Despite her efforts, she couldn't shake the feeling that Clara suspected something amiss.

When she finally paused for breath, Clara seized the opportunity to speak. "I stopped by to check on Polly earlier," she said gently. "You'll be pleased to know she's progressing nicely."

A wave of shame washed over Emmeline. She hadn't visited Polly since their arrival at Hollybrook Manor, and Clara's kindness only heightened her neglect. "Thank you," she said earnestly. "I'll make sure to visit her as soon as I can."

Clara smiled and returned to the kitchen, leaving Emmeline free to make her escape. She hurried upstairs, her heart thudding in her chest. Pausing at the door to Lord Hawthorne's chamber, she cast a quick glance over her shoulder. Satisfied she was alone, she slipped inside, shutting the door softly behind her.

"What the devil!" His lordship's eyes flew open, his voice a hoarse rasp. He groaned, sinking back against the pillows. "Oh, it's you again."

"So much for a mission of mercy," Emmeline snapped, setting the jar and bottle she carried on the bedside table.

"Well, how the deuce am I supposed to recover if you keep popping in uninvited? You promised to give me time, remember?"

"Oh, do be quiet. Believe me, this is the last place I'd choose to be if I were rational. But I can't just let you die of blood poisoning without lifting a finger, now can I?"

"Ah, well. I am touched, Miss St. Clair."

"You needn't be. I'd do the same for a spaniel."

"Damn it, woman!" he swore, hissing as she began unwrapping the old bandage without preamble.

"Do be still," she admonished sharply. "Someone might hear you. Besides, it can't be *that* bad."

"Easy enough for you to say!" he bit out, his knuckles whitening as she peeled away the last of the dressing. "Good God!" He flinched as she applied the cool salve to the inflamed skin. "I really do rue the day I splattered you with mud. The Inquisition could have used your talents."

"Don't be such a baby," she retorted, dipping her fingers back into the jar. Yet her movements softened as she spread the salve over the wound, her lips pressing into a thin line. "If Miss Clara swears by this, it must be effective."

"Miss Clara?" His eyes narrowed. "You told Clara Hollybrook about me? Damn it all, I should have known no woman could keep a secret."

"I don't recall promising you anything of the kind. And no, I didn't tell Clara about *you*. She thinks the salve's for me."

His brow furrowed. "Oh? And what ailment did you invent to justify your theft of her apothecary stores?"

"Boils," she replied primly.

A MARQUESS FOR CHRISTMAS 113

"Boils, Miss St. Clair?" he murmured, a faint chuckle escaping despite his discomfort. "Of all the maladies you might have chosen, you've saddled me with boils and measles. Really, your imagination deserves applause."

"I fail to see any humor in the situation," she said coldly, though the corners of her mouth twitched despite herself. She poured a measure of laudanum into the glass by his bedside and thrust it toward him. "Drink this."

"What is it?"

"Laudanum. To help you sleep."

He downed it in one swallow, grimacing as he set the glass aside. "Are you sure you're finished?" he drawled sweetly as she capped the jar. "You could always bleed me, you know."

"Don't tempt me, Lord Hawthorne," she shot back, rising from her seat.

"Good day, Miss St. Clair," he murmured, his voice already thick with drowsiness.

She hesitated at the door, watching him for a moment longer than was strictly necessary. As the lines of tension eased from his face, a faint pang of something unfamiliar stirred in her chest. Compassion, surely—that was all.

Chapter Twelve

"We must send for Dr. Wickham immediately."

Though she had often read of it, Emmeline had never actually seen anyone wring their hands until her aunt did so. The dramatic gesture, combined with the tremor in her voice, spoke volumes about Lady Hollybrook's agitation. She seemed wholly unconcerned with the presence of her niece as she swept into the great hall, Gabriel close on her heels. Her sudden arrival interrupted the anecdote Sir Edmund had been relating to his sister and Emmeline, drawing the attention of every guest gathered before dinner.

The disagreement was apparent even before Lady Hollybrook began her tirade. "Edmund, you must make him see reason," she declared, clutching at her ostrich-feathered fan as if to emphasize her distress. "Lord Hawthorne's severe case of the measles demands immediate medical attention."

Gabriel, already bristling, interrupted before his father could respond. "Papa, you must not. Hawthorne made me swear not to call in a quack. He loathes them. Said so himself."

"I should hardly term Dr. Wickham a quack," Sir Edmund replied mildly, swirling the brandy in his glass.

"No, indeed," Lady Hollybrook agreed, nodding vehemently. "If anything, Dr. Wickham is as competent as any London physician. Better, in fact. His treatment for my staggers was far more effective than Dr. Philpott's syrup ever was."

Gabriel visibly fought the urge to roll his eyes. "Mama, that's not the point. I've told you a hundred times—Hawthorne made me give my word. No doctors. That's final."

"But what if he dies here?" Lady Hollybrook clutched her chest dramatically, her voice rising enough to draw curious glances from the guests. "What would everyone say? What would *become* of us?"

"Come now, my dear," Sir Edmund soothed, ever the diplomat. "Surely the likelihood of such a fate befalling a young man in the pink of health is exceedingly slim."

"But it *does* happen! And if it *should* happen while Lord Hawthorne is under my roof, I would be ruined! Absolutely ruined! Society would cut me dead!" She turned to Gabriel, her voice taking on a pleading note. "And you too, Gabriel. Do you not see?"

Gabriel crossed his arms, his expression as unyielding as granite. "I'll be cut either way, Mama. Hawthorne swears that if I so much as call for a doctor, he'll disown me."

"Oh, my heavens!" Lady Hollybrook gasped, clutching her fan so tightly Emmeline feared it might snap. The ostrich feathers atop her brassy coiffure quivered violently with her distress. Emmeline exchanged a quick glance with Clara, both women struggling to suppress their mirth.

"How could his lordship say such a thing?" Lady Hollybrook wailed, her eyes brimming with unshed tears. "Does he not consider

Gabriel's feelings? Not to mention mine! Oh, Edmund, what shall we do?"

"For the moment, my dear," Sir Edmund said, gesturing toward the dining room where Riggs stood waiting, "we shall go into dinner. We can address this crisis afterward."

"But—" Lady Hollybrook began, only to falter as Sir Edmund raised a placating hand.

"To set your mind at ease," he continued, "Clara can look in on Lord Hawthorne directly after dinner. You don't mind, do you, Clara?"

The question had clearly been rhetorical, for Sir Edmund didn't pause for an answer. Instead, he turned to his wife with a calming smile as he offered her his arm. "You know how greatly Dr. Wickham respects Clara's nursing skills. She'll be able to determine what's best. And if, in her opinion, his lordship requires a physician's care, then we'll have no choice but to override his wishes. In the meantime, however—" He cast a meaningful glance toward Riggs, who hovered by the dining room entrance, clearly anxious. "Let's not allow the soup to cool."

Dinner was a formal affair, complete with three removes that Emmeline barely registered. The conversation around her ebbed and flowed, punctuated by polite laughter and the clink of silverware against porcelain. She nodded when expected and murmured the appropriate responses, but her thoughts were elsewhere—specifically, upstairs in Lord Hawthorne's chamber. She had agreed to Clara's involvement, but what if Clara's nursing led to more questions?

When the ladies retired to the drawing room, Emmeline's nerves reached a breaking point. She excused herself under the pretense of needing air, but only managed to make it halfway to the corridor leading to Hawthorne's room before turning back. Clara would see to him. She had no reason to interfere further—or so she told herself.

Clara reappeared just as the gentlemen began rejoining the ladies. Emmeline, seated beside a chatty elderly widow on the sofa, entirely lost track of the anecdote being shared. Her gaze remained fixed on her aunt, uncle, and cousin, who had formed a tight circle around Clara at the far end of the room. *What are they saying?* She wondered, her frustration mounting. Clara's expression remained composed, unreadable as ever, but the relief that softened her aunt Arabella's face was unmistakable.

"I don't think you've heard a single word I've said," the widow remarked crossly, drawing Emmeline's attention back with a sharp nudge.

"Oh, indeed I have," Emmeline replied hastily, though she wasn't entirely sure she had. "You were describing your youngest child's horrendous case of the measles. It must have been dreadful."

"*Next-to-youngest,*" the widow corrected with great severity. "The baby, of course, caught it as well." And with that, she launched into an excruciatingly detailed account of spots, fevers, and remedies, her voice rising theatrically to emphasize the direst moments.

As the widow droned on about spots and remedies, Emmeline struggled to keep her expression composed. Her mind, however, betrayed her. The dull rise and fall of the woman's voice seemed to blend with another—deeper, richer, with that maddeningly sardonic edge. Hawthorne's voice. She could almost hear him now, laughing softly at some private jest, the sound low and warm enough to send an unwelcome shiver down her spine.

Her gloved hand tightened against the armrest, her thoughts spiraling further against her will. The feel of his fevered skin—so shockingly firm despite his condition—lingered in her memory. She had only meant to help him out of his coat, but her fingers had brushed against the hard planes of his chest, and the memory burned far longer than she cared to admit.

By the time the widow began listing the poultices she'd used, Emmeline was hardly listening. Her gaze fixed on the flames in the hearth, she inwardly cursed her own treacherous mind. What business had she remembering such things? And why, oh why, did the mere thought of him leave her palms feeling absurdly warm?

Emmeline's grip on her teacup tightened as she fought the urge to scream. Was this to be her evening? Trapped listening to tales of childhood illnesses while her aunt, cousin, and uncle discussed the very thing she most needed to know?

A general restlessness began to affect the company, particularly among the younger ladies. Suggestions for dancing were met with murmurs of disinterest, and a few of the elder guests drifted toward the card tables. Emmeline, thankful she wasn't needed to balance the numbers, allowed herself a brief sigh of relief. It was short-lived, however, for no sooner had she settled back than Mr. Moorefield appeared at her elbow, hovering like a particularly persistent gnat.

"Miss St. Clair," he began. "I do hope you aren't feeling unwell. You seemed rather preoccupied earlier."

Emmeline mustered a tight smile, privately lamenting her inability to escape him. "Not at all, Mr. Moorefield. I assure you, I am perfectly well."

"Excellent." His smile widened, and he seated himself uninvited. "I thought I might keep you company. It's always a pleasure to converse with someone of your intelligence."

The compliment, while likely sincere, only made his presence more unbearable. Emmeline nodded politely, all the while searching for some excuse—any excuse—to extricate herself. Yet Moorefield remained steadfast, deftly cutting off her attempts to drift toward Clara, who had returned to the sofa nearest Sir Edmund.

Lady Hollybrook, sensing the lull in energy among her guests, clapped her hands together with forced cheer. "Perhaps we might enjoy some music! Surely among us there must be a few talented musicians willing to entertain?"

Reluctant daughters, no doubt volunteered by ambitious mothers, rose one by one to perform. Piece after piece filled the room, ranging from trembling pianoforte renditions to overly earnest vocal performances. The evening stretched interminably until Emmeline began to think her sanity migabouttht give way entirely. When the tea tray finally appeared—mercifully early—it was as though the entire company exhaled at once.

It was going to be a long night. Emmeline sighed as she dismissed the maid who had helped her prepare for bed. She couldn't possibly wait until morning to discover Lord Hawthorne's condition. Then again, wasn't this hypocrisy at its finest? She wasn't truly concerned for his health. No, what gnawed at her was her own involvement in his situation. If it came to light that she had aided a lawbreaker, what would the consequences be? The scandal alone could topple Hollybrook Manor—and perhaps her family along with it.

Just as she was about to reluctantly climb into bed, a soft knock at the door startled her.

"May I come in?" Clara's voice preceded her entrance.

"Oh, yes, of course," Emmeline said, inwardly grateful for the distraction.

Clara entered, closing the door behind her, and motioned toward the fire. "I thought I'd better check on all my patients." She smiled as they settled into two wingback chairs, pulling them closer to the warmth of the blaze. Her gaze settled on Emmeline with a knowing glint. "Your boils—how are they?"

Emmeline flushed. "Oh, that... Can you believe I'd nearly forgotten them?"

"Oh, I can absolutely believe it," Clara replied.

"Your salve is miraculous," Emmeline babbled. "The moment I applied it, I felt instant relief. It's almost unbelievable, but my boil—there was only one, you see," she added hastily, "has completely disappeared."

"How extraordinary," Clara said, her lips twitching. "I can't say the comfrey's effect on Lord Hawthorne has been quite so dramatic, but you'll be pleased to hear his wound appears to be healing nicely. I take it there was real cause for concern?"

"Oh, dear." Emmeline sank back in her chair, her hands fluttering in her lap. "You know, then."

Clara tilted her head slightly. "Let's just say I suspected. Your story about needing the salve for yourself didn't quite ring true, though your agitation certainly did. And, of course, I saw you helping his lordship into the house earlier. Had his wound become putrefied?"

"Oh, yes. It looked dreadful." Emmeline shuddered at the memory. "But he made me promise not to tell anyone, so I felt I had to do something myself."

Clara nodded, her expression calm and measured. "I see. Well, let me congratulate you. You may soon eclipse my own reputation as a healer. I thought your bandaging was quite skillfully done—though it's a pity about his lordship's neckcloth."

Emmeline huffed. "Not in the least. The conceited dandy must have two dozen of the things, all starched to perfection. They were devilishly difficult to tie, but they held the dressing in place. I used a strip from his shirt for the rest," she added, folding her arms. "It was quite soft, actually."

Clara laughed softly. "So I noticed. His lordship does dress exceptionally well, doesn't he? Poor Gabriel is positively green with envy. I do hope he never learns you ripped up one of those fine cambric shirts. That might be the most expensive wound dressing in history."

"Oh, as to that," Emmeline replied with a sharp tilt of her chin, "I wasn't the one who destroyed the shirt. Lord Hawthorne had already ripped it up to bandage himself—not that I'd have minded in the least."

"You really don't approve of him, do you?" Clara asked, her amusement lingering.

"I don't approve of his *type*," Emmeline corrected firmly. "Men who care for nothing beyond their tailoring, their horses, and their clubs. Fobs, quizzing glasses, gaming, boxing, racing—it's all so *frivolous*." She waved a hand, as if dismissing an entire class of men. "They're parasites, the lot of them."

"Goodness," Clara chuckled. "I do think you've just described your cousin, Gabriel."

Emmeline let out a short laugh. "No, Gabriel is worse. At least Lord Hawthorne is an original. Gabriel is nothing more than a toadeater."

Clara shook her head, still smiling. "Tell me, Emmeline—may I call you that?"

"Oh, yes, please do."

"And you must call me Clara. But what I'm curious about is this: Given your strong dislike of his lordship—or his type, at any rate—what compelled you to help him?"

"To tell the truth," Emmeline began, staring into the fire as if it held the answers she couldn't seem to find within herself, "I hardly thought about it. I just…did what seemed necessary."

Clara tilted her head, studying her. "Most people would have fetched a doctor. Or, at the very least, laid the matter at my brother's feet."

"And ensured his arrest?" Emmeline turned sharply toward her friend, her voice rising. She caught herself and softened her tone, though her hands tightened in her lap. "I couldn't do that. Even though I don't...particularly approve of him, I couldn't—" She broke off, shaking her head. "I just couldn't."

Clara didn't respond, and Emmeline felt her throat tighten under the weight of her words. She pressed on before Clara could probe further. "But honestly, it wasn't about him. It was for Rosalind. If he were arrested, then Christopher Langford would surely be discovered. That would be...disastrous."

Clara's silence lingered for a moment longer before she finally spoke. "You've realized, of course, that Lord Hawthorne rescued Mr. Langford?"

"I..." Emmeline faltered, torn between what she had said aloud and what she knew to be true. Her fingers twisted in the folds of her dressing gown. "Yes, I suppose I have. Though he hasn't exactly admitted it outright."

"No?" Clara asked.

Emmeline blinked, the memory rising unbidden—the raw tension in his voice when he'd said, *There's Chris to consider. He's depending on me.* An admission, plain as day, and yet she hadn't pressed him on it. She had been too focused on his fevered state, on the sheer closeness of him as she helped him out of that confounded coat.

Her breath hitched at the memory—the feel of his hard chest beneath her hands, the way the muscles shifted under his fevered skin, the heat of his lips when he'd kissed her. She knew the kiss was meaningless, a rouse, only to feel that treacherous, lingering warmth whenever she thought of it. As she did now.

"Perhaps he has," she murmured, more to herself than to Clara.

Clara didn't press her, but gave a small nod of understanding. "And you wonder why," she said softly. "Why he'd take such a risk."

Emmeline's eyes widened slightly. "Yes," she admitted, her voice dropping to a whisper. "Why would he? He and Mr. Langford aren't particularly close—at least, that's what he claimed. Yet he called him...Chris." The name felt intimate on her tongue, even now. "That doesn't sound like the distant acquaintance he made him out to be."

"No, it doesn't," Clara agreed, her voice calm. "But then, men are often less forthcoming than women about their affections. Perhaps their bond runs deeper than he let on."

Emmeline nodded absently, her mind churning. If Hawthorne and Langford truly were close friends, then his criminal act—well, it could be defined as heroic, could it not? Admirable, at the least. *Emmy, what in the damnation is wrong with you? The man is a criminal! A rakehell! And yet...*

Clara broke the silence. "You've surprised me, Emmeline."

"Surprised you?" Emmeline turned to her, startled.

"Yes," Clara said with a small smile. "You're hardly seem the type to involve yourself in such a risky affair. Especially for a man you claim not to like."

"I *don't* like him," Emmeline said quickly, too quickly. "He's everything I dislike in a man. Vain. Reckless. Arrogant. Useless to society. I would never..." Her voice trailed off as Clara's smile deepened.

"Never fall for him?" Clara finished for her, one brow arching knowingly.

"Exactly," Emmeline said, her cheeks flaming. "There's no need for a warning. I'm quite immune."

Clara chuckled softly. "You're many things, my dear, but immune is not one of them."

Emmeline turned back to the fire, unable to meet Clara's gaze. She clenched her hands in her lap, willing away the conflicting emotions roiling within her. She wanted to argue, to insist that her feelings toward Lord Hawthorne were nothing more than irritation, disdain, and a touch of pity. But the truth—the unspoken, undeniable truth—burned hotter than the flames before her.

"Clara," she said after a moment, her voice quiet but steady. "Do you think I should tell my uncle?"

Clara's expression sobered. "No. Edmund has enough to contend with. And if it does come out, his ignorance will protect him. No one would question his innocence."

"Well, let's hope Mr. Moorefield doesn't share any more of his suspicions with him," Emmeline said, biting her lip. "He believes capturing Mr. Langford will make his political career."

"Did he actually say that?" Clara asked, her expression sharpening.

"Not in so many words," Emmeline admitted, "but he certainly implied it."

"Well, he's likely mistaken," Clara said. "As I said, I doubt the Regent wants this affair dredged up further. And implicating Lord Hawthorne? That would create a political storm. His family is far too powerful, far too admired. The Regent has enough enemies without making them his foes as well. So you see, by keeping Hawthorne's secret, we might even be doing Mr. Moorefield a favor. How's that for wrapping our sins in clean linen?"

Emmeline nodded, relieved by the certainty in Clara's voice. "I suppose you're right. Still, I can't help but worry."

"As do we all," Clara said, rising with a soft sigh. "But worrying won't solve anything tonight. Rest, Emmeline. And try not to overthink what cannot be undone."

Clara stood, wincing slightly as she stretched. "If only everyone continues to believe the measles story."

Emmeline followed Clara to the door, her mind still churning. As her friend stepped into the corridor, she hesitated. "Clara?"

"Yes?"

Emmeline paused mid-step, her thoughts suddenly turning. "He will get well, won't he?"

"There's no reason he shouldn't," Clara reassured her. "He's young, healthy, and his wound is improving. He was sleeping soundly when I last checked."

"Oh, that must be the laudanum," Emmeline said with a sheepish smile.

Clara's brow furrowed. "How much did you give him?"

Emmeline hesitated. "Oh...about a third of a tumbler?"

"Good God!" Clara exclaimed, her eyes wide. "No wonder he didn't stir. He'll sleep splendidly, Emmeline. I won't be the least bit surprised if he sleeps straight through Christmas."

Chapter Thirteen

Emmeline passed a restless night, tossing and turning in a haze of guilt and absurd imaginings. When she did drift into a fitful sleep, it was to find herself standing trial before a corpulent, wigged judge who bore an uncanny resemblance to the Prince of Wales. "I meant it for the best!" she cried, clutching a laudanum bottle as the prince glowered down at her. "Poisoning him was purely accidental!"

At the first hint of dawn, she threw back the covers, shivering as her bare feet met the icy floor. The dream lingered uncomfortably in her mind, and no amount of rationalizing seemed to ease the knot in her stomach. She wrapped herself in her dressing gown, slipped on her slippers, and cautiously opened her door. The hallway was empty, cloaked in the hushed stillness of early morning. With a determined nod, she tiptoed toward Lord Hawthorne's chamber.

Relief washed over her the moment she stepped inside. He was breathing deeply, his chest rising and falling in a steady rhythm. She tiptoed closer, her gaze sweeping over him. His face, shadowed with stubble, bore a healthier color than the day before. Emmeline exhaled, the tension in her chest easing.

"Good," she murmured to herself. "Still alive."

Careful not to wake him—though Clara's assurance about playing bagpipes in his ear crossed her mind—she unbuttoned his shirt and loosened the dressing. Her lips parted in a pleased gasp. The angry streaks around the wound had subsided, and the edges were no longer red and inflamed. He was healing. Gently, she applied more of the comfrey salve and secured a fresh bandage in place.

Her hand lingered a moment longer than necessary against his chest, her fingertips brushing over the warm, steady rise and fall beneath her palm. The warmth of his skin startled her, sending an unwelcome jolt through her. Beneath the layers of cloth and mischief lay a man of maddening contradictions—a rake, a rogue, a criminal, and yet... a rescuer. How infuriating it was to feel that traitorous flutter low in her stomach when she ought to be thinking about how to avoid further scandal, not how soft his skin was beneath her touch.

With the medical portion of her mission accomplished, Emmeline stepped back to survey her patient. Her eyes wandered over him with a reluctant curiosity—his long lashes resting against his cheeks, the relaxed line of his mouth, and the hint of a smile that made him appear maddeningly endearing in repose.

She caught herself leaning in slightly, her gaze lingering too long on that mouth. Had his lips really been that soft? The memory of his fevered kiss swept through her, and she gave herself a firm shake. *Good heavens, Emmy. Pull yourself together.*

No time for woolgathering. She reached for the rouge pot she'd brought, uncapped it, and dabbed at its contents with her finger.

"What the devil—!"

Lord Hawthorne shot upright with a groan, flailing wildly and sending the rouge pot flying from her hand. It hit the floor with a muffled thud and rolled under the bed.

"Oh, heavens, hold still!" Emmeline dove after it, crawling on all fours beneath the bed. "Now, where did that blasted thing go?"

Hawthorne groaned again, pressing his palms to his temples. "Miss St. Clair," he said through gritted teeth, "would you kindly explain why you're in my chamber? And, for that matter, why my skull feels as though it's hosting a blacksmith's competition?"

Emmeline emerged triumphantly, holding up the pot. "Ah, found it! And you can thank the laudanum for the headache. Perhaps I overdid the dosage—only slightly."

His glare was withering. "Overdid it? Woman, I feel as though I've been run over by a team of horses."

"Well, you should count yourself lucky," she said, unfazed. "Your wound is healing splendidly."

"Is it?" He peered under the edge of the bandage and let out a reluctant grunt of approval. "So it is. Well done, Nurse St. Clair. Now, if you'll kindly remove yourself from my—" His words cut off as he caught sight of her hand, now smudged with rouge. "What the devil are you doing with that?"

"Spots," Emmeline replied matter-of-factly. "You can't very well have measles without them. Hold still a moment."

"Spots?" he spluttered, grabbing her wrist before she could dab his cheek. "You've lost your wits!"

"Oh, blast! Look what you've made me do," she grumbled, inspecting the smear on his jawline. "It's uneven now."

"You're painting *spots* on me?" he barked. "This is—this is madness!"

"This is necessary," she corrected, wrenching her wrist free. "If you're to play the part of a measles-ridden invalid, you need to look the part."

"Play the part? Have you—"

"Shh!" Emmeline froze, her eyes darting to the door. "Someone's coming. Hide me!"

Without waiting for a reply, she dove under the bed, her skirts swishing audibly against the wooden floor. She yanked the dust ruffle into place just as the door creaked open.

Emmeline froze beneath the bed as the door creaked open, heart pounding against the floorboards.

"Oh, it's you, Gabriel," Hawthorne drawled, his voice suddenly weak and pitiful. He cleared his throat for good measure. "Best not come too close, old boy. Highly contagious."

Gabriel's footsteps halted a safe distance from the bed. "Contagious? Good heavens, Hawthorne, you've come out in spots."

"Have I?" Hawthorne's fingers brushed his cheek with feigned surprise. "Oh, well then, that's an excellent sign."

"An *excellent* sign?"

"Most assuredly." Hawthorne leaned back against the pillows, his expression solemn. "It means the worst is over. Textbook Hawthorne recovery, you see. The spots appear, and then, just like that—" He snapped his fingers weakly. "Gone."

Gabriel squinted at him, his doubt practically radiating across the room. "I've never heard of such a thing."

"An old family trait," Hawthorne said smoothly, his lips twitching with barely suppressed amusement. "The Hawthornes are renowned for their swift recovery from measles. Once the blasted spots break out, we're practically cured."

Gabriel's skepticism remained intact. "I don't know, Hawthorne. If you don't mind my saying so, you look like the devil's warmed-over breakfast."

"I don't doubt it," Hawthorne replied dryly. "But I assure you, Gabriel, there's no need to fret. In fact, you'd best take yourself off before you infect that fine constitution of yours."

Gabriel hesitated, then shifted uneasily. "Well, I suppose you'd know best. Though I still feel rather responsible for all this. After all, it was my ninnyhammer of a cousin who brought the plague into the house."

Under the bed, Emmeline stiffened, her teeth clenching at the insult.

"Your cousin, eh?" Hawthorne's voice was laced with exaggerated curiosity. "Bit of a calf, is she?"

Gabriel snorted. "A proper one. You've met her. Surely you've noticed how she tongue-bangs anyone who crosses her path?"

"Ah, yes," Hawthorne murmured, stroking his chin thoughtfully. "Like a regular fishwife, isn't she?"

"Always has been. Why, when we were only six, the little hoyden shoved me into the ornamental lake."

Hawthorne chuckled, a low, indulgent sound. "Well, Gabriel, we all have one of those unfortunate relations we'd rather keep locked in a closet—or under the bed, as the case may be."

Emmeline pressed her hand over her mouth to stifle the noise bubbling in her throat, caught somewhere between indignation and the need to sneeze. Insufferable as he was, at least Hawthorne managed to turn Gabriel's insults into a shared jest. But she would not forgive the "fishwife" remark so easily.

"Still, decent of you to look in on me," Hawthorne said. "But truly, there's no need to hover. I'm already feeling much better."

"You're certain?" Gabriel still sounded doubtful. "There's nothing else you need?"

"Well," Hawthorne said with a sigh, pressing a hand dramatically to his temple. "If you're offering, I wouldn't say no to a pot of coffee. Very strong. I seem to have the headache of all headaches—feels as though an anvil is being pounded inside my skull."

"Right. I'll see to it immediately." Gabriel promised with a nod before slipping back out of the room, the door clicking shut behind him.

As the silence settled once more, Emmeline finally sneezed, the sound exploding into the room like a trumpet blast.

"God bless you," Hawthorne said smoothly, leaning over the edge of the bed with a grin.

Emmeline crawled out in a huff, her skirts tangling beneath her. "And the devil take you, sir," she snapped, brushing herself off. "A fishwife, am I?"

Hawthorne's grin widened. "Only in the most charming sense."

Hawthorne grinned, leaning back against the pillows. "Oh, come now. Surely you've been called worse?"

She glared at him, swiping one of the biscuits from his plate and biting into it with relish. "You are impossible."

"Help yourself, why don't you?" he called after her, laughter lacing his voice.

"I already have," she replied, her tone sharp as she glanced back over her shoulder. "Oh, and your Lordship—please inform the chambermaid that the dust under your bed is appalling. She's clearly shirking her duties."

Hawthorne's laughter followed her as she slipped out of the room, darting down the hallway and back to her own chamber. Once safely inside, she closed the door and leaned against it, her heart pounding in her chest.

Arrogant... insufferable... ungrateful... argh!

Chapter Fourteen

Emmeline had only crawled into bed to chase away the morning chill, but sleep overtook her almost immediately. As a consequence, she overslept and entered the dining chamber much later than usual, only to find the table already bustling with conversation.

"Ah, Emmeline," her uncle teased warmly as she filled her plate and took a seat beside him. "You've turned into quite the slug-a-bed this morning. No walk? No horseback ride? I certainly hope you're not sickening for something. But no, I won't hear of it—you look positively radiant, my dear."

"And speaking of the sick," Gabriel interjected, his voice muffled slightly by a mouthful of pound cake, "I'm happy to report that Benjamin—Lord Hawthorne, I mean—is greatly improved. It wouldn't surprise me in the least if he rejoins us today."

This announcement electrified the company, particularly the ladies, who suddenly seemed to come to life with a renewed interest in their breakfast.

Not everyone shared their enthusiasm. Mr. Moorefield frowned deeply, looking skeptical. "Well, if he's so improved, he can't possibly have had the measles."

"Oh, he most certainly had them," Gabriel countered. "I grant you measles don't seem the sort of malady to afflict a man like Hawthorne, but when I looked in on him early this morning, he was as spotted as a speckled hen. Measles. No doubt about it."

"Then he won't be joining us," Moorefield concluded.

"Oh, but that's the remarkable thing," Gabriel continued, his face alight with wonder. "Hawthorne claims that in his family, once someone blossoms, the disease is over and done with. Says he could be cured at any moment."

Moorefield sniffed, unimpressed. "Sounds utterly far-fetched. If measles defer to the peerage, it's the first I've heard of it. Are you certain that's what he had?"

"Absolutely certain," Gabriel insisted. "His face looked like someone had embroidered it with little red dots."

Emmeline, caught off guard, choked on a mouthful of roast beef and had to take a hasty sip of water. The other guests looked at her with varying degrees of amusement and concern, though Gabriel plowed on without noticing.

"I don't see why you're so keen to argue, Moorefield," he added crossly. "If you don't believe me, ask Maggie. She said she was half afraid to hand him his coffee for fear she'd catch them herself."

"Well, now I am sorry for having struck terror into the poor girl's heart," drawled a familiar voice from the doorway.

All heads turned as Lord Hawthorne entered, moving with his characteristic ease despite his apparent recent illness. Though faint lines around his eyes hinted at lingering discomfort, there was no trace of a measles sufferer in his appearance. Quite the contrary—he dazzled. His maroon superfine coat, fastened with sterling buttons, perfectly complemented a snowy cravat tied in the elegant waterfall style. Dove-gray pantaloons hugged his muscular thighs and calves before disappearing into gleaming Hessians adorned with silver tassels. The entire ensemble was so impeccable that it momentarily silenced the room.

"There," Gabriel crowed, shooting a triumphant look at Moorefield. "What did I tell you?"

The gentlemen regarded Hawthorne with ill-disguised suspicion. Moorefield, however, broke the silence. "Gabriel was just enlightening us about your miraculous recovery, Lord Hawthorne."

"Ah, nothing miraculous about it," Hawthorne replied, piling his plate with ham as though he hadn't a care in the world. "Measles simply take our family that way. Days of torment, then we blossom, and presto—it's all over. My sister, as I recall, had only three spots in total. Fortuitous, considering it was the eve of her come-out."

A sudden giggle from Emmeline drew the room's attention. She pressed her napkin to her lips in a futile attempt to suppress her laughter. "That was certainly... fortuitous," she managed to say, her voice trembling with mirth.

"Quite," Hawthorne replied, a glimmer of amusement in his dark eyes.

"Oh, Lord Hawthorne," one bold schoolroom miss leaned forward eagerly, her cheeks pink with the effort of her daring. "We were just scolding Sir Edmund for not having mistletoe anywhere in the house. Christmas isn't Christmas without mistletoe, is it?"

Hawthorne merely smiled, his silence doing nothing to dampen the young lady's enthusiasm. Emboldened, the rest of the table joined in teasing their host about his oversight.

"Must be getting on in years, Sir Edmund, to forget mistletoe," an elderly gentleman joked with a broad wink. "Thank God, I still remember what it's good for."

Laughter rippled through the group as Sir Edmund held up his hands in mock surrender. "Yes, yes, I grant you, it's a grievous oversight. But if the gardeners couldn't find any, there's little I can do."

"We used to gather it ourselves," Gabriel said with nostalgic enthusiasm. "Remember, Papa? The best mistletoe always grew near Hollingsworth Manor."

"Oh, do let's go!" the schoolroom miss clapped her hands, and a chorus of young voices joined her in pleading for an expedition.

Sir Edmund raised a placating hand. "We can't trespass on private land."

"But is there a law against mistletoe poaching?" another guest quipped, setting off another round of laughter.

Eventually, Sir Edmund agreed to an expedition—on Hollybrook land only. Excitement buzzed around the table as plans began to form.

"You'll come, won't you, Lord Hawthorne?" Miss Lydia Evans asked with a coquettish dimple. Her question was met with a surprising interruption from Gabriel.

"I don't think that's a good idea," Gabriel said quickly. "It's quite a tramp. Wouldn't want you to relapse, old man."

"Of course," Sir Edmund interjected. "We could drive near the wood. That way, the walk wouldn't be too strenuous. If you're up for it, that is."

"Oh, do say you'll come," Miss Evans pleaded. "And do drive your curricle. Mr. Hollybrook assures me it's all the crack. I'd simply adore a ride in it."

A MARQUESS FOR CHRISTMAS   139

The blatant hint drew a few raised eyebrows, but Hawthorne only smiled. "I'd be delighted. But I'm afraid you'll have to wait your turn, Miss Evans. Miss St. Clair has already claimed the first spin in my rig."

The entire table turned to Emmeline, whose expression rapidly shifted from shock to outrage. Her protests died in her throat as Hawthorne fixed her with a look—one that might have been pleading, if not for the unmistakable glint of mischief behind it.

Emmeline swallowed hard, her cheeks flaming as the company murmured their astonishment. She didn't trust herself to speak, but one thing was certain: Hawthorne had just secured her presence on this ill-advised expedition.

Thirty minutes later, Emmeline stood beside a visibly disgruntled Miss Evans at the main entrance to Hollybrook Manor, her gaze fixed on the circular carriage drive. Her irritation deepened as a sleek black-and-red curricle, drawn by a pair of perfectly matched grays, swept into view with a theatrical flair. The vehicle came to an elegant halt directly before her.

"Do you think you might manage to admire it?" Lord Hawthorne inquired in a low, sardonic tone as he descended to assist her, his voice rich with amusement.

"I don't see why I should," she replied curtly, keeping her voice just as low. "If admiration is what you're after, why don't you take Miss Evans?"

"And cut out my good friend, Gabriel?" His dark eyebrows rose in mock indignation. "What kind of cad do you take me for?"

"I don't think you truly want me to answer that," she shot back as he helped her into the curricle. Once she was settled, he cracked the whip with a deft motion, springing his horses into a brisk trot. Gabriel, arriving moments later in a slightly less impressive vehicle, followed in their wake.

"Tell me," Emmeline asked as the countryside blurred around them, "is that what you told my cousin? That you gave Miss Evans a turn for his sake?"

Hawthorne adjusted the reins with practiced ease, his expression impassive. "I don't consider giving Miss Evans a 'turn.' But to answer your question—yes, I let Gabriel know I was aware of his... tenderness for the young lady. Otherwise, I'd have been delighted to enjoy her company myself."

"And you expect me to believe that?"

"Of course. Why wouldn't you?"

"Well then, he's an even bigger fool than I thought," she muttered, clutching at her bonnet as the wind tugged insistently at its ribbons.

They swept through the main gates, and onto the highway, the curricle's pace quickening. Hawthorne's grin widened as Emmeline tightened her grip on the armrest. "Do you mind telling me why you singled me out?" she demanded.friend

The look he cast her was one of feigned innocence. "Why, you asked me to ride in my rig, didn't you?"

"You know perfectly well I didn't."

"Are you certain? That's strange. I distinctly recall our first meeting—you talked at great length about my curricle. Are you quite sure you didn't request a ride, then?"

Her glare was pointed and unamused.

"Oh, well," he continued, undeterred. "My mistake, then. But you must admit, it's a natural assumption. Most young ladies can't resist. It simply didn't occur to me that you might be the exception."

"You aren't going to tell me why you brought me along, are you?"

"I believe I had the impression," he mused, "that you'd ask fewer questions."

Before she could retort, he glanced back toward Gabriel's curricle, a mischievous spark lighting his eyes. "Hold on, Miss St. Clair," he said abruptly, his grip tightening on the reins.

"What are you doing?" she asked, alarmed, as his whip cracked sharply over the horses' backs.

"Outrunning Gabriel," he replied, grinning wickedly.

Her heart jumped into her throat. "Oh, my heavens, are you stark raving mad?"

Their already swift pace became a blur of motion. The wind whipped fiercely around her, snatching the bonnet from her head as the ribbons tugged painfully against her neck before giving way entirely. She released a strangled cry, her hands gripping the armrest for dear life.

"Slow down, you idiot!" she shouted, her voice nearly lost in the wind. "Are you trying to kill us?"

Behind them, she could faintly hear Gabriel's panicked cries, but Hawthorne remained utterly unfazed. His focus was fixed ahead, his jaw set with a determination that sent a chill down her spine.

"Slow down, you fool!" she bellowed again. "You can't manage this with one good arm!"

"Oh, no?" he drawled, flashing her a quick, reckless smile. "Just watch me.

To her horror, the curricle veered sharply off the highway toward two crumbling stone pillars marking the entrance to a neglected estate. The vehicle tilted precariously onto two wheels, threatening to overturn entirely.

"Good heavens, slow down, you madman!" she cried, clutching the side rail for dear life.

Hawthorne, utterly unfazed, flashed her a wicked grin. "Where's your sense of adventure, Miss St. Clair? Surely you're not afraid of a little speed."

"A little speed?" she snapped, her voice rising in panic. "I'm afraid of you breaking your neck—and mine!"

The horses thundered on, their hooves pounding the earth in a relentless rhythm. The wind tore at her bonnet, her hair whipping free in wild tendrils, but Emmeline barely noticed. Her entire world had narrowed to the jolting curricle, the dangerously close treeline, and the infuriating man at the reins.

Her grip tightened on the armrest as the curricle swerved again, throwing her dangerously close to Hawthorne's side. Without thinking, her hand shot out and latched onto his sleeve. "For heaven's sake, Hawthorne, stop this insanity!" she pleaded, her voice cracking with unguarded fear.

Hawthorne's grin faltered, just for a moment, his dark eyes flicking to her hand on his arm. His tone softened, though his grip on the reins remained firm. "Do you trust me, Emmeline?"

The question was so unexpected, so disarmingly sincere, that she blinked in shock. "Trust you?" she echoed. "After this? Absolutely not!"

"Then I suppose you'll have to pretend," he said lightly, though something in his expression shifted—a flicker of vulnerability so fleeting she might have imagined it. "I won't let anything happen to you."

Her heart thudded painfully against her ribs, her anger momentarily eclipsed by something far more unsettling. The reckless gleam in his eyes remained, but beneath it was a steadiness, an assurance that rooted her in place. Against her better judgment, her grip on his sleeve loosened, though her fingers lingered for a heartbeat longer than necessary.

The curricle hit a bump, jostling her back into her seat. "If we survive this," she muttered darkly, "I'll kill you myself."

Hawthorne's laughter rang out, rich and unrestrained. "I wouldn't expect anything less."

Emmeline squeezed her eyes shut, her knuckles white against the armrest. "Oh, dear Lord, please don't let me die like this," she prayed silently, bracing herself as the world tilted and the curricle hurtled forward into the unknown.

Chapter Fifteen

"You can open your eyes now," Lord Hawthorne chuckled.

Emmeline did so, realizing that the curricle had somehow righted itself and passed cleanly between the gateposts. They were now traveling up a weed-choked lane, the tension of the ride gradually giving way to a prickling irritation.

"I was right the first time, wasn't I?" she remarked dryly, calmly despite the faint tremor in her hands. "You really should be banned by law from driving. There's something about holding a pair of reins that transforms you from a tolerable human being into a mindless menace."

"A tolerable human being?" Hawthorne tilted his head, feigning astonishment. "Coming from you, Miss St. Clair, that's high praise indeed."

"Don't pretend you missed my point," she snapped as they rounded a bend in the driveway and the grays finally slowed. "By the by, you do realize you're trespassing?"

"How else was I to shake Gabriel? Besides, this is where the mistletoe is, isn't it?"

"Yes," she admitted, her gaze sweeping over the grounds, "and I expect that's not all there is here either."

They had entered what remained of Hollingsworth Park. Once a grand estate, it was now overrun with weeds and tangled undergrowth that encroached on every corner of the decaying grounds. The signs of past grandeur were evident but overwhelmed by neglect. Emmeline's brow furrowed as she surveyed the ruins of order.

"What are you doing?" she demanded, as Hawthorne guided the team off the road and into a grove of overgrown trees.

"We'll walk from here," he replied, climbing down and retrieving a napkin-covered basket from the curricle. Turning, he extended a hand to help her disembark.

She eyed him suspiciously as she accepted his assistance. "Been here before, have you?"

"Don't ask so many questions," he said lightly, setting the basket down to adjust his gloves. "Now, let's see. The woods Gabriel mentioned should be that way." Without waiting for her, he set off across the uneven terrain, moving with surprising confidence.

Emmeline trailed after him, struggling to keep up as the undergrowth clutched at her skirts. "Wait! I'm caught!" she called out, her voice tinged with frustration.

Hawthorne let out a long sigh as he crouched to free her from the tangled blackberry brambles. How the devil did she manage to get herself into such scrapes? The faint line of frustration on her brow and the sharpness in her tone suggested she wasn't enjoying the walk any more than he was—but she hadn't turned back. That stubbornness of hers... Maddening. And oddly admirable.

"You might try looking where you're going," he grumbled.

"How could I?" she shot back. "I was too busy watching *you*. Heaven forbid I take my eyes off you—you've no sense of direction, and I forgot to pack breadcrumbs to mark the trail back to your curricle."

"You do have a flair for dramatics, don't you?" He yanked his glove off, wincing as he pricked his thumb on a particularly wicked thorn. But his irritation quickly dissipated as he glanced at her. The sunlight filtering through the trees cast golden highlights in her hair, and even as she muttered something biting about his sense of direction, her lips curled just slightly in a way that softened the barb. What was it about this woman that made her so confounding? She was clearly trying to distance herself, but every word she threw at him only drew her closer.

Sucking the drop of blood away, he gave her a pointed look. "Come along. It's not much farther." He pulled the last thorn from her hem. Best not to linger on such thoughts. He couldn't afford the distraction—especially not with Langford still tucked away in a borrowed attic.

As Emmeline brushed her skirts down with a huff, she muttered, "I suppose I should thank you, though I doubt you'd have returned the favor had the brambles caught you."

Hawthorne smirked, slipping his glove back on. "I'm not entirely devoid of chivalry, Miss St. Clair."

"Ah, yes. How could I forget? You're the paragon of gentlemanly virtues, Hawthorne." she quipped.

For a moment, he hesitated, his gaze fixed on hers. "You know," he began, his voice quieter now, "you don't have to call me Hawthorne."

She blinked, caught off guard. "Pardon?"

"Hawthorne," he repeated, adjusting his gloves unnecessarily. "It's formal, impersonal—suits the House of Lords, perhaps, but not..." He trailed off, his jaw tightening briefly before softening again. "Not this."

"What should I call you, then?" she asked, her brow arching skeptically.

He smiled faintly, his tone almost self-deprecating. "Ben."

Emmeline tilted her head, studying him as though trying to gauge his sincerity. "And here I thought you relished the title."

"I relish it when it keeps the world at a distance," he replied, his voice quieter still. "Not when I'm untangling you from brambles."

"Oh... well, I suppose you may call me Emmeline—she hesitated—that is, if you wish."

For a fleeting moment, the lightness between them gave way to something warmer, more intimate. But Hawthorne—or Ben, rather—cleared his throat abruptly and gestured toward the woods. "Shall we, Emmeline?"

Still processing the shift in his demeanor, Emmeline nodded and followed him, the new name lingering on her lips. *Ben.* It felt strange—yet not unwelcome.

"Remind me to come back with a pail next summer," she muttered, plucking at her snagged hem. "There's no shortage of blackberries here."

Her musings were cut short when she nearly collided with Haw—Ben, who had come to an abrupt halt behind a massive oak tree. He was peering across what once must have been a pristine expanse of lawn, but was now an unruly tangle of weeds and overgrowth. Beyond it, perched on a slight rise, stood the crumbling remains of a once-stately manor house.

The sight gave Emmeline pause. The roof sagged ominously, its shingles cracked and weathered by time. Ivy grew unchecked, clinging to the stones as though to keep them from crumbling entirely. A Corinthian column from the portico had fallen, replaced by a rough-hewn wooden post. The entire structure seemed held together by little more than stubborn defiance.

"They say it's haunted," Emmeline whispered, her voice barely audible over the rustle of the wind through the trees.

"I can believe it," Hawthorne murmured, his gaze fixed on the decaying edifice.

"Would you like to see inside?" came a third voice, startling them both. They spun around, hearts pounding, to find a man standing a short distance behind them.

"Mr. Hollingsworth!" Emmeline exclaimed, clutching a hand to her chest. "You frightened me."

The man, clad in a fisherman's garb that had seen better days, regarded them with a mild, almost amused expression. An ancient flintlock gun rested comfortably on his shoulder, more an accessory than a threat.

"I apologize," he said with a polite incline of his head. "I didn't mean to startle you. I heard noises and expected to find gypsies." His demeanor was calm, but there was an unmistakable note of curiosity in his gaze.

Emmeline, unsure how to respond, fell back on her drawing-room manners. "Mr. Hollingsworth, may I introduce Lord Hawthorne? He is staying at Hollybrook Manor. Lord Hawthorne, Mr. Hollingsworth, is the owner of this property."

"I've heard of you, of course," Hollingsworth said after the two men exchanged brief nods. "You won that infamous curricle race to Brighton a few years back. Unfortunately," he added with a rueful smile, "I had my blunt on some other fellow."

"Then you clearly hadn't heard much about Lord Hawthorne," Emmeline remarked with a pointed look.

"No, I suppose not," Hollingsworth agreed, his smile unflappable. "You must have just come down from Oxford then. Now, of course, your reputation as both a boxer and a bruising rider precedes you—it's practically a legend."

Hawthorne, to his credit, inclined his head slightly at the backhanded compliment, though his gaze remained sharp. Emmeline couldn't help but wonder what game he might be playing, or whether the dilapidated Hollingsworth Hall held more secrets than either man would admit.

Up until now, Emmeline had considered Mr. Hollingsworth a sensible man. Yet as she listened to Gabriel in stoking Lord Hawthorne's already overblown ego, she began to have her doubts.

"You really must forgive us our trespasses," she interjected sharply, cutting short the exchange. "It seems our illustrious nonesuch here has managed to get us completely lost."

"Oh, indeed?" Mr. Hollingsworth replied, tilting his head with mild curiosity.

"Yes," she said firmly, "we left his famous curricle—or what's left of it—a few miles back. We were looking for mistletoe and seem to have lost our way."

"That, Miss St. Clair, is an outright falsehood," Hawthorne said with infuriating calm, ignoring her glare. "The truth, Mr. Hollingsworth, is that we are blatant trespassers. We heard the best mistletoe could be found on your property."

"Well," Mr. Hollingsworth said with a small smile, "that's quite true, and you're welcome to it. But I'm afraid you're nowhere near the right spot. Come along, I'll show you."

As their impromptu guide led the way, Emmeline noticed how Hawthorne's gaze lingered on the decaying manor house. His expression revealed none of the turmoil she suspected brewed beneath the surface, but his silence was telling.

They trudged through the undergrowth for nearly a mile, Emmeline regretting her choice of delicate half-boots instead of the stout pair she had left at home. Meanwhile, Hawthorne and Mr. Hollingsworth fell into an easy conversation about London life. To her relief, Hawthorne refrained from making any of his usual barbed remarks that might embarrass their host. Instead, he seemed oddly congenial, steering the conversation toward lighter topics.

At last, Mr. Hollingsworth stopped and gestured grandly toward a towering grove of trees. "Here we are—mistletoe!" he declared.

Emmeline squinted up into the treetops, where clumps of green nestled high in the bare branches. "So that's what all the fuss is about," she muttered, brushing a leaf off her pelisse.

They weren't alone for long. From across a nearby field, Gabriel and Miss Evans came into view, their expressions a mix of indignation and accusation. The pair stormed toward them, boots crunching through the frosted grass.

"Where the devil did you get to?" Gabriel demanded, his usual deference to Hawthorne conspicuously absent. Emmeline found she liked him better for it.

"We wondered if you were deliberately trying to get away from us," Miss Evans added, equally aggrevatedaggravated.

"Oh, not at all," Hawthorne said smoothly, his face the picture of innocence. "Miss St. Clair insisted I show off my grays' paces, and then, I'm afraid, I took a wrong turn onto Mr. Hollingsworth's property. My sincerest apologies." He turned toward their host with a gracious nod. "Mr. Hollingsworth, may I present Miss Evans and Mr. Hollybrook?"

Miss Evans murmured a barely audible "How do you do," but Gabriel's thunderous reply was less polite. "We know each other," he said stiffly.

"Your servant, madam." Mr. Hollingsworth bowed lightly in Miss Evans's direction before casting a cool, appraising glance at Gabriel. "Well, Gabriel, I see you've grown into a man since last I saw you. Though perhaps I should say Mr. Hollybrook now?"

"Come on," Gabriel said abruptly, ignoring the civility. He jerked his head toward the direction they had come. "We're trespassing. My father made it clear we shouldn't be here."

"Actually, the spot you're looking for is in the other direction," Hawthorne said casually. "We must have gotten turned around."

"Now, now," Mr. Hollingsworth interrupted. "Since you're already here, it seems rather silly to leave without taking some mistletoe. I assure you, Mr. Hollybrook, it's perfectly uncontaminated. No one need know where it came from." He paused, his eyes twinkling. "Though I do wonder—how exactly do you plan to get it down?"

"Well," Hawthorne said with a sudden grin, "I had intended to send Miss St. Clair shimmying up the nearest tree. She's an absolute marvel at climbing, though her descent technique could use some work. What do you say, Miss St. Clair? Practice makes perfect." He gestured grandly toward a towering oak, its mistletoe hanging tantalizingly out of reach.

Emmeline glared at him. "Your sense of humor, my lord, is yet another thing in need of practice."

"If it's no trouble, allow me," Mr. Hollingsworth offered. He raised his ancient flintlock, taking careful aim. With a deafening crack, a clump of mistletoe tumbled through the branches and landed on the ground.

"Well done!" Emmeline cheered, running to gather the greenery.

Mr. Hollingsworth repeated the process several times, their collection quickly growing into an impressive pile. Unfortunately, none of them had considered how to transport the mistletoe back to the carriages. A spirited debate ensued, with Gabriel adamantly refusing Emmeline's suggestion to use his lavender greatcoat as a makeshift hammock.

"It's perfectly clean," Emmeline pointed out. "And the rig is only a short distance away. You'll neither freeze nor ruin your precious coat."

Even Miss Evans joined in, siding with Emmeline. With a disgruntled sigh, Gabriel reluctantly spread his coat on the ground to carry the mistletoe.

As the group prepared to part ways, Mr. Hollingsworth turned to Gabriel. "By the way, has your bailiff mentioned anything about gypsies in the area?"

"No. Have you seen any?" Gabriel asked.

"Not seen, no," Mr. Hollingsworth replied. "But someone broke into my house yesterday. Not that they had to break in—it's never locked. They cleaned me out of food. Strange, really. The locals might help themselves to the game, but roasted chicken and bread? That's unusual."

Gabriel thanked him stiffly, while Emmeline offered her own profuse gratitude for the mistletoe. With that, the party went their separate ways, though Emmeline couldn't shake the feeling that the mysteries of Hollingsworth Hall were far from over.

"Well, it looks as though you lugged that basket for nothing," Emmeline remarked, watching Ben deposit it back in the curricle with a disgruntled air.

"The crowd spoiled my private picnic." He said with a flash of genuine irritation as he brushed an invisible speck from his coat.

"Poppycock. You didn't bring all that food for us. Why not admit it?"

"I admit nothing," he replied smoothly, climbing into the driver's seat and expertly maneuvering the curricle out of the thicket.

Emmeline refused to let the subject drop. "Well, at least you know your friend isn't starving," she observed a little while later, as the team trotted down the highway at a mercifully sedate pace—a pace she hadn't realized he was capable of maintaining. "Though, of course, he's likely to be arrested for theft at any moment."

"Again, what a Job's comforter you've turned out to be," he drawled, though there was a thread of weariness beneath the sarcasm. "Not that I've the faintest idea what you're talking about."

"Oh, rubbish." She turned in her seat to face him, her eyes sparking with exasperation. "Why even bother with this ridiculous charade? Ever since Mr. Moorefield mentioned the rescue, I've known it was you who freed Mr. Langford. I saw you were bleeding. I heard what you said about 'Chris,' and I certainly noticed how you've maneuvered us into delivering supplies to a supposedly deserted estate."

"My, aren't you clever?" He tilted his head. "Bow Street would love you."

"I'm not trying to be clever," she snapped, crossing her arms. "Clever doesn't even come into it. The facts are plain as day. What is the point of your persistence with this pea-brained pretense?"

He exhaled sharply, his grip on the reins tightening. "The point, *Emmeline*," he said, his voice clipped, "is that I'm trying to keep you out of this."

She snorted, unamused. "It's a bit late for that, don't you think? If Bow Street comes knocking, do you honestly believe they'll leave me out of it? 'Oh, pay no attention to the lady helping Lord Hawthorne deliver bread and wine to a haunted estate.' Really, my lord?"

"You could walk away from all of this right now," he said, low but insistent. "Plausible deniability, St. Clair. If I confirm what you suspect, you're implicated. Every bit of it sticks to you, too."

"Well, it's a bit late for that, isn't it? The only real question is—what do you plan to do now?"

"How the devil should I know?" he muttered. "Maybe if I had a moment's peace, I could figure something out."

"Surely you must have *some* plan of action."

"My plan of action," he said bitterly, "was to get Christopher to France. I thought a deserted, haunted estate was the perfect place to leave him temporarily while I made arrangements. But I didn't count on being shot, or on having the ubiquitous Mr. Moorefield breathing down my neck, and most especially"—his jaw tightened—"I didn't count on the 'deserted' estate suddenly becoming occupied. By the by," he added with deliberate casualness, "how is it you're so well-acquainted with Mr. Hollingsworth?"

Emmeline explained how he'd driven her to the court after her coach accident. "And then I ran into him again on the beach, where he was working on his boat."

He stiffened slightly, his eyes narrowing. "What sort of boat?"

"How should I know? I'm no expert. A fishing boat, I suppose."

"Large or small?"

"Must you snap at me? Isn't that purely relative? It's larger than a rowboat but smaller than a Channel packet, if that helps."

"Does it have sails?"

"Yes, definitely sails," she replied, exasperated.

He fell silent for a moment, as if weighing this information. "What's your impression of Mr. Hollingsworth?"

"If you mean, do I think he's the sort of man to smuggle Mr. Langford into France? Frankly, I doubt it."

"Oh?" His brows rose. "The risk wouldn't have to be enormous, and I'd pay him handsomely. He certainly appears to need the blunt."

"Money's your answer for everything, isn't it?" she snapped.

"No, not everything. But it does tend to smooth out the rough edges. Now tell me—why don't you think it would work with Hollingsworth?"

"Because he's just come from prison. And unless I miss my guess, no power on earth could make him risk going back."

"My God!" Hawthorne's genuine shock caught her off guard. "So *that's* why Gabriel was so insufferably rude to the man."

Emmeline let that pass. She wasn't inclined to reveal there might be a more personal reason for Gabriel's hostility.

"Do you know what his crime was?"

"Failure to pay his debts. His family has apparently been addicted to gambling for generations, or so he said."

"He told you that? You two seem to have become bosom friends in record time."

"Mr. Hollingsworth thought it only fair to warn me about his reputation. After all, he didn't know I was accustomed to consorting with criminals."

"Touche." He gave her a wry glance, but lapsed back into thoughtful silence.

Emmeline broke the spell as they approached Hollybrook Park. "Tell me," she asked, her voice quieter now, "what is Mr. Langford like?"

"Christopher?" He blinked, as if pulled from a reverie. "What's he like?" A rueful smile tugged at his lips. "I'll tell you this much. He's about the last man in England who'd be capable of borrowing a beached fishing boat and sailing himself to France."

Chapter Sixteen

Lady Hollybrook reclined on a Grecian couch, her dressing gown falling in carefully draped folds as though she had posed for a portrait rather than spent the morning lounging. A recently discarded copy of *The Ladies' Magazine* lay open on a side table, its pages ruffled by the faint breeze filtering through the cracked window. Her sharp eyes, however, were fixed squarely on her niece, and their gleam held none of the warmth one might expect from family.

"Emmeline," she began, her voice clipped and brimming with disapproval, "I am shocked. No—mortified. Humiliated beyond measure. To think a niece of mine could conduct herself in such a brazen manner." She sat up slightly, the better to cast her judgment like a thunderbolt. "Throwing yourself at Lord Hawthorne's head like some... some common lightskirt! You may rest assured, young miss, that I intend to write your mother a full account of your wanton behavior."

Emmeline's fingers tightened imperceptibly at her sides, but her expression remained composed. "If you truly intend to write Mama such nonsense, Aunt Arabella, I'll have no choice but to correct you. You have misunderstood entirely."

"There is no misunderstanding," her aunt snapped, punctuating the denial with a dismissive wave of her hand. "Miss Evans was kind enough to inform me of your shamelessness. As bold as brass, she said, you invited yourself into Lord Hawthorne's curricle."

"Well, now." Emmeline's smile didn't reach her eyes, though a dangerous glint sparked within them. "That was indeed kind of Miss Evans. Did she also inform you that she asked for the same privilege?"

For the briefest moment, Lady Hollybrook faltered. "No," she admitted, her voice slower now, "but even if such a thing occurred—which I find doubtful—the two situations could hardly be considered the same."

"Oh?" Emmeline's eyebrow arched in polite challenge. "And why not?"

Her aunt sniffed, gathering her composure. "In the first place, it is common knowledge that Gabriel and Miss Evans have an understanding. Lord Hawthorne would not misconstrue her request as anything beyond genuine interest in his rig."

"And I could not share such an interest?"

Lady Hollybrook pressed on, ignoring her niece's interruption. "Furthermore, Miss Evans is a young lady of considerable fortune and impeccable social standing. Even if she did display some curiosity about Lord Hawthorne, which I do not for one moment believe, he would treat her with respect. Whereas in your case..." She leaned forward slightly, her expression pitying and predatory all at once. "Not to put too fine a point upon it, but the only thing you might expect from a gentleman of his sort is a slip on the shoulder."

Emmeline's spine straightened, her voice cold and clear. "You are offensive, madam."

A MARQUESS FOR CHRISTMAS

"Good," her aunt shot back, her voice rising. "Perhaps a little plain speaking will do you some good. And I am not finished with you yet, young lady." She sat up fully now, the rustle of her dressing gown sharp in the otherwise still room. "There is one more matter I feel compelled to address. Miss Evans also informs me that you had the audacity to enter Hollingsworth Estate this morning—after your uncle expressly forbade it."

Emmeline's lips twitched, though not in amusement. "Surely, Aunt Arabella, you cannot hold me solely responsible for that. If anyone deserves your scolding, it is Lord Hawthorne. Perhaps you'd prefer to summon him here and read him the riot act."

"Don't be impertinent," her aunt snapped. "You could have prevented it."

"Could I?" Emmeline tilted her head, her voice sweet with mock innocence. "You've already made it abundantly clear that Lord Hawthorne holds me in such contempt. How, pray tell, would I have controlled him?"

Lady Hollybrook ignored the pointed logic, her focus shifting to another sore point. "There is also Mr. Moorefield to consider."

"Oh, indeed?" Emmeline's tone sharpened. "I fail to see what he has to do with the matter."

"A great deal," her aunt said sharply. "It would be far too easy for you to sink beneath his contempt as well—and after all your uncle has done to promote a match between you."

"Between him and Rosalind, surely," Emmeline countered, though she could feel the familiar stirrings of frustration.

"Between him and one of my widowed sister's daughters," her aunt corrected, her voice brimming with righteousness. "And given his political prospects, he would be a fine match for you. Your uncle has even considered—though he wouldn't want me to say so—offering a small dowry under favorable circumstances. You would do well to watch your behavior, Emmeline. It would not do for society to develop a disgust for you. Be warned."

"Oh, I am, Aunt Arabella," Emmeline replied coolly. "Now, is there anything else you wish to say?"

"Yes, as a matter of fact, there is something more." Lady Hollybrook's said coldly, her disdain sharpening like the point of a blade. "Miss Evans also mentioned that you appear to be on quite familiar terms with Mr. Hollingsworth. That will not do." Her lips curled as if the name itself left a bitter taste. "Our family is not, nor shall we ever be, on speaking terms with that—that reprobate. I trust you will remember this while you remain under this roof." With a dismissive wave of her hand, she reached for her magazine, her attention already shifting away. "You may go now."

As Emmeline left the chamber, her vision was so blurred with angry tears that she nearly collided with Miss Clara in the corridor. Her breath hitched as she hurriedly swiped at her cheeks, desperate to maintain her composure. But the sting of her aunt's words lingered, curling around her chest like a vise. As her aunt's voice echoed in her mind, Emmeline's thoughts flickered briefly to Lord Hawthorne—Benjamin, she corrected herself. He, at least, had never spoken to her with such condescension. It was maddening to think that someone so infuriating could also seem... reliable, in his own way. The thought brought no solace, only a fresh wave of frustration.

"Oh, I'm sorry," she mumbled, ready to flee, but Clara gently placed a hand on her arm to stop her.

"Please, may I have a word?" Clara whispered, glancing toward the closed door of Lady Hollybrook's room as if ensuring her presence wouldn't be noticed.

For a moment, Emmeline hesitated, torn between the urge to crumble into her room and the gnawing sense of duty to not appear rude. She bit the inside of her cheek, her frustration threatening to bubble over, but Clara's gentle expression softened her resolve.

"Of course," she murmured, managing a polite nod despite her frayed nerves.

Once they were safely inside Emmeline's chamber, with the door closed behind them, Emmeline exhaled sharply. "You'll have to excuse me," she said, sitting heavily on the edge of her bed. "I've just endured the most unpleasant interview with my aunt. I feel... utterly battered." The admission slipped out, unbidden, and her shoulders slumped as the fight drained from her posture.

"I know," Clara admitted softly as she limped to the dressing table stool and settled herself with care. Her soft understanding tugged at something fragile in Emmeline.

"I'm sorry to add to your distress, but I overheard part of the conversation." A faint, self-conscious smile flickered across her face. "The truth is, I was about to knock when I heard Mr. Hollingsworth's name. After that... well, I confess I listened rather shamelessly. Tell me, Emmeline, is it true you've made his acquaintance?"

"Yes," Emmeline admitted with a small sigh, before recounting her three encounters with Mr. Hollingsworth.

Clara listened intently, her hands folded tightly in her lap. "So you know he's been in prison?"

Emmeline nodded. "I do."

She hesitated, unsure how much to say, before continuing. "Tell me... how does he seem to you?"

"Well, you must realize I have no basis for comparison," Emmeline replied, floundering slightly. "I've never seen him dressed like a gentleman, for instance. But I... I quite liked him."

Clara's lips curved into a bittersweet smile, her gaze distant for a moment. "I'm very glad to hear it. I had hoped prison life hadn't changed him overly much. Of course, it's bound to leave its mark."

The next question burst out of Emmeline before she could stop herself. "You're not bitter?"

Clara blinked, then gave a soft laugh. "I see you've heard the story of my elopement."

"In part," Emmeline admitted cautiously. "I assume Mr. Hollingsworth was the man involved. Am I correct?"

Clara nodded, her expression calm but guarded. "It's natural enough that you'd wonder about my feelings on the matter. To answer your question: no, I'm not bitter in the least. Unlike my brother, I never found it shocking that a gentleman might be interested in more than my fortune."

She raised a hand to silence Emmeline's attempt at protest, effectively closing the topic. "But that's not the only reason I wished to speak with you. I have some Christmas baskets to deliver to the tenants and wondered if you'd like to come along. Of course, since you've been out all morning, you might prefer to rest."

"Rest?" Emmeline's laugh was short and humorless. "After that unpleasantness with my aunt, I think a breath of fresh air would be just the thing. I'd be delighted to join you."

Clara smiled warmly, and soon the two women set out in a well-loaded gig, the brisk winter air a welcome balm to Emmeline's frayed nerves.

Clara proved to be a remarkably skilled driver, expertly navigating the narrow and winding lanes that led to the tenant cottages. Emmeline accompanied her into each home, carrying the weighty baskets brimming with food and gifts. She quickly noticed how warmly each tenant welcomed Clara, their eyes lighting up with gratitude and affection. Though Lady Hollybrook might officially be the lady of the manor, it was clear Clara's genuine concern for the sick and elderly had earned her the loyalty of the people. Clara didn't just deliver provisions—she delivered comfort.

"Would you like to drive along the beach?" Clara asked as they left the last cottage, where the rhythmic sound of the surf filled the air. "I love the sea in winter. Then again," she laughed, "I suppose I love it just as much in spring, summer, and autumn."

Emmeline smiled, her spirits lifting at the suggestion. "I'd like that very much."

As they approached the pebbled shore, Clara skillfully guided the gig along a precarious precipice that had Emmeline clutching the edge of her seat and holding her breath. Once the beach came into view, she wasn't entirely surprised when Clara turned the horses toward the direction of the Hollingsworth estate.

Clara seemed to sense Emmeline's unspoken question. "I thought I might leave a basket for Mr. Hollingsworth," she said, her tone a touch too casual. "A sort of welcome-home present. That is, if you don't mind delivering it. The hall isn't far from here—we can see it from the beach."

Emmeline hesitated, the words to explain that Mr. Hollingsworth wasn't currently living in the hall hovering on her lips. But then she thought better of it. Someone was living there—someone who needed the food more urgently. If Clara's basket could spare him from exposing himself to gather supplies, it seemed the kinder course to let the matter rest.

Her moral dilemma was swiftly resolved when Clara stiffened beside her, her gaze fixed on a figure down the beach. Following Clara's line of sight, Emmeline recognized Mr. Hollingsworth at once. Dressed in the same patched and weathered clothes, he appeared to be mending his sails. At the sound of the gig's approach, he straightened, turning toward them.

Emmeline kept a close eye on Clara, watching her pale slightly. Yet her hands remained steady on the reins, and when she spoke, her voice betrayed no hint of unease. "Hello, Graham," she called as she reined in the horses. "It's nice to see you again."

Emmeline might as well have disappeared into the sea spray for all the notice Mr. Hollingsworth paid her. His attention was entirely fixed on Clara as he walked slowly toward them, his expression a mixture of surprise and something softer. "Clara," he said, his voice warm with familiarity. "How have you been? But there's no need to ask. You're even lovelier than before."

Clara laughed lightly, and for a moment, Emmeline could see the girl she must have been when she ran off with him. "Oh, Graham," she said, her tone half-amused, half-reprimanding. "Prison hasn't changed you a bit. You're as free with your Spanish coin as ever."

"Spanish coin? I think not, Clara," he replied, his voice more serious now, his gaze searching. "I'm not proud of everything I did back then, but I always told you the truth about yourself."

Clara straightened slightly, meeting his gaze with a levelness that Emmeline hadn't seen before. "Perhaps," she said, though her voice carried a quiet strength, "but the truth was never the problem, was it, Graham? It was what we did with it that left the scars." Her words hung in the air, weighty and unflinching, and for a moment, Graham looked as though she had struck him.

Clara shifted, her discomfort clear as she gestured toward Emmeline. "I believe you've already met my friend, Miss St. Clair."

At last, Mr. Hollingsworth turned his gray eyes toward Emmeline, flashing a disarming smile. "Indeed, we have. In fact," he added with a playful gesture to his buttonhole, where a sprig of mistletoe was tucked, "I even kept a souvenir."

Emmeline returned his smile, explaining to Clara how Mr. Hollingsworth had retrieved the mistletoe for them earlier.

"You've lost none of your skill, Mr. Hollingsworth," Clara said with a faint smile. "The nemesis of all the local rabbits. Are you settling in well, Graham? I hope things haven't been... awkward for you."

"Not at all," he replied lightly. "Oh, I'll grant you, the neighbors haven't exactly been queuing up to call, but after my time in the Fleet, I find solitude quite bearable. Not that I've been entirely alone. After this morning's adventure and now your visit, I had another visitor just a little while ago."

"Who was it?" Clara asked, her voice carefully even, while Emmeline strove to appear no more than politely curious.

"Mr. Moorefield," Graham said with a faint, wry smile. "Most polite fellow, though rather intense. He asked quite a few questions."

"Questions about what?" Clara pressed.

"Gypsies, mostly. Gabriel must have mentioned the food I lost. Moorefield seemed keen to know if I'd seen any strangers about. He even hinted he'd like a tour of the hall. I think he's heard the ghost stories and wanted to investigate, though he hardly strikes me as the type to believe in such things. Still, I had work to do, so I didn't entertain him long." He chuckled. "Not that it matters. No self-respecting ghost wanders about in broad daylight."

"It is a fascinating place," Emmeline remarked, her gaze drifting to the crumbling manor towering above the cliff. "I wouldn't want to meet your ghost, but might I take a closer look at the house? That is, if you're not in a hurry, Clara."

Her offer was transparent, and she knew it, but Clara seemed to accept it without protest. "Of course. Leave the basket, would you?"

"Basket?" Graham asked, his brow lifting.

"It's just a few things from the kitchen," Clara said. "Christmas pudding and the like—a welcome-home gift."

His expression softened as he took her hand briefly. "Please don't look like that, Clara. I was only teasing. Thank you for thinking of me."

As Graham lifted the basket from the gig and carried it toward the hall, Emmeline climbed down and wandered toward the manor. Neither Clara nor Graham seemed to notice her departure, too absorbed in their quiet exchange to care.

Chapter Seventeen

Emmeline was breathless by the time she reached the top of the steep cliff path, the crisp winter air stinging her lungs. She set the basket down on the frosted grass with a small huff of relief and straightened, her gaze sweeping over the looming facade of Hollingsworth Hall. The manor was a decaying relic of a bygone age, its filthy, cracked, and broken windows reflecting the pale winter light like a hundred unblinking eyes. A shiver rippled through her as she imagined someone—perhaps Christopher Langford himself—watching her from the shadows. The thought was both comforting and unnerving.

Determined to shake the feeling, she squinted and forced her gaze to travel systematically over the entire face of the building. The windows betrayed no movement, but the layers of grime could easily conceal prying eyes. She half-wished there were curtains to twitch and give her some sign of life within. Even without tangible proof, an inexplicable certainty settled over her: she was being observed.

Would Christopher know her intentions if he were there? The thought gave her pause. Calling his name seemed the most direct solution, but she dismissed it as quickly as it occurred to her. He had no way of knowing she meant him no harm, and she could hardly blame him if he kept to the attic or the cellars, avoiding discovery at all costs. Worse still, if Graham Hollingsworth appeared and overheard, it would raise far too many questions.

Her brow furrowed as she considered her options. Simply leaving the basket where it was and hoping Christopher would retrieve it wasn't feasible. If Hollingsworth discovered the basket missing, he'd likely conclude his elusive "gypsies" were camped inside and call for the authorities. No, she had to ensure the provisions reached Christopher without arousing suspicion.

Her fingers brushed the basket's linen covering as inspiration struck. Of course! Graham hadn't cataloged the contents of the Christmas basket—it was unlikely he'd notice if most of it went missing. She could make a smaller bundle for Christopher using the napkin and leave it inside the house. But first, she needed to signal her intent to anyone watching.

Stepping into full view of the windows, she raised the basket and waved it like a signal lantern, the absurdity of her actions not lost on her. She then set it down and shook out the napkin with deliberate movements, as though brushing off imaginary crumbs. If Christopher were watching, surely he'd understand the message. For good measure, she tucked the napkin into the collar of her pelisse, peering into the basket to assess its contents.

A feast awaited inside: chicken, ham, beef, cheese, cakes of all sorts, and a generous Christmas pudding. She couldn't resist helping herself to a ginger nut, the spicy sweetness momentarily lifting her spirits. Feeling a touch theatrical, she exaggerated her movements as she wrapped the smaller bundle, imagining herself as some improbable heroine in a gothic tale.

"Miss St. Clair, what are you doing?"

The sharp voice startled her so thoroughly that she choked on the ginger nut, spinning around to find Mr. Moorefield watching her with a mixture of curiosity and suspicion.

Emmeline's startled shriek was muffled by the ginger nut still in her mouth, and she coughed, sputtering as she spun around to face Mr. Moorefield. "You—you shouldn't creep up on people like that!" she managed, her voice hoarse from choking.

"I wasn't creeping," he said evenly, his brow raised in mock innocence. "I was here before you."

"Then why didn't you make your presence known?" she snapped, her indignation barely masking her embarrassment. "You nearly scared me out of my wits!"

"I was curious about your strange behavior," he replied, folding his arms. His piercing gaze swept over her, making her feel entirely too scrutinized.

"Strange behavior?" Emmeline shot back. "If you mean helping myself to a ginger nut, then yes, I confess to being a little peckish after climbing that cliff. Perhaps I shouldn't have taken it, but Miss Hollybrook does tend to play Lady Bountiful, and there's enough in this basket for an army. I doubt it will be missed." She attempted a sheepish smile, though her hands clutched the basket protectively.

"And for whom is this Christmas basket intended, Miss St. Clair?" he asked.

"For Mr. Hollingsworth, naturally," she replied, lifting her chin. "I've been helping Miss Hollybrook deliver gifts to the tenants, and since she couldn't manage the climb, I brought this one myself." She paused, her mind racing for a way to steer the conversation. "And I fully intended to tell her I helped myself to a ginger nut," she added, hoping to distract him.

"Hmm." He didn't look convinced. "It seems rather odd—not to mention entirely inappropriate—that Miss Clara should include Mr. Hollingsworth in her charitable endeavors."

"I don't find it odd at all," Emmeline retorted, standing straighter. "It's the season of goodwill, after all. Mr. Hollingsworth is my uncle's closest neighbor, and judging by the state of his property, he could use a bit of charity."

"I doubt Sir Edmund's Christmas spirit extends that far," Moorefield replied dryly. "I suspect he doesn't even know of his sister's generosity."

"Then I won't mention it," Emmeline said briskly, her patience wearing thin. "And now, Mr. Moorefield, would you mind explaining why you're skulking about?"

"Skulking?" His brows rose, affronted. "I assure you, I was doing no such thing."

"Well, you certainly sneaked up on me," she accused.

"I've already told you I was simply standing here," he replied.

"Behind a bush?" she pressed, her voice tinged with triumph.

He shifted uncomfortably, suddenly on the defensive. "I was merely curious to see Hollingsworth Hall," he said, recovering his composure. "It has historic significance, you know. It's one of the oldest estates in the area—or so I've been told."

"No doubt about that." Emmeline cast a critical eye over the crumbling facade. "But I wouldn't call it a showplace. Of course, it's reputed to be haunted, which adds a certain fascination. Frankly, though, Mr. Moorefield, I'm surprised that sort of thing appeals to you."

"I have no interest in the supernatural," he replied stiffly. "There's always a rational explanation."

"Gypsies, perhaps?" she ventured, tilting her head. "Mr. Hollingsworth did mention them when we met him this morning—when we were looking for mistletoe."

"Did he?" Moorefield's seemed skeptical. "I believe Mr. Hollingsworth merely wondered if there were gypsies in the area."

"Well, perhaps I misunderstood," Emmeline replied, her voice light and pointed. "You seem remarkably well-informed for someone who wasn't there."

He ignored her jab. "What I find curious is how your party ended up on Hollingsworth land when Sir Edmund explicitly forbade it."

"Oh, that was entirely accidental," Emmeline said breezily, lifting the basket and walking toward the manor's crumbling marble steps. Moorefield trailed her closely. "Lord Hawthorne was showing off his team's pace and took a wrong turn. That's all."

"A remarkable coincidence," he sneered, standing over her as she set the basket down.

"Not so remarkable," she replied evenly. "We're both strangers to the area. I assure you, there was no intention of defying my uncle's wishes."

"Not on your part, perhaps," he muttered.

Ignoring the insinuation, Emmeline continued, "And though I would never wish to disobey my uncle, no harm was done. We gathered a prodigious amount of mistletoe—with Mr. Hollingsworth's permission, I might add. So, all's well that ends well, wouldn't you agree?"

"No, Miss St. Clair, I wouldn't," he said darkly. "Nothing has ended."

"I'm sure I don't know what you mean," she replied, feigning confusion.

"You can't have forgotten," Moorefield said, his voice low and deliberate. "I warned you once to steer clear of Lord Hawthorne."

"Well, that's rather difficult," she countered. "Considering we're both guests at the same house."

"Many people are guests," he said sharply. "But you were alone with him this morning."

"I hardly think anyone could object to that," Emmeline said, her confidence faltering as she recalled the objections already raised. "This is 1817, after all."

"Let me say it plainly," Moorefield continued, his tone that of a weary tutor addressing a slow pupil. "Lord Hawthorne would never take a proper interest in a woman of your station."

"Let me assure you, Mr. Moorefield," Emmeline replied icily, "I have no desire for such an interest."

"Then take heed," he said, his voice hardening. "The kind of proposal you might expect from his lordship would be of an entirely different nature."

"Well, now you have, Mr. Moorefield," Emmeline retorted. "But you'd have done better to save your breath to cool your porridge. Oh, I don't doubt that his lordship is every bit the rake you say he is. But I sincerely doubt he would dare attempt anything untoward with Sir Edmund's niece while under Sir Edmund's roof. That would require an even blacker character than the one you paint." She paused. "Besides, I don't believe Hawthorne has the slightest interest in me. After the opera dancers and other...exotic company he's used to, I expect I must seem rather like an antidote."

"I doubt that."

"Goodness, Mr. Moorefield," Emmeline said, feigning a light laugh. "I can hardly tell whether I've just been complimented or insulted."

"Neither," he replied curtly. "You're being warned."

"Again?" she asked, arching an eyebrow. "How many times do you intend to repeat yourself?"

"Until you heed me," he snapped. "Do not allow his lordship to use you as a cat's paw. Hawthorne has a knack for keeping his hands clean while others bear the consequences. If Langford is involved, you'll be the one facing Bow Street, not him." He gestured pointedly toward the basket.

Emmeline blinked. "Entirely too cryptic, sir. I fail to see how he could possibly do so. The notion is, frankly, ludicrous."

"Is it?" Moorefield's brow lifted, his expression quietly triumphant. "I hope you're right, Miss St. Clair. But that would rather depend, would it not, on who the intended recipient of that basket truly is."

"I've already told you," she said firmly, her patience thinning. "It's for Mr. Hollingsworth. Pray pay attention. And now, if you'll excuse me..." She rose, lifting the basket as she crossed the flagstones to the tarnished knocker on the manor's door. A hollow echo rang out as it struck, and she couldn't help but wonder how the sound might carry inside—if Mr. Langford was, indeed, within those walls.

"Mr. Hollingsworth is not home," Moorefield volunteered, his voice carrying just enough smugness to make her teeth grind.

Good, she thought, relief washing over her. *At least he doesn't know Mr. Hollingsworth isn't actually living here.* Aloud, she asked, "Then why didn't you mention that before I knocked?"

Without waiting for his reply, she tried the door, fully expecting it to be locked. Instead, it groaned open on creaking hinges. "In that case, I'll just set the basket inside," she announced briskly. "He's sure to find it when he returns."

She stepped into the dim entryway, placed the basket carefully on the nearest table, and shut the door behind her with a reverberating slam. Turning back to Moorefield, she smoothed her skirts. "Well, I must be going," she said politely. "By now, Miss Hollybrook must be wondering what's become of me. Would you care to catch a ride back with us? I'm sure we could squeeze three in the gig."

"No, thank you," he replied. "I came on horseback."

"Indeed?" Emmeline glanced around pointedly. "And where, pray, is this animal?"

Moorefield reddened faintly, gesturing toward the woods with a stiff motion. "I tethered it back there."

"How very considerate," she remarked, her voice faintly mocking. "Well, then, I shall see you back at the manor—unless, of course, you plan to explore the haunted house after I'm gone."

"Of course not," he said stiffly. "Hardly seems worth entering when Mr. Hollingsworth isn't here."

Ah, so he's afraid, Emmeline realized with sudden clarity, a flicker of amusement sparking within her. *Or perhaps he has every right to be. If Mr. Langford is desperate, who could blame him for keeping his distance?*

"I think I'll wait here a bit, though," Moorefield continued, his voice measured. "Have a word with Mr. Hollingsworth when he comes back. That way," he added pointedly, "I can be certain that Miss Clara's Christmas bounty falls into the proper hands. Good day, Miss St. Clair."

Emmeline kept her expression neutral, nodding briskly before turning back toward the cliff path. Her mind whirled as she hurried back, barely noticing the precarious footing beneath her. There was no doubt about it—Moorefield was convinced Christopher Langford had gone to ground inside Hollingsworth Hall. She had to inform Lord Hawthorne immediately, though what he could do about it—short of fleeing for France himself—she couldn't fathom.

Her preoccupation was so complete that she failed to notice Clara and Mr. Hollingsworth until she was nearly at the gig. When she finally looked up, she saw them standing together, locked in deep and earnest conversation. The intensity of their exchange struck her as odd; they seemed even less aware of the world around them than she had been a moment before.

Chapter Eighteen

The mistletoe had transformed the house party into a lively spectacle. The younger guests, with no shortage of holiday mischief, had taken it upon themselves to distribute the festive greenery throughout the manor. No doorway or chandelier was safe from their efforts, and those who passed beneath the sprigs often paid the traditional consequences.

Emmeline was struck by how the sight of the house—alive with merriment and mischief—offered both charm and chaos. The holiday spirit was infectious, yet for her, the room felt like a maze of schemes and secrets. Every clump of mistletoe, every burst of laughter, seemed to mask some ulterior motive.

Her gaze swept the lively crowd, seeking Lord Hawthorne, whom she spotted at last in the midst of a foreign group dominated by her aunt's pointed commentary. She was just about to make her approach when she felt an arm clasp firmly around her waist and a loud, enthusiastic kiss land squarely on her cheek.

"Caught you, Miss St. Clair!" crowed an elderly gentleman, leaning heavily on his cane as the nearby guests erupted into laughter and applause. His cheeks were flushed with wine and triumph, and Emmeline's indignation warred with amusement at his audacity.

Despite her urgent need to speak with Hawthorne, Emmeline found herself momentarily diverted by the old man's antics. With remarkable vigor, he stationed himself strategically by the doorway, his sharp eyes gleaming with mischief as he waited to ambush every unwary lady who dared pass beneath the mistletoe.

Each time he struck, his laughter rang out louder, the joy of the room swelling with every stolen kiss. The air itself seemed charged with the anticipation of his next victim.

The old gentleman's enthusiasm quickly proved infectious. Before long, the younger men turned into merry predators, eager to prey upon unsuspecting women who wandered into their reach. Emmeline watched with growing amusement as Miss Evans, strolling with calculated ease, "accidentally" positioned herself beneath a clump of mistletoe. Gabriel seized the opportunity, stepping forward to claim a kiss, though it was impossible to miss the faint look of disappointment that crossed Miss Evans's face. Her subtle glance in Lord Hawthorne's direction revealed her true target.

The realization sparked an idea in Emmeline's mind. Miss Evans wasn't the only one casting out lures tonight, and perhaps the mistletoe offered the perfect excuse for a discreet assignation. Moving nonchalantly across the room, she feigned a search for someone. When she came within earshot of Lord Hawthorne, she added strength to her ruse, inquiring in a carrying voice whether anyone had seen Miss Clara. After receiving the expected negative replies, she continued her circuit, finally positioning herself beneath the same sprig of mistletoe Miss Evans had abandoned moments earlier.

As she waited, her pulse quickened. There was something exhilarating, even daring, about orchestrating such a public maneuver. Yet beneath the thrill lay a quiet desperation. She needed to speak with him, needed to confirm her fears—or dismiss them outright.

Catching Hawthorne's eye was no challenge; he had been watching her with a puzzled yet intrigued expression since she entered. Emmeline met his gaze and shot him a pointed look. After a brief hesitation, he gave the smallest of nods, signaling that he understood her intention.

She waited, heart thudding with a mixture of nerves and anticipation, but as she saw Hawthorne move toward her, her moment was stolen yet again. An arm encircled her waist from behind, and before she could react, she felt another kiss pressed soundly to her opposite cheek.

The intrusion shattered the fragile anticipation, and Emmeline's frustration flared.

"Really, Mr. Moorefield?" she exclaimed, spinning to face him with a glare.

"Really, Miss St. Clair," he replied, his smirk infuriatingly smug as he gestured upward. "The mistletoe, you see.

Emmeline's eyes darted to the offending greenery, and she all but stamped her foot. Her irritation only deepened as she caught sight of Hawthorne, striding past without so much as a glance in her direction, already drawn into a group surrounding her uncle.

In that moment, she hated the smirk on his face, and the presumptuous familiarity in his tone. Yet she forced herself to maintain composure. Anger would only feed his ego.

Her carefully laid plan lay in ruins, all thanks to Moorefield's interference.

"I've been wishing to speak to you, Emmeline," Mr. Moorefield said, his voice pulling her reluctant attention back to him. "You don't mind me making free with your first name, do you?"

She did mind, actually, but thought it more politic not to say so. Instead, she offered a faint smile. "Not at all."

"Good," he said, his satisfaction making her regret her civility. "Then you must call me Alistair."

"Alistair?" she repeated, raising a brow. "Oh, are you perhaps part Welsh, then?"

"Yes, as a matter of fact," he replied, his expression briefly softening. "But I do wish you wouldn't change the subject."

"What subject? I thought we were merely making conversation," she countered lightly. "I wasn't even aware that one had been introduced."

"I am trying to tell you something," he said, turning impatient. But before he could continue, a loud chime announced dinner. "Oh, bother," he muttered.

Emmeline bit back a triumphant smile, grateful for the reprieve. Yet as they moved toward the dining room, her relief was short-lived. Moorefield remained fixed to her side, and she couldn't shake the sense that his persistence would soon lead to a revelation she wasn't prepared to face.

The vicar, invited to dine with them, began the evening meal with a lengthy blessing. As the dishes were served, Emmeline turned politely to her partner. "You mentioned you had something to tell me, Alistair," she said, hoping to draw him out.

"Not here," he whispered, glancing around and lowering his voice further. "This is hardly the setting for such a conversation."

Her stomach tightened. *Surely he can't be about to propose.* The thought sent a wave of dread washing over her. She knew Mr. Moorefield would go to great lengths to curry Sir Edmund's favor, but matrimony? On such a short acquaintance? She tried to steady her breathing, wondering what her answer would be if he truly asked.

The weight of her family's expectations pressed down on her. Her mother had made no secret of her desire to see her daughters settled, and Emmeline's older sister, the family's hopeless romantic, had already caused enough scandal by falling for a fugitive from justice. Mr. Moorefield—or rather, Alistair—might not be her ideal match, but what choice did she have? Her frazzled thoughts were interrupted by an unwelcome realization: Lord Hawthorne's eyes were fixed on her from his seat above the salt.

The meal dragged on interminably. As Christmas approached, even Lady Hollybrook's modestly situated friends and poor relations seemed to lose their initial awe of the grand surroundings. The wine flowed freely, and the footmen refilled glasses with alarming alacrity, fueling the room's rising merriment.

Laughter rippled through the crowd, much of it spurred by the old gentleman who had made himself the life of the mistletoe escapades. Now, at the dinner table, he held court with increasingly ribald anecdotes, his wit drawing gasps and giggles from the assembled guests. One particular tale—concerning a fresh-faced curate and a sharp-tongued spinster—sent a young schoolgirl into such fits of laughter that she developed a case of the hiccups. Her sharp squeaks punctuated the room's mirth, much to the dismay of her mother, who frowned sharply from across the table.

At last, the signal was given for the ladies to retire, but Emmeline found little relief in the drawing room. The wait for the gentlemen to rejoin them stretched on, each moment further taxing her nerves. Her growing headache threatened to become a convenient excuse to escape to her room, but she dismissed the thought. Fleeing would only postpone the inevitable, and the suspense was already unbearable.

When the gentlemen finally filed in, their jovial chatter filling the room, Emmeline's heart sank. Her eyes flitted over the crowd, searching anxiously for Mr. Moorefield and Lord Hawthorne. Neither was among the company.

Her breath quickened, unease creeping into her chest. Where were they? Had something transpired? Her mind raced with possibilities, each more unsettling than the last.

She was still puzzling over the curious absence when, at last, the two men entered together. Both immediately sought her out, but it was Mr. Moorefield who made his way straight toward her, leaving Hawthorne to join the larger group.

"I'm sorry to have kept you waiting," Moorefield said, lowering his voice as he settled into a chair beside hers. "But I needed to keep an eye on a certain individual. Now, perhaps there's still time to say what I wish before Lady Hollybrook organizes us for entertainment."

"You wish to speak to me *here*?" she asked, her nerves jangling.

"Yes," he said firmly. "No one is paying us any mind, and it would look far stranger if we left the room together. Don't worry," he added with a reassuring smile.

But Emmeline felt no reassurance. Instead, a knot tightened in her chest, her dread mounting as his eyes gleamed with suppressed excitement. Whatever he was about to say, she knew it would change everything.

"I suppose so," Emmeline said, casting a sidelong glance at him. He was practically bursting with the desire to speak, his eyes alight with suppressed excitement.

"I want you to be the first to hear," he whispered, leaning in conspiratorially.

"Well, yes, I suppose I should be the first, since Mama isn't available," she replied lightly, hoping to deflect whatever seriousness loomed in his tone.

"What the devil—err, deuce, I mean—does your mother have to do with the matter?" he sputtered, caught off guard. "What I have to say is for your ears alone. For the moment, at any rate. But once this evening's drama has played itself out, well, then everyone will know."

"I see," Emmeline murmured, though in truth, she saw nothing of the sort. "Mr. Moorefield, what on earth are you talking about?"

"Alistair, please," he corrected with a faint hint of exasperation.

"Very well," she said with a sigh. "But do come to the point before my aunt corrals us all into the quadrille or some other dreadful activity."

"Very well," he said, straightening with an air of great importance. "First, I must offer my deepest apologies for suspecting you—only briefly, you understand—of being involved in the Christopher Langford affair. My reason for this suspicion, slight though it was, is rooted in ample observation of how easily females lose their heads over Lord Hawthorne. I thought, perhaps, he might be using you to further his dubious schemes."

"Ah, so you said," she replied, striving for offense rather than guilt. "And what, pray tell, caused you to change your mind?"

"The fact that Mr. Hollingsworth confirmed Miss Clara had prepared a basket for him, which you were entrusted to deliver. I must admit, up until then, I had entertained the faintest notion that the provisions were intended for someone else."

"Surely you didn't imagine I had developed a peculiar soft spot for gypsies?" she asked, arching a brow.

"Of course not," he replied impatiently. "What I imagined, for instance, was that Lord Hawthorne had persuaded you to carry provisions to Christopher Langford, who, I am quite certain, is holed up inside Hollingsworth Hall."

"Oh, really?" she managed, though her throat tightened with the effort. "And why, exactly, would you think that? The Dover Channel?"

"No," he said with a dismissive wave. "His rescuers would know the authorities are watching every ship that sails. I suspect the plan is to hide Langford away until the hue and cry dies down, then book passage elsewhere. And what better place to conceal a wanted felon than an estate everyone assumes is deserted?"

"Not Hollingsworth Hall," Emmeline said firmly. "You can't seriously believe Mr. Hollingsworth is involved."

"No," he admitted reluctantly. "While Graham Hollingsworth's character is questionable, I doubt he knows anything of this affair. I questioned him—subtly, of course—and I'm convinced he hasn't even heard of Christopher Langford, let alone become a party to his escape. You must remember, Miss St. Clair, that Mr. Hollingsworth has only just been released from prison himself, and no one in these parts was aware of his release beforehand. As far as anyone knew, Hollingsworth Hall would be unoccupied—a perfect hiding place."

"Who in London would have known that?" she asked, her voice carefully neutral.

"Hawthorne, for one," Moorefield replied.

"But I thought you'd finally concluded he couldn't be involved," Emmeline pressed. "You listed so many reasons only recently."

"I was mistaken," he said, his eyes gleaming with fervor. "The witnesses must have been confused in the chaos. I now believe the guard who fired his weapon missed his target entirely or aimed at Langford instead of his rescuer. Perhaps the story was fabricated to save face. Either way, the truth will soon come to light."

"And how do you intend to uncover this truth?" she asked, dread coiling in her stomach.

"The magistrate," Moorefield said triumphantly. "I've spoken to him, and he's organized a party to search Hollingsworth Hall tonight. In fact..." He glanced at the mantel clock, a gleam of pride in his eyes. "The raid should be underway at this very moment."

"The magistrate will handle this properly," Moorefield said, his tone carrying the weight of authority. "If Christopher Langford is truly hiding at Hollingsworth Hall, bringing him to justice will be a significant victory—not just for the local authorities, but for the community as a whole. We cannot let criminals believe they can evade the law so easily."

He paused, straightening his shoulders as though imagining himself at the center of applause. "These are the sort of actions that inspire trust in leadership. A decisive hand, a clear vision—essential qualities in a man of standing."

Emmeline's pulse raced. She felt as though the room had tilted, the ground beneath her shifting precariously. Christopher was in danger—real, imminent danger—and she had precious little time to act.

Chapter Nineteen

"Oh, my heavens!" Emmeline choked, her hand flying to her mouth.

Fortunately, her aunt Arabella chose that exact moment to swoop down upon them. Her voice, sharp with the importance of mediating a household crisis, cut through the tension. "Mr. Moorefield, I must consult you immediately regarding the rules of snapdragon. There seems to be some contention among the younger set about who has earned the most points."

Emmeline seized the opportunity to excuse herself, retreating toward the far end of the drawing room. She had hoped this would provide a chance for a private word with Lord Hawthorne while Mr. Moorefield was otherwise occupied. However, much to her dismay, his lordship had become the center of attention for two giggling schoolroom misses.

She stood nearby, her arms folded, barely concealing her impatience as she waited for Hawthorne to disentangle himself. Her foot tapped against the polished floorboards as the laughter of the young ladies grated on her nerves. At last, she caught his eye, but his expression—one of deliberate indifference—made her long to scream.

"Well, you certainly took your time," she hissed as he finally moved toward her. "I need to talk to you—it's most—"

Her words were abruptly cut off as he pulled her close, his arm wrapping firmly around her waist. Before she could protest, his lips descended on hers, silencing her completely. A thousand thoughts raced through her mind in that brief, overwhelming moment. Anger. Shock. And beneath them, something unbidden—a traitorous spark of warmth she immediately tried to smother. How dare he! How could he? And yet... how could her heart betray her so thoroughly by skipping a beat?

Later, it occurred to her that it was a pity so much expertise had to go to waste. But even as she tried to frame the moment with wry detachment, her thoughts betrayed her. Why had it unsettled her so deeply? It wasn't just the impropriety—or the audience. It was something far more dangerous, something that whispered she wasn't entirely indifferent to his touch. And that frightened her more than any of Moorefield's accusations or the looming scandal at Hollingsworth Hall.

But as it stood, she had no difficulty finding her indignation. After a long moment spent regaining her composure, she shoved his chest with both hands, forcing him to release her. She stepped back, her cheeks blazing. "Have you entirely lost your mind?" she demanded, her voice trembling with fury.

In reply, he pointed upward. Following his gaze, she saw the chandelier above them, its crystal prisms glittering in the candlelight—and adorned, much to her mortification, with sprigs of mistletoe. Around them, the other guests were tittering, their amusement making her blood boil.

"Oh, blast!" she muttered, her mortification boiling over.

Hawthorne raised a brow, his smirk maddeningly insouciant. "A strange reaction, Miss St. Clair, considering you've been trying to lure me under that stuff all evening."

Her eyes narrowed. "I've been trying to have a private word with you all evening—by hook or by crook," she hissed through clenched teeth. "But now there's no time to waste on this sort of foolishness. Mr. Moorefield has sent the authorities to search Hollingsworth Hall."

His expression sharpened immediately. "Good God!" he whispered, his voice urgent. "I must get out of here and warn Christopher."

"It's too late for that," Emmeline said, glancing anxiously around the room. "The search is already taking place. What you'd best do is take to your heels while you still can."

"Now that would be damn stupid," he muttered, shaking his head.

"And waiting here to be arrested is intelligent?" she countered, her voice rising slightly before she forced it back down.

"It won't come to that," he said firmly. "Christopher won't implicate me. You can rest assured of that. And as for Moorefield's suspicions—no one will take his word over mine."

Emmeline considered this, her brows furrowing. "No, I don't suppose they will," she said slowly. "Which doesn't seem fair, I don't mind saying."

"Agreed," Hawthorne replied, his gaze steady. "Nor is it fair that Christopher Langford faces prison for daring to speak his mind. But that's the way of the world, Miss St. Clair." His eyes softened as he studied her face. "Of course, you could always even the score by turning me in yourself."

"You know I won't do that," she said quickly, the words coming without hesitation.

"Well, actually, your principles left me somewhat uncertain." His voice was calm, but his gaze bored into hers, as if searching for something deeper. "Do you mind explaining just why you won't inform on me?"

She swallowed hard, her throat constricting. What she wanted to say—to hurl back at him with righteous fury—was that it wasn't for the reasons he was imagining. She wasn't some foolish woman swayed by a handsome face and a noble title. She wasn't like Miss Evans or the countless other women who had fallen prey to his effortless charm. But the words stuck.

Finally, she lifted her chin. "I don't like sending anyone to prison," she said simply. But as she spoke, she couldn't ignore the deeper truth lurking beneath her words. Hawthorne had tested her resolve, her principles—and perhaps even her heart—in ways no one else ever had. The thought of betraying him felt not only wrong but strangely unbearable, as though doing so would shatter some fragile, unspoken understanding between them.

For a moment, he regarded her in silence, his expression unreadable. Then, his lips curved into the faintest of smiles—one that held no trace of mockery. "Fair enough, Miss St. Clair," he said softly.

Before she could respond, the sound of her aunt's voice rang out, drawing the attention of the room. Lady Hollybrook was sorting guests into various entertainments, and Emmeline watched as Hawthorne excused himself from dancing, claiming he had not yet recovered sufficiently for such strenuous activity. Instead, he joined a group forming at the card tables, leaving Emmeline to take her place at the pianoforte.

A MARQUESS FOR CHRISTMAS 191

As her fingers moved mechanically over the keys, her mind raced. No matter how she tried, she couldn't shake the thought of what might be happening at Hollingsworth Hall—and what it might mean for Lord Hawthorne if Moorefield's accusations gained any traction.

Moorefield had stationed himself uncomfortably close to Emmeline at the pianoforte, insisting on turning the pages of her music. His efforts, however, left much to be desired. His nervous energy betrayed him—he kept glancing at the clock, his ears straining for the sound of approaching horsemen, and his fingers flipping the pages too early or too late. The result was a stuttering melody that caused the dancers to stumble in their steps.

"Really, Mr. Moorefield, just let me do it," Emmeline said sharply, her patience at its limit.

Chastened, he withdrew to a nearby chair, but he was far from still. He tapped his foot absently in time to the music, his gaze fixed intently on the drawing-room door, as though willing it to burst open with news.

The evening dragged on until the guests began exchanging their goodnights. It was then, just as Emmeline thought the night might finally end in peace, that the expected interruption came.

The butler entered the room, followed closely by a towering man clad in riding clothes. His cheeks were puffy and red from the cold, his nose matching the bright cherry hue. The stranger strode in with an air of urgency that silenced the room.

"Mr. Carter!" Sir Edmund exclaimed, rising from his seat, his surprise evident. "What brings you out at this hour? Come, stand by the fire, man. You look frozen. Riggs, fetch a brandy."

"Apologies for the intrusion, sir," Mr. Carter said, rubbing his hands briskly as he approached the hearth. "Your man offered to have me wait in the hall, but I thought it better to come straight in. I need a word with two of your guests—and I reckoned this would be quicker so we can all get to our beds. God knows I need mine."

Emmeline, along with the rest of the company, leaned in with curiosity. The murmured farewells were forgotten as all attention turned to the unexpected visitor. Mr. Carter, however, appeared in no hurry to satisfy their curiosity. He accepted the glass of brandy from Riggs, took a generous mouthful, savored it with an exaggerated smack of his lips, and then, to everyone's exasperation, followed it with another.

"You were saying?" Sir Edmund prompted, his tone clipped with impatience.

"I need a word with your secretary and Lord... Lord Hawthorne, is it?" Carter asked, his memory clicking into place with a triumphant nod.

"Yes, Lord Hawthorne," Sir Edmund confirmed, though his brows furrowed in concern.

"And," Carter continued, his gaze sweeping the room, "anyone else who might shed light on this business." He let the words hang tantalizingly in the air, clearly enjoying his moment as the center of attention. "Because, I'll not lie, Sir Edmund, I've no idea what to make of it. The fact of the matter is, a good number of men—good men—who'd have preferred to spend this evening with their families have been dragged out for what seems to be nothing more than a wild goose chase."

The magistrate's reproachful gaze landed squarely on Moorefield, whose eager expression abruptly drained of color. His face, so animated just moments ago, now took on a waxy pallor, his discomfort plain for all to see.

Emmeline was struggling to keep her expression under control, willing her face into a mask of polite neutrality. She avoided looking at Lord Hawthorne, knowing full well that his reaction would only stoke the tumult of emotions she was working so hard to suppress. But despite her best efforts, her gaze strayed to him, and what she saw left her both infuriated and begrudgingly impressed.

There he was, lounging casually against the mantel as though entirely unaffected by the storm brewing in the room. The sight infuriated her—how could he remain so maddeningly calm? Yet, beneath her irritation, she couldn't help but marvel at his confidence. He seemed untouchable, as though no accusation, no danger, could rattle him. Was it arrogance? Or something more—a certainty in his own honor that she couldn't help but admire, despite herself?

His posture was one of effortless grace, his gaze directed at Mr. Carter with mild curiosity. As Emmeline watched, he even stifled a yawn, the very picture of nonchalance.

"What do you mean, 'wild goose chase?'" Moorefield blurted, his voice cracking slightly under the strain of his agitation.

"I mean, sir," Mr. Carter replied with deliberate calm, "that we searched Hollingsworth Hall from attic to cellar not once, not twice, but three times, and found no sign whatsoever of your fugitive. That, Mr. Moorefield, is what I call a wild goose chase."

"Searched Hollingsworth Hall?" Sir Edmund echoed, his expression a mix of shock and disbelief. Beside him, his sister turned an alarming shade of pale, clutching the back of a chair for support. "Why would you do such a thing?"

"Ask him." Mr. Carter jerked his thumb toward Moorefield, his voice heavy with reproach. "Your secretary here was positively convinced that a certain Mr. Christopher Langford—escaped felon, mind you—was hiding out there. But now, I'm forced to wonder just what made him so certain."

"He was there! I know it!" Moorefield sputtered, his face growing increasingly red as all eyes turned toward him.

The room seemed to collectively hold its breath.

"He had to be!" Moorefield continued, his voice rising in desperation. "It's the only logical place Hawthorne could have hidden him!"

A cacophony of voices erupted in response.

"Oh, I say!"

"Mr. Moorefield!"

"Alistair!"

"How dare you!"

"He can't mean it!"

So many people spoke at once—Sir Edmund, Lady Hollybrook, Gabriel, and others—that Emmeline could barely make sense of the bedlam. Amidst the chaos, however, one sound stood out to her: Lord Hawthorne's low, dry chuckle.

Mr. Carter turned his sharp gaze on Hawthorne. "And what do you have to say to that, sir? You are Lord Hawthorne, I presume?"

Lord Hawthorne's raised brow and faintly amused expression seemed to imply that there could be no doubt of his identity. But before he could speak, Gabriel burst out indignantly.

"Now, look here, Carter, you've no right to—"

"Of course he has, Gabriel," Hawthorne interrupted smoothly, his tone as soothing as a balm. Turning back to the magistrate, he inclined his head politely. "Am I to understand, sir, that Mr. Moorefield here"—he cast a contemptuous glance toward the secretary—"has attempted to implicate me in Christopher Langford's disappearance? I was aware, of course, that he's harbored this peculiar obsession for some time, but I confess I didn't think he would take his absurd suspicions to such extremes."

Hawthorne folded his arms and continued, his voice calm but laced with irony. "As far as I can tell, Mr. Carter, Moorefield's basis for his accusations is twofold: firstly, that Langford and I were schoolmates, and secondly, that I would be pleased—very pleased, in fact—if Langford has indeed escaped. On the latter point, I make no apology. I think most Englishmen would agree with me, for I can scarcely conceive of a more unjust conviction."

"Well, I'll not argue with that, sir," Mr. Carter said, though he added with a faint smile, "though in my position, I suppose I ought to."

The magistrate's gaze then swung back to Moorefield, his demeanor darkening. "And is that truly all you had to go on, sir?"

"No, it isn't!" Moorefield thundered, his voice trembling with rage. His face was suffused with color, his eyes wild with frustration. "His curricle was seen near the site where Langford was taken! And he may claim he had the measles, but I happen to believe that he was shot!"

By this time, everyone in the room was staring at Moorefield as though he had grown a second head. Mr. Carter regarded him with raised brows, his voice dry when he finally responded. "Measles or a gunshot wound, eh? Well, I'd wager that most folk could tell the two apart."

His remark drew a ripple of laughter from the more irreverent members of the company, but the tension in the room was far from diffused. All eyes remained fixed on Moorefield, whose desperate fervor now bordered on the unhinged.

While some of the company tittered at the magistrate's dry wit, Gabriel stepped forward, his indignation palpable. He was trembling as he spoke, his voice a mix of fury and exasperation. "I don't know why Moorefield here is so hell-bent on vilifying Hawthorne, but he's been at it ever since he arrived! I, for one, am thoroughly sick of it. The truth is, Carter, that whereas his lordship would never stoop to such a shocking thing as taking a prisoner at gunpoint, the fact remains that he *couldn't* have done so. He was on his way here at the time. Frankly, I see no need to dignify the ravings of a jumped-up, underbred secretary who's clearly jealous as anything—"

"That will do, Gabriel," Sir Edmund interjected, his voice sharp with reproach. He turned to the magistrate with an expression of weary regret. "Mr. Carter, I must extend my sincerest apologies that your evening has been wasted in this absurd manner. The fault lies entirely at my door. Please convey my apologies to your men as well. And now, unless you have further questions, I will not detain you any longer from your much-deserved rest."

Riggs stepped forward to escort Mr. Carter out, the room abuzz with shocked murmurs. Guests exchanged scandalized whispers, their gazes flickering furtively toward Mr. Moorefield, whose complexion had turned a blotchy shade of crimson. His expression teetered between outrage and humiliation, his fists clenched at his sides.

As the company slowly dispersed, bidding each other good night, Emmeline joined the reluctant exodus. She kept her eyes fixed straight ahead, determined not to look at Lord Hawthorne. Yet, despite her resolve, curiosity won out, and she cast a furtive glance in his direction.

He was still lounging against the mantel with an infuriating air of ease, his lips curled in the faintest of smirks as though entirely untouched by the evening's drama. The sight sent a wave of both irritation and admiration through her. How could he remain so unruffled in the face of Moorefield's hysteria?

The answer came moments later when Moorefield suddenly wheeled around to face Hawthorne, his voice rising to a near-shriek. "You needn't think for one minute that this is finished, Hawthorne!" he spat, trembling with rage. "No, not by a long shot! I'm on to you, and you won't be able to lift a finger to help Langford escape—not one finger! I'll be watching you like a hawk every single moment. You may depend on it!"

A hush fell over the room, broken only by the sound of the old gentleman's booming voice. "My God, the fellow's *dicked in the nob*!" he declared with what was perhaps meant to be a whisper but carried easily to every corner of the room. "Why, the man's a regular Bedlamite if ever I saw one!"

The ripple of laughter that followed was restrained but unmistakable. Even Sir Edmund's lips twitched, though he quickly schooled his features into a mask of authority. Moorefield, however, looked ready to explode, his eyes darting wildly as though seeking some form of retribution.

Lord Hawthorne, unperturbed, gave an elegant shrug and adjusted his cuffs as though the entire scene had been nothing more than a mild inconvenience. "How fortunate for me, then," he drawled, "that I have no intention of lifting even a finger for you to watch. Good night, Mr. Moorefield."

With that, he turned on his heel and strode from the room, leaving Moorefield spluttering in impotent fury and the rest of the company exchanging wide-eyed glances. Emmeline, despite herself, found her lips twitching in the beginnings of a smile. Whatever else Lord Hawthorne might be, he certainly had a flair for the dramatic.

But as she watched him stride from the room, unruffled and self-assured, a nagging unease coiled in her chest. He was playing a dangerous game, and she couldn't shake the feeling that she was being drawn into it—whether she wanted to be or not. What frightened her most wasn't the risk to his reputation, but the risk to her own heart.

Chapter Twenty

As Emmeline left the drawing room, she saw Sir Edmund draw his secretary aside, presumably to reprimand him in private. Taking advantage of Moorefield's distraction, she hurried to her chamber and left the door slightly ajar, just enough to watch for Lord Hawthorne without being seen herself.

"Psst!" she whispered sharply when she spotted him in the hall. His head turned, brows raised in curiosity, but before he could react further, she opened the door wide and practically yanked him inside by the sleeve.

"We need to talk," she hissed, her voice low.

"Not as much as I need to get out of here while Moorefield is distracted," he replied with maddening patience, even as his eyes scanned the room. "I've got to find Christopher. God knows what kind of trouble he might be in by now."

"Don't be ridiculous! How do you expect to find him out there in the pitch-dark? There's not a sliver of moonlight, and you can't exactly wave a lantern around and call his name, can you?"

"Look," he said tightly, "I don't need your sarcasm. I have to do what I—"

Before he could finish, the door opened with a creak, and both Emmeline and Hawthorne froze.

Her heart leapt into her throat. *Oh, dear God, what have I done?* For the first time, the full implications of her impulsive act hit her like a slap. She had dragged a gentleman—unmarried, titled, and notorious, no less—into her private chamber. What if it wasn't Clara who entered but her aunt, or worse, Mr. Moorefield himself? The impropriety of the situation was damning enough to ruin her reputation entirely, and she could already hear the whispered accusations spreading like wildfire through the household.

But it was not Moorefield who entered. Miss Clara Hollybrook stepped inside, the hem of her gown swishing softly over the floor. Her normally gentle features were tight with anger, her eyes burning with an emotion so foreign to her usual demeanor that Emmeline hardly recognized her friend.

"I thought I might find you both in here," Clara said, her voice quivering, not with nervousness but with unmistakable fury.

Hawthorne tilted his head, his lips curving into the faintest smirk. His expression seemed to say, *Et tu, Brute*? But he spoke with studied calm. "And what, may I ask, have I done to earn your displeasure this time, Miss Hollybrook? Surely you don't take Moorefield's nonsense seriously."

"Don't fence with me!" Clara snapped, her voice shaking. "I'm not concerned with whether what you did was right or wrong. What enrages me is that you dragged Graham Hollingsworth into this mess! Hiding Langford on his estate was despicable, Hawthorne! If you're discovered, with your family's influence, you might escape unscathed.

But Graham? He's only just been released from prison! You've risked putting him away for life."

Her voice cracked as her eyes welled with tears, the full weight of her anger and worry crashing down on her.

"Oh, God," Hawthorne muttered, dragging a hand through his hair, leaving it charmingly tousled in the process. "Let's all just sit down and try to discuss this rationally, shall we? You're right, Miss St. Clair," he added, casting a rueful glance at Emmeline, "there's nothing I can do about Christopher tonight. Emmeline, bolt the door, would you? I'd rather not have this little gathering interrupted by Moorefield—that would truly put the cat among the pigeons."

"Please believe me, Clara," Hawthorne said earnestly as they settled into chairs by the fire, the flickering light casting shadows across his face. "I never intended to involve Mr. Hollingsworth—or anyone else, for that matter—in this business. Moorefield's suspicions, of course, were inevitable. But the Hollingsworth estate?" He exhaled heavily, running a hand through his already disheveled hair. "That was pure chance. Gabriel happened to mention the place—the emptiest estate bordering his land, abandoned and infamous for being 'haunted.' It sounded perfect, the last place anyone would think to search. Believe me, it was a shock to learn the owner was back in residence. One of several shocks," he added bitterly, shifting in his chair. "The first was the unscheduled bullet in my arm."

Clara flinched at his words, her face pale but stern. Emmeline, however, found her voice edged with disapproval. "Well, it seems to me," she said pointedly, "that you might have expected that sort of thing when you took on three armed guards."

"The devil bit I did," he replied. "What kind of fool do you take me for? I made sure they were bought off well in advance—more than enough blunt to ensure their shots went wide."

Emmeline blinked, caught off guard. "You mean you bribed the guards?" Her shock was evident, her lips parting as though she couldn't quite believe it.

"Of course I did," he said matter-of-factly. "Sorry to shatter your illusions, Miss St. Clair, but I'm no hero."

Emmeline was momentarily silenced, grappling with the bluntness of his confession. Clara, however, pressed on, her tone sharp and acidic despite her effort to keep her voice low. "We're straying from the point," she said crisply. "What's done is done. The real question is: what do you plan to do now?"

Hawthorne leaned forward, resting his forearms on his knees as he stared into the fire. "That's the rub, isn't it?" he said quietly. "I have to contrive some way to leave in the morning without Moorefield seeing me. If I can't walk out the front door in plain sight, well, there's always the window."

"The window?" Emmeline repeated incredulously. "A sheer drop of three stories? You're hardly in any condition to stage an escape worthy of a gothic novel. Remember, you're no hero."

"She's right, you know," Clara added. "Not about the heroics, but about your arm. It's nowhere near healed enough for a rope descent—or whatever harebrained scheme you've cooked up."

"Besides," Emmeline continued, folding her arms, "if you're seen climbing out the window in the dead of night, it will only look like an admission of guilt."

Hawthorne slumped back in his chair, his expression dark with frustration. "Then what do you propose I do, Miss St. Clair? Sit here and twiddle my thumbs while Langford—God knows where he is—faces the wolves alone?"

"No," Clara interjected firmly, her composure returning. "You will stay here, and *we* will find Mr. Langford at first light. It's the only reasonable course of action. You're in no state to act, and you'll only make matters worse if you're caught."

The room fell silent for a moment, the crackle of the fire filling the space as Hawthorne stared at them both, the weight of their words sinking in.

"No, may I remind you, you are *not* above suspicion," Hawthorne said firmly, his gaze locking on Emmeline. "I cannot allow it."

"Well then, you'll just have to lead Mr. Moorefield astray on his own wild goose chase," Emmeline retorted, her chin lifting defiantly. "If Moorefield follows you, he'll be too occupied to interfere while Clara and I search for Mr. Langford on the Hollingsworth lands."

"*We'll* be free?" Clara interjected quietly, her voice carrying a note of caution. "It would look peculiar—not just to Moorefield but to everyone—if you were gone for any length of time on your own. But if we were seen delivering Christmas baskets together, no one would think twice about it." She managed a faint, wry smile. "This might just end up being the most generous Christmas our tenants have ever had."

Hawthorne opened his mouth to object, but Clara cut him off with a determined look. "You can't do this alone, Hawthorne. Let us do our part."

The following morning, Emmeline and Clara waited near an upstairs window overlooking the stables, their breaths fogging the frosty glass. Below, they watched as Hawthorne excused himself from the breakfast table and made his way toward the stable yard with an air of calculated nonchalance.

The moment he stepped outside, their patience was rewarded. Mr. Moorefield emerged almost immediately, skulking along behind him, attempting—and failing—to blend into his surroundings. Hawthorne, in turn, threw occasional furtive glances over his shoulder, clearly aware of his unwanted shadow.

"He mustn't overdo it," Emmeline murmured, half-amused. "He's no more an actor than he is a hero."

Clara, stifling a nervous laugh, pointed toward the secretary, who was crouching awkwardly behind a shrub. "It might take more acting ability for Hawthorne to *pretend* he doesn't notice that."

They exchanged a brief moment of mirth, though their unease lingered beneath the surface.

Once Moorefield and Hawthorne were well out of sight, Clara and Emmeline made their way toward the beach, a basket laden with provisions perched innocently on the gig beside them. Clara gave a final caution as they approached the familiar stretch of sand. "You'll have to be the legs of this operation," she said, handing the basket to Emmeline. "Try to find Graham and tell him I need to see him. If Mr. Carter's men are still lurking about, you can always say the basket is for Mr. Hollingsworth. Let's hope they won't remember we brought one yesterday."

To their relief, no such encounter was necessary. Hollingsworth was at the beach once again, absorbed in his work on a small boat. He straightened as the gig rolled to a stop behind him, brushing sawdust from his hands as he approached.

"Charity, ladies?" he asked with a sardonic grin. "Or have you come chasing after your fugitive?"

"In a way," Clara replied, her face edged with concern. "Have you seen him, Graham?"

He leaned lightly on the gig's shaft, his gaze softening as it met Clara's. "Now, do you truly expect me to answer that, Clara Hollybrook?" he said gently. "Don't you think I'd feel a touch of sympathy for some poor devil being hounded into prison?"

"That's exactly what I've imagined, Hollingsworth," Clara said, her voice trembling but resolute. "And I'm here to tell you I don't give a—" she hesitated for a split second before spitting the words, "tinker's damn—about Mr. Langford. It's you I'm concerned with. I won't have you dragged into this. You've suffered enough already. This is no concern of yours."

Graham raised both hands in exaggerated astonishment, his brows shooting up. "By George, I think you really mean it. Clara Hollybrook swearing? I never thought I'd live to see the day."

"Don't make jokes, Graham," she snapped, her voice thick with emotion. Tears glistened in her eyes, threatening to fall. "This isn't a laughing matter."

Before Clara could continue, Emmeline stepped in. "Look, Mr. Hollingsworth, you've got it all wrong if you think we're here to turn Mr. Langford in. We're trying to help him."

"We?" Clara said, brushing at her cheeks with a handkerchief. "Let's be clear—I want to help him. You've just been dragged along."

Disillusionment hung heavy in the air. Emmeline, who had always seen Clara as a tower of strength, was stunned to see her friend so visibly shaken. But she didn't let it deter her. "Have you seen Christopher Langford, Mr. Hollingsworth?" she asked bluntly, meeting his gaze head-on while Clara worked to compose herself.

"Yes," Hollingsworth admitted after a moment's pause. "As a matter of fact, I have. After meeting you both yesterday and speaking with that insufferable Mr. Moorefield, I put two and two together. It didn't take much to figure out that all that food wasn't meant for me and that your supposed 'gypsy' was something else entirely. So, after you left, I searched my house thoroughly and found your Mr. Langford hiding in my attic."

"Good thing I did, too," he added with a touch of pride. "I convinced him the house was likely to be searched by the authorities—which, as it turns out, was exactly the case."

"And where is he now?" Emmeline pressed her voice tight with urgency.

Hollingsworth's expression hardened. "I think it's best that you remain ignorant of his whereabouts, Miss St. Clair," he said firmly. "But rest assured, he's safe enough and little the worse for wear, thanks to the provisions and a few old blankets."

Clara's shoulders sagged with visible relief, but her voice carried a bitter edge as she spoke. "You just couldn't stay uninvolved, could you?" she accused.

"No, I couldn't," Hollingsworth replied evenly, his voice softening. "It hardly seemed possible, Clara. It's not as though Langford is one of those hardened criminals I've had the misfortune of meeting over the years. And God knows I'm something of an authority on *those* types. Why would you believe it? The poor cove doesn't even owe anyone money." He cracked a wry grin, but it quickly faded under Clara's disapproving glare.

"This isn't a laughing matter," she snapped.

"Perhaps not," he conceded, his expression sobering. "But to give you a straight answer—no, I couldn't leave him to the wolves. Any more than you could, with your tender heart."

Clara straightened, her chin lifting defiantly as she met his gaze head-on. "But that's exactly what I *will* do, Graham Hollingsworth, before I allow you to risk going back to prison on his account."

Hollingsworth stared at her, his jaw tightening. "Clara..." he began, but the words faltered, and for a moment, the tension between them was palpable.

"Have no fear on that score. I've no yearning myself to repeat the experience," Graham said, his tone light but his eyes shadowed with something far darker.

"Don't try to pull the wool over my eyes, Graham," Clara snapped, her voice sharp enough to cut. "I saw the supplies in your boat when we drove up. You're planning to take that man across the channel, aren't you?"

"Now, couldn't I just be planning a fishing trip?" he countered, the faintest smile tugging at his lips.

"I know what you're up to, and I will *not* allow it," she shot back, her eyes flashing with determination.

Graham sighed, running a hand through his hair. "Come now, Clara, be reasonable. Even if the 'rat,' as you so kindly call him, were capable of sailing himself—" he gestured toward his modest craft—"and believe me, he isn't, I couldn't just donate my boat, now could I? Fishing has become an important part of my livelihood, you know."

Clara's voice rose in fury. "I meant what I said. I'll suggest to the authorities that they do well to keep an eye on your boat if you persist in this madness."

"That's harsh, Clara," Graham said quietly, his usual glibness stripped away. "God knows I appreciate your concern. But honestly, the risk is minimal. After last night's debacle, the authorities are convinced Langford is nowhere within miles of here."

"*Stop it!*" Emmeline interjected sharply, cutting through their argument before it could escalate further. Both Clara and Graham turned to her, startled by the force of her voice. "This is getting us absolutely nowhere. Clara is right, Mr. Hollingsworth—you shouldn't be involved in this. You're already under enough scrutiny. But you're also right when you say that Mr. Langford is no sailor." She turned her gaze pointedly to Clara. "Lord Hawthorne, however, is—or at least claims to be," she amended with a small, wry twist of her lips, recalling his boasts.

Clara crossed her arms, her expression skeptical. "And how exactly does that help us, Emmeline?"

"Well," Emmeline said, thinking aloud, "we all agree that Mr. Langford is Lord Hawthorne's responsibility. So, it seems to me that Lord Hawthorne should simply *borrow* the boat—unbeknownst to Mr. Hollingsworth, of course—and then return it. And," she added, her voice lowering as she glanced at Graham, "it wouldn't hurt if you went to stay with friends while all this is going on. That way, if anything does go wrong—" she shivered, "you won't be implicated."

Graham's laugh was short and humorless. "Thank you for your concern, Miss St. Clair, but an ex-convict doesn't exactly have a wide circle of friends to call on."

Emmeline flinched at the bitterness in his voice, but pressed on. "Then—"

"And how, pray tell," Clara interrupted, her voice cutting, "do you expect Lord Hawthorne to manage such an escape with Mr. Moorefield following his every move? The man's practically a shadow at this point."

"That," Emmeline admitted, her brows furrowing in frustration, "is a very good question."

"By the by," Mr. Hollingsworth interjected, "where is Hawthorne at this moment? Needless to say, Mr. Langford is anxious to contact him."

The ladies exchanged a glance before Clara explained. "He's decoying Moorefield as far away as possible. The idea is to give us the time to figure out what's become of Langford."

"Not that it's a perfect plan," Emmeline added with a sigh, brushing a strand of hair from her face. She began describing Moorefield's dogged pursuit of Hawthorne when suddenly, her hand shot up to her forehead. "Of course! That's it! Why didn't I think of it sooner?"

Clara frowned. "What are you scheming now, Emmeline?" Her expression held equal parts exasperation and unease.

Emmeline's eyes gleamed with sudden inspiration. "It's so obvious. I can't believe we didn't consider it before! As I was saying, Mr. Hollingsworth here shouldn't sail the boat himself because of his... er..."

"Criminal record?" Graham supplied with a wry smile.

"Well, yes," she admitted, flushing slightly. "That would put you in too much jeopardy. And Lord Hawthorne can't sail the boat because Moorefield's always breathing down his neck. So the obvious solution is for them to trade places. Mr. Hollingsworth here will have to *be* Lord Hawthorne for a while."

"*That's* your obvious solution?" Clara's voice was dry enough to parch a desert. "And just how do you intend for that to work? They hardly look alike."

"Just hear me out," Emmeline pressed, undeterred. "It's simple, really. Lord Hawthorne sneaks to the stables—with Moorefield close behind, of course. He takes out his famous curricle—"

"Which is instantly recognizable," Clara interrupted, her brow arching higher.

"Yes, yes," Emmeline conceded, waving her hand impatiently. "That's the point. He wears his coat, his jaunty, curly-brimmed beaver hat—everything that screams 'Hawthorne.' Then he sets off down the road at a decent pace—not too fast, not too slow, just enough to keep Moorefield on his trail. Meanwhile," she turned to Hollingsworth, "you'll be waiting at a designated spot. Once Hawthorne gets there, the two of you switch places. Coats, hats, the whole lot. Then *you* drive the curricle and continue down the road as if you're him."

Graham leaned back against the gig, arms crossed, a bemused expression on his face. "And Moorefield's none the wiser?"

"Exactly!" Emmeline declared, clearly pleased with herself.

Clara, however, looked less convinced. "And what, pray tell, happens when Moorefield finally catches up to *Graham*?"

"The object," Emmeline said firmly, "is for that not to happen."

"And if it does?" Clara pressed, her skepticism palpable. "Then it will look very much like Hawthorne has successfully smuggled Langford out of the country. The only variation from the truth is that Moorefield will believe they sailed from Dover, not here."

"Oh." Emmeline paused, the first crack appearing in her confidence. "I suppose that's true."

"Exactly."

"Well," Emmeline said, recovering quickly, "then Moorefield will simply *have* to catch up to Graham, eventually. The trick is to keep him occupied for long enough that Hawthorne and Langford are well out of reach. Once Moorefield realizes his mistake, it will be far too late."

"And when this happens," Clara said, her voice tight with exasperation, "just how is Graham supposed to explain why he's driving Hawthorne's rig? Not to mention why he's wearing his coat and hat. Do you have an explanation ready for that?"

Emmeline hesitated, her brow furrowing. "Well..."

"Exactly," Clara said, throwing up her hands. "This plan of yours has more holes than a fishing net."

"We'll just have to come up with a good explanation, that's all!" Emmeline insisted.

Graham chuckled softly, shaking his head. "Oh, that should be easy enough, then. There must be *loads* of perfectly logical reasons why a recently released convict would be gallivanting down the Dover road at midnight in a marquess's rig, dressed like him to boot."

"Exactly!" Clara said triumphantly, crossing her arms.

"Wait!" Emmeline's eyes lit up again, and she clasped her hands together as the beginnings of a new idea formed. "What if—what if it's an elopement?"

Both Clara and Graham blinked at her in stunned silence.

"An *elopement*?" Clara repeated flatly.

"Yes! It's perfect!" Emmeline's voice rose with excitement. "Think about it—no one would question why Mr. Hollingsworth was racing down the road in Hawthorne's rig. They'd just assume he'd borrowed it in his desperation to elope in secret! It's a perfect cover."

"Except for one small detail," Clara said, her voice dripping with sarcasm. "Who exactly is Graham eloping *with*?"

"Why..." Emmeline faltered, realizing the flaw in her plan. "Well, he'd... that is to say, someone could... oh, blast."

"Precisely," Clara said victoriously.

"If it's any help," Mr. Hollingsworth offered with a perfectly straight face, "I do happen to own a curly-brimmed beaver hat. Not quite as elegant as his Lordship's, but its silhouette at night should pass muster. Unfortunately, my greatcoat can only hold three capes, but in the dark and at a distance, Moorefield likely won't count them. That just leaves the rig to be explained."

Emmeline straightened her spine, determination gleaming in her eyes. "I'll come with you," she declared. "That is to say, I'll be waiting with you when Lord Hawthorne drives up. Let's see now—I'll need to wear a greatcoat or something bulky enough to disguise me as a man. Why, this is perfect. It never made much sense for you to be driving to Dover alone, Graham. I had hoped Moorefield would be distracted long enough to believe Mr. Langford was hidden here, but this is much better. Brilliant, in fact."

"It really isn't, you know," Hollingsworth replied gently, a faint smile tugging at his lips. "We cannot allow you to ruin yourself. Your reputation would be in shreds, and Mr. Langford certainly wouldn't wish that. I'm certain Lord Hawthorne would never agree to such a reckless enterprise."

"But—" Emmeline began, only to be cut off by Clara's calm, steady voice.

"Do you know, Graham?" Clara interjected, "I really think it could work—with one small adjustment. You won't elope with Emmeline. You'll elope with me."

Emmeline's mouth fell open. "What?" she managed to stammer. "But, Clara, I—"

"No one will find it unbelievable," Clara continued, ignoring Emmeline's protests. "Nor will they connect it to Mr. Langford. We'll simply borrow Hawthorne's curricle for speed—though I should very much like to avoid being overtaken a second time. It's entirely plausible, and," she added, tilting her head at Graham with a faint smile, "I'm game if you are."

"Oh, no, Clara," Emmeline stammered. "You can't. I didn't mean—I never intended for you to—"

"It could be most unpleasant for you," Graham finished for her, his expression conflicted.

"Not in the least," Clara replied firmly. "I'm quite accustomed by now to being the subject of gossip. But Emmeline is young and marriageable. An elopement with you would sink her prospects entirely. I, on the other hand, have little to lose."

"Besides," Clara added with a touch of dry practicality, "Emmeline has no fortune. No one would believe in our elopement, let alone approve of it."

Graham, however, smiled faintly, his eyes gleaming with amusement. "Well, Miss St. Clair, if you're volunteering to play the part of my runaway bride, I suppose we could make it work."

Emmeline flushed scarlet, stammering in protest, while Clara muttered something decidedly unladylike under her breath.

After a spirited exchange of ideas, objections, and counterarguments, the group finally settled on the details of the audacious scheme. Each role was defined, each step meticulously planned, and every potential snag accounted for—at least as much as haste and nerves would allow. Now, the only task remaining was to bring Lord Hawthorne into the fold and convince him to play his part.

Chapter Twenty-One

Emmeline and Clara had been home for the better part of two hours before Lord Hawthorne returned to the manor. The front door banged open, letting in a rush of icy air that swirled through the hall like an unwelcome guest. Ben strode in, his boots leaving wet marks on the polished floor as he unwound his scarf.

"Oh, leave the door open," he called to Riggs, who was already rushing to close it. "I expect Mr. Moorefield's right behind me, skulking as usual."

Emmeline, who had been loitering at the top of the stairs under the pretense of examining a vase on the banister, caught his eye as he ascended. She waited until he was nearly level with her before turning and walking past him with exaggerated nonchalance.

"Meet me in the library as soon as you can," she murmured, just loud enough for him to hear. Without waiting for his reply, she disappeared down the corridor, her heart pounding with anticipation.

When he finally joined her in the library, Emmeline was already seated by the fire, arms crossed and fuming. He had taken the time to change into a rustic-colored coat and tight-fitting white pantaloons that clung to his legs in a way she found disconcertingly... noticeable. She couldn't help but glance down at her own dull brown round gown and wish she'd worn something else. Anything else.

"For heaven's sake, was it necessary to change?" she snapped as he approached, her irritation sharpened by her sudden self-consciousness.

"I did rather smell of the stables," he said defensively as he crossed the room. "Besides, aren't we trying to appear normal? A gentleman doesn't loiter in his riding clothes all evening."

Without waiting for her response, he wandered to the nearest shelf, plucking a book at random and thumbing through its pages. Then, with studied carelessness, he settled into the chair across from her.

"'*A Treatise on the Propagation of Turnips,*'" Emmeline read aloud, her lips quirking into a wry smile. "Do you call *that* normal?"

"Normal enough for a library conversation. Now get on with it before someone walks in. Did you find Christopher?"

"I know where he is, in general terms," she replied, leaning forward conspiratorially. "And he's to be rescued." She paused, allowing herself a brief, smug smile before launching into the details of the plan.

As she spoke, his expression shifted, first from skepticism, then to reluctant approval, and finally to something that looked alarmingly like admiration. When she finished, he sat back in his chair, arms crossed, his gaze fixed on her with newfound respect.

"You know," he said after a moment, "that's really brilliant. Was it your idea?"

"Mostly," Emmeline admitted, her attempt at modesty undermined by the slight tilt of her chin.

"Of course, there's one thing," he mused, his brow furrowing. "I'll be missed. Still, it doesn't really matter what anyone suspects, so long as nothing can be proved."

"We thought of a plan to cover the night of the elopement," Emmeline began, her words brisk as though she were detailing a military maneuver. "It involves you getting sick again right away, I'm afraid. Do you think you can manage a relapse?"

"Absolutely not," He replied, recoiling in mock horror. "No more spots, thank you. Once was quite enough, and besides, no one would believe it."

"Well, they might," she countered with a grin, "considering the bizarre course your measles seemed to take. But no, a second round of spots isn't what I had in mind. You simply got up too soon after your so-called recovery, so now you've come down with the grippe—or something equally convincing. We'll have Polly, my maid, take your place in bed with a nightcap. As long as no one leans in to inspect your face too closely, they'll think it's you."

"Good God," Ben muttered, leaning back in his chair as though physically grappling with the absurdity of the plan. He was silent for a moment, his expression thoughtful as he stared at her. Finally, he spoke, his voice softer and tinged with curiosity. "There's one thing I still don't understand, Emmeline. Just why are you doing all this?"

She hesitated, glancing away as if the bookshelves held the answer. "I'm not really doing anything at all," she said, her voice betraying a note of regret. "My original idea was to elope with Mr. Hollingsworth myself, but they insisted it wouldn't do."

"I should think not," He said dryly, his lips twitching with amusement.

"Well, it probably wouldn't have been convincing anyway," she admitted, brushing a loose strand of hair behind her ear. "Though

I don't see why I couldn't get to Dover, then pretend to change my mind. That's what Clara plans to do. But she doesn't think I could pull it off the way she can."

"You still haven't answered my question," he pointed out.

"Why am I involved?" She sighed, tapping her fingers against the arm of her chair. "Mostly because of my sister. She idolizes Mr. Langford, you see." A small smile softened her features as she added, "By the way, what's he like? Is he married?"

"Good Lord, no," He chuckled. "To tell you the truth, I think Christopher is a bit frightened of women. He's only a firebrand with his quill in hand, and only after the Regent has done something particularly outrageous."

"Well, no one could possibly be frightened of Rosalind," Emmeline said with a wistful smile. "Not that they're ever likely to meet."

"You never know," Ben mused, leaning forward. "If we manage to save his neck, France isn't a million miles away. Perhaps in a year or so, Georgie Porgie might even be prevailed upon to forgive him. The Regent's not really such a bad sort, you know."

Emmeline tilted her head, studying him. "Right," she said, steering the conversation back to his earlier question. "You said you didn't understand why I became involved. Well, yes, it's mostly because of my sister." Her voice faltered slightly as his gaze grew more intense. "But there's... another reason."

His brows arched. "And what would that be?"

Emmeline's cheeks flushed, and she shifted uncomfortably in her chair. "I... I really don't wish to say."

"Come now, Emmeline," he coaxed, his voice low and teasing. "Surely, after all we've been through, there's no need for coyness."

Her lips pressed into a thin line, but she finally relented, her words tumbling out in a rush. "Fine. If you must know—it's because I didn't want to come here at all."

His surprise was evident. "Didn't want to come? Why?"

"As you know," she continued, looking anywhere but at him, "they asked for Rosalind. And while Mama thought it perfectly fine to send me in her place, I knew it would put Aunt Agatha and Gabriel in an awkward position. We've never gotten on, you see."

"I noticed," he said dryly, his mouth twitching in amusement. "But your mother insisted?"

"She thought it would be an opportunity to broaden my horizons," Emmeline said, rolling her eyes. "By which, of course, she meant I should meet an eligible suitor."

"And that suitor turned out to be Mr. Moorefield?"

"Precisely," she replied, her voice heavy with disdain.

"How ghastly for you."

"Quite," she said, her lips curving into a rueful smile. "But as it happens, none of that really mattered."

"And why is that?"

Emmeline's eyes sparkled with unexpected excitement. "Because this has all been the most incredible adventure! You can't imagine how dreadfully dull my life is at home. Nothing ever happens. Absolutely nothing. But since I've been here, I've been in a coach wreck—oh, I was furious at the time, but if it hadn't happened, I wouldn't have met Mr. Hollingsworth. Then there was the excitement of realizing you'd been shot—"

"Glad you found that exhilarating," Ben interjected, his voice laced with irony.

"Oh, don't be so touchy," she said, waving a dismissive hand. "I didn't mean it like that. All I'm trying to say is that a visit I thought would be tedious beyond measure has turned into a glorious adventure. So that's why I've involved myself. For the excitement of it all. Surely, you can understand that."

Ben's gaze softened as a small, knowing smile crept across his lips. "I'm beginning to," he said quietly.

It was her turn to study him now; her gaze narrowing with pointed intensity. "Oh, for heaven's sake," she said, her voice laced with incredulity. "You thought I'd done it all for you, didn't you? Go on, admit it."

His mouth quirked into an amused smile. "And would that be so terrible?"

"Evidently not," she said. "Ever since I arrived, everyone seems to expect me to make a complete fool of myself over you. So I don't know why I imagined you, of all people, might be an exception."

His brow furrowed, his pride visibly pricked. "And what, pray tell, do you mean by 'you, of all people'?"

"Well," she said, waving a dismissive hand, "you're accustomed to having women fall at your feet by the dozens, aren't you?"

"Certainly," he replied dryly. "I simply step over them or kick them aside—whichever seems most expedient."

"There's no need to take offense," she said, her eyes glinting with mischief. "It's an inevitable state of affairs, I imagine. At least, it must be for someone as wealthy as Croesus and of such an incorrigibly rakish disposition."

"Which, of course, I am."

"Well, aren't you?" she pressed. "That's what everyone says about you." She blurted the next words before she could stop herself. "Do you have a particular mistress you've given carte blanche to, or do you simply play the field?"

His jaw tightened, and his voice lowered, suddenly more severe. "Do you have any notion of propriety at all?"

"Well, you did say there was no need for us to stand on ceremony," she replied, though her cheeks flushed. "But if I've been offensive, I do beg your pardon."

"You have," he said flatly. "To answer your question, I've never been fool enough to establish a love nest. I prefer to avoid complications."

"Wise of you," she said, her voice suddenly brisk. "That's why I thought it absurd that everyone kept warning me you might try to sweep me off my feet. You must be used to the crème de la crème, after all."

"If you're fishing for compliments, Emmeline, I refuse to rise to the bait."

Her cheeks reddened further, and she glanced away. "That did sound rather like fishing, didn't it? Believe me, it wasn't intentional."

"Oh, what the devil," he said with a resigned sigh. "Just because you've trampled on my self-esteem doesn't mean I need to tear you down. For the record, when it comes to looks, Emmeline, you are very much the crème de la crème."

Her breath caught at the unexpected compliment, but before she could respond, he added with a wry grin, "Your disposition, of course, is quite another matter. You are, without a doubt, the most irritating, contrary, impossible woman I've ever met."

"Still," he murmured, his gaze turning speculative, "I can't help but wonder how things might have gone if we'd met under more normal circumstances."

Emmeline scoffed, though her voice wavered slightly. "Oh, I'm sure if you'd made me one of your flirts, I'd have swooned at your feet like all the rest. There's no need to concern yourself with your appeal."

"You know," he said pleasantly, leaning back in his chair, "I'm astonished no one has throttled you by now."

"I assure you," she replied, her voice rising, "that I'm not usually thought of as—" She stopped herself mid-sentence, visibly reigning in her temper. "Well, we've certainly wandered off the subject, haven't we? Shall we get back to the matter at hand? Are you quite sure now that you know exactly what to do?"

Ben straightened, saluting her with mock gravity. "Yes, General," he said. "The moment I leave here, I'll go into a rapid decline and take to my bed. I'll manage to rise bravely for dinner, though I'll still look a bit peaked. After cigars and brandy, I shall declare that I need a breath of fresh air, but intend to return to bed afterward."

He paused. "God forbid it should rain, but I'll go to the stables, get my rig, and drive like the devil himself is chasing me. At this point, Moorefield—who will naturally have followed me—will be compelled to give chase. Meanwhile, Graham and Miss Clara will be lurking behind the gate pillars, ready to take my place. I'll jump out, Graham will leap in, and they'll drive off just slowly enough for Moorefield to catch a glimpse of two people in my rig. Ha! He'll think he's chasing Hawthorne and Langford to Dover."

"And you?" Emmeline asked, though her expression betrayed a faint unease.

"I'll make my way to the beach on foot," he said, his tone turning grim. "Christopher will be hidden in Hollingsworth's boat, under canvas or something, and we'll push off for France. I'll see him settled there and return with the tide."

Emmeline's face paled slightly as she considered the enormity of the plan. "You certainly make it sound simple," she said softly, though her voice lacked its usual confidence. "But... what if something goes wrong? I'd never forgive myself if you were caught."

Ben smiled, a faint, lopsided thing meant to reassure her, but it only deepened the gnawing unease in her chest. What if something did go wrong?

The thought struck her like a thunderclap. She could picture it all too vividly—Ben's small boat tossed like a toy in the dark, freezing waters of the Channel, the canvas cover ripped away by the wind, his strong, sure hands struggling to steady the tiller as waves crashed over the bow. And then—no. She couldn't bear to imagine more. But the image was there, stark and unrelenting, and it twisted something deep inside her. It wasn't just the plan she feared losing.

Her breath caught, the realization dawning with chilling clarity: she couldn't bear to lose him. The enormity of it made her dizzy. She clenched her hands tightly in her lap, as though willing the tide of emotion to ebb, but her heart refused to be silenced.

"You've asked me why I'm involved, and I've told you. But there's something I still don't understand."

Ben's eyebrow raised. "Only one thing? I must be slipping."

"Oh, stop it. I mean it. Why are you doing this? Why are *you doing this*? Why risk so much for someone who's not even your family? Is it really just the thrill of adventure?"

At first, Ben tried to deflect with his characteristic humor but gradually realize that Emmeline deserves the truth.

Ben's smirk faded. "You have a way of cutting through defenses, don't you, Emmy?"

"I'm serious. You must have a reason, and I'd like to know it."

Ben sighed, his expression softening as he stared into the fire. His usual glibness gave way to something more vulnerable.

"Christopher Langford is more than just an old school friend, you know. He's my oldest friend—the kind of man who could make the worst day bearable with a clever quip or a ridiculous scheme. He's also, for all his faults, the most honest man I've ever known. The kind who'd rather starve than compromise his principles."

He ran a hand through his hair. "When he came to me, unsure whether to publish that damned article, I... encouraged him. Told him to speak his mind, that it was the right thing to do. And it was—but I never imagined the Regent would be so vindictive, so petty as to arrest him. And then..." His jaw tightened. "Botany Bay..."

"You blame yourself."

"I pushed him into the fire, Emmeline. And now he's paying the price for my conviction. Do you have any idea what they do to men in Botany Bay? What kind of life that is?"

He shook his head, his voice rough with emotion. "I can't let that happen to him. I won't. Not while there's still a chance to set things right."

"That's not your fault. Christopher made his own choice, and it was the right one. The real fault lies with the Regent—and anyone who stands by while injustice prevails." She hesitated before adding. "But I think Christopher is lucky to have a friend like you. Most people wouldn't risk so much."

"Oh, don't make me out to be a hero. I'm just trying to clean up my own mess."

"No. You're trying to save someone who matters to you. That's not a mess—that's loyalty."

Ben studied her. "You're full of surprises, Emmeline. I expected a lecture on foolhardy schemes, not... "

"I suppose you've managed to surprise me too."

"So no second thoughts, General?" He teased, though his gaze softened as he noted the genuine worry in her eyes.

"Absolutely not, but... are you sure you're up to it? The arm, I mean."

Ben tilted his head, a soft smirk playing at his lips. "Except for being a bit stiff, I'm perfectly fine. But thanks for asking. And don't fret—it's a good plan. I'm an excellent sailor. Your part is over. You can just relax and enjoy Christmas Eve."

"Unlikely," she replied, though a faint smile tugged at her lips. She stood, smoothing her skirts as she carried her book back to the shelf. "Don't you want to take something to read? You're going to be in that bed for quite some time, you know."

"Perhaps you're right," he said, coming to stand behind her, his warmth radiating close enough to send a faint shiver down her spine. "What do you suggest?"

Emmeline turned her head slightly, startled to find him leaning so near. Her fingers danced over the spines of the books, stopping when her eyes lit on a familiar title. "Have you read *Roderick Random*?" she asked, pulling the volume free. "It should take your mind off—"

Before she could finish, the book tumbled from her grasp as she was spun abruptly around, her breath catching in her throat. She found herself pressed against the solid wall of his chest, his super-fine coat soft beneath her fingertips. Her words evaporated when his mouth descended, silencing her with a kiss that left no room for protest or thought.

The world seemed to tilt as his lips claimed hers with a fervent, undeniable heat. His hand splayed against the small of her back, pulling her closer, while his other hand rose to cradle her cheek. His touch was both firm and achingly tender, as though he'd been holding back some great storm of feeling and could no longer contain it.

Her senses ignited all at once. The faint spice of his cologne teased her nose, mingling with the wood smoke and leather that clung to him. The rasp of his thumb brushed her jaw, igniting a trail of heat that spread through her body. His lips were warm and commanding, coaxing a response from her that she had no strength—or will—to deny. She felt herself yielding, her knees weak as her hands found their way to his shoulders, clutching at him for support.

Her heart thundered in her chest, each beat echoing in her ears as the kiss deepened. His lips moved against hers with a skill that left her breathless, every stroke and caress sending molten fire coursing through her veins. The world outside the library ceased to exist; there was no plan, no Moorefield, no danger—only the overwhelming force of him and the sensations he evoked.

When he finally drew back, the separation was torturous, and Emmeline realized she was clinging to him, her breath coming in shallow, unsteady gasps. For a moment, she rested her forehead against his chest, her mind too fogged to form a coherent thought.

After a deep breath, she tilted her head to look up at him. His eyes smoldered with a mixture of triumph and something deeper, something that made her pulse skip. "What brought that on?" she whispered, her voice barely audible.

"Mistletoe," he replied wickedly, a grin tugging at the corners of his mouth. "What else? Merry Christmas."

Her lips parted in shock as he bent to plant a chaste kiss on her forehead, as if to mock the passion they'd just shared. Before she could find her voice, he turned and strode toward the door, his stride as confident as ever. He paused, only to glance back with a knowing smile. "Goodnight, Emmeline."

She stared after him, rooted to the spot, her thoughts a tangled, frenzied mess. Slowly, her gaze drifted upward to where he'd claimed mistletoe had been. But the doorframe above her was empty.

"Blast his eyes!" she muttered, her cheeks flaming as she realized the ruse. But even as indignation bubbled up, it was accompanied by the lingering warmth of his touch. His kiss seared into her very bones.

The library door clicked shut, and Emmeline remained standing there, her fingers lightly brushing her lips as a treacherous smile began to form.

Chapter Twenty-Two

The cold bit through Ben's coat like a pack of sharp teeth. Each wave that struck the boat sent icy spray lashing against his face, numbing his cheeks and soaking through his gloves. The small craft groaned under the strain of the tide, its timbers creaking ominously as he adjusted the tiller. Overhead, the stars were veiled by thick, shifting clouds, and the inky blackness of the water stretched endlessly in every direction.

Christopher Langford sat across from him, his arms crossed tightly over his chest, his breath visible in the frosty air. He glanced at him with a faint, wry smile that cut through the gloom. "Tell me, Ben, how did you sell me on this ridiculous plan again?"

Hawthorne snorted, his jaw tightening against the ache in his arm as he steered the boat away from a jagged swell. "I don't recall you putting up much of a fight. Don't tell me you've developed a sense of self-preservation at this late hour."

Chris chuckled softly, his teeth chattering between words. "I suppose it's my fault for trusting you. 'Brilliant plan,' you said. 'Piece of cake,' you said. I didn't realize 'brilliant' involved risking hypothermia in the middle of the Channel."

"You're welcome to take the tiller if you'd like," Ben shot back, nodding toward the rudder. "Of course, when the boat capsizes, you'll have to explain to the fish how you steered us straight into oblivion."

Chris held up his hands in mock surrender. "Far be it from me to interfere with the captain's genius."

The silence between them stretched, broken only by the rhythmic slap of waves against the hull and the groan of the oars as Ben worked them. Each stroke sent a deep ache through his injured arm, but he refused to let it show. He had already put his friend in enough danger—his pain was irrelevant.

Chris's voice cut through the quiet, softer now. "You know, Ben, I didn't expect you to come for me. Not after everything."

Ben glanced up, his brow furrowing. "What the devil are you on about?"

Chris shrugged, his gaze fixed on the dark horizon. "You've got your own life—your title, your estates. I thought I'd burned that bridge when I sent you that article to read."

Hawthorne's grip on the tiller tightened, the wood cold and unyielding beneath his fingers. "You mean when you asked for my advice and I told you to do the right thing? I don't regret that, Chris. Not for a moment."

"Even now?" He asked quietly, his eyes narrowing. "Even after the Regent put a price on my head and made you an accomplice just by association?"

Ben exhaled sharply, his breath fogging in the frigid air. "Yes, even now. You spoke the truth, and the truth needed saying. That the Regent chose to punish you for it says more about him than it ever will about you."

Chris studied him for a moment, his expression inscrutable. Then, with a faint smile, he said, "You still blame yourself, don't you?"

Ben didn't respond immediately, focusing instead on guiding the boat through a particularly rough patch of water. The waves hissed and surged around them, each crest threatening to spill over the side. When he finally spoke, his voice was low and edged with regret.

"I pushed you to publish it," he admitted. "Told you it was the right thing to do, that the Regent couldn't touch you if you stood your ground. I didn't think he'd..." He trailed off, shaking his head. "Botany Bay isn't a punishment—it's a death sentence."

"You weren't wrong," Chris said after a pause. "About doing the right thing. I'd do it again if I had to."

Ben's gaze snapped to his friend's face, his expression incredulous. "Do you have any idea what they'd do to you in that hellhole? You'd never survive it."

"Perhaps not," Chris said. "But I'd rather die standing for something than live cowering in silence. You're the one who taught me that, remember?"

Ben let out a low laugh, though there was little humor in it. "You've always been better with words than I am. Maybe that's why I've spent so much of my life cleaning up your messes."

Chris' grin widened despite the cold. "And here I thought you just liked having an excuse to play the hero."

"Hero, my foot," Hawthorne muttered. "This isn't heroics, Christopher. This is loyalty. Plain and simple." Emmeline's words echoed in his ears.

Chris leaned back slightly, his arms draped over the oars. For a moment, he didn't reply, his expression unusually solemn as he gazed out over the dark, churning water. Finally, he spoke, his voice quiet but firm. "You know, Ben, this plan of yours—it's brilliant. I mean that. I wouldn't have made it this far without you."

Ben let out a soft, humorless laugh. "The plan wasn't mine."

Chris glanced at him sharply, his brow furrowing in confusion. "What do you mean?"

"It wasn't my plan," he repeated, his grip on the tiller tightening as he adjusted their course. "Not entirely, anyway. Most of it came from someone else."

"Who?"

"Miss St. Clair," Ben admitted, his tone grudging but tinged with something else—something almost like admiration. "Emmeline St. Clair. She's... remarkable."

Chris blinked, his surprise evident. "Miss St. Clair? You're telling me that some young lady came up with this entire scheme?"

"Not just any young lady." A faint smile tugged at the corners of his mouth despite the gravity of their situation. "She's clever, resourceful, stubborn as hell—and apparently has no sense of self-preservation. If she did, she wouldn't have thrown herself into this mess to begin with."

Chris let out a low whistle, shaking his head. "Well, I'll be damned. And here I thought you were the brains of this operation."

"Don't let her fool you. She's more than just brains. She has this... way of cutting through the nonsense, of seeing what needs to be done and doing it—consequences be damned."

Chris studied his friend closely, a knowing gleam in his eye. "Sounds to me like she's made an impression."

Hawthorne's jaw tightened, but he didn't deny it. Instead, he kept his gaze fixed on the horizon, the lines of his face taut with focus. "She's made more than an impression. She's the reason we're here."

"Ben Hawthorne, taking orders from a lady. Now that's something I'd have paid to see."

"If we make it out of this, you owe her your thanks. And a hell of a lot more."

Langford smiled faintly, his expression thoughtful as he turned his attention back to the dark sea. "I'll thank her, all right. But, Ben—just make sure you don't let this one slip away."

Ben shot him a sharp look, his brows drawing together. "What's that supposed to mean?"

"It means she sounds like someone worth holding on to. Don't be a fool."

"That's absurd," Ben replied curtly, though his pulse quickened.

Chris' grin turned knowing. "Is it? Tell me, old friend, how many women have you met who'd go to such lengths for a marquess with a flair for trouble?"

Ben's jaw tightened, but he said nothing.

"Don't let that one get away."

Before Hawthorne could respond, a sudden gust of wind sent the boat rocking violently, and the oars slipped from Chris's grasp. The sky darkened further as clouds thickened overhead, and a distant rumble of thunder sent a shiver down Ben's spine.

"Steady!" he barked, his hands gripping the tiller with renewed urgency.

Chris scrambled to retrieve the oars, his movements hurried but efficient. "I suppose this is the part where you tell me everything's under control?" he quipped, though his voice was tight with tension.

Ben didn't answer, his focus locked on the horizon as the first fat drops of rain fell. The waves grew rougher, their peaks crashing against the boat with increasing force.

"Hold on," he muttered, his voice grim. "This is going to get worse before it gets better."

"Just like old times, eh?"

"Let's hope not." His jaw set as he fought to keep the boat steady. "I'd rather not add 'drowning' to our list of shared adventures."

The wind howled, rattling the small boat like a toy as the waves rose higher around them. Hawthorne gripped the tiller with white-knuckled determination, his fingers stiff from the cold. Every muscle in his body strained as he fought the churning water, but his mind... his mind was somewhere else.

Emmeline. Damn her and her infernal cleverness.

He hadn't thought about her, not truly, until this moment. Oh, he'd appreciated her wit, her courage, her maddening determination to insert herself into every dangerous situation. But now, with the freezing spray stinging his face and Langford murmuring worriedly at his side, he realized the truth that had been creeping up on him since she'd yanked him into that library.

She wasn't just clever. She wasn't just resourceful. She was... vital. Essential. The kind of woman who could unravel him with a smile and rebuild him with a single glance.

The realization hit him with all the subtlety of a cannonball, and he swore under his breath, his grip tightening on the tiller. What kind of fool allowed himself to get distracted by a woman in the middle of a channel crossing, of all things? He needed to focus. Lives were at stake.

And yet, her face lingered in his mind's eye: the spark in her eyes when she'd challenged him, the way her lips curved when she thought no one was looking, the way her voice softened when she let her guard down. He had to get back to her. He couldn't explain why, not yet, but the thought of her waiting, uncertain of their fate, was enough to set his jaw with fresh resolve.

"Ben," Langford's voice cut through the storm. "Are we off course?"

Hawthorne glanced up, his heart lurching. The coastline was no longer visible, swallowed by the roiling black of the sea and sky. His pulse quickened as he adjusted the tiller, his stomach knotting at the realization of how precarious their position was.

"Hold steady," he barked, though the words sounded more like a command to himself than Langford.

A wave crashed against the bow, sending icy water cascading over them. Langford cursed, grabbing for the oars as the boat tilted violently to one side. Hawthorne threw his weight against the tiller, his breath hissing between his teeth as he fought to right them.

"Damn it, Ben, this isn't looking good," Langford muttered, his usual sardonic tone replaced by genuine concern.

"We'll make it," He snapped, though his voice wavered. He wasn't sure if he was trying to convince Langford or himself.

Another wave loomed ahead, taller than the last, its crest glowing faintly in the dim light of the lantern strapped to the mast. Ben's heart thundered as he adjusted their course, aiming to cut through the swell at an angle. The boat shuddered violently as they rose, the wave's roar deafening in his ears.

For one terrifying moment, the world seemed to hang suspended. Hawthorne felt the boat tilt precariously, the tiller slipping in his frozen hands. A single thought flashed through his mind: *If we capsize, we won't survive.*

And then, beneath that, another thought—quieter but no less urgent: *I can't leave her.*

The boat plunged down the other side of the wave, slamming into the trough with a force that left both men gasping. Langford clutched the oars, his face pale, but Hawthorne's gaze remained fixed on the horizon—or what little he could see of it.

He couldn't leave her. Not like this. Not ever.

"Ben," Chris said again, his voice trembling with the strain of keeping the oars steady. "We're losing control."

Ben opened his mouth to reply, but the words froze on his tongue as another wave rose before them, even larger than the last. His stomach dropped as the lantern's faint light revealed a shape in the distance—a ship, its dark silhouette cutting through the storm like a phantom.

"Brace yourself," he shouted, his voice barely carrying over the roar of the sea.

Chris's eyes widened as he followed Ben's gaze. The ship's prow gleamed like a specter in the storm, and for one heart-stopping moment, it appeared it would bear down on them, swallowing their tiny craft whole.

Chapter Twenty-Three

Under normal circumstances, it would have been a marvelous Christmas Eve. Sir Edmond had gone to great lengths to ensure it. The company gathered in the grand hall before dinner, marveling at the massive Yule log that crackled merrily in the oversized hearth. It had taken four men to haul it in, and the hearth grate had to be removed entirely to accommodate its girth. In the dining chamber, tall Christmas candles blazed with an almost supernatural cheer, their golden light outshining the ordinary tapers. Mince pies held pride of place among the bountiful spread on the groaning board—a sight that would have ordinarily made Emmeline's mouth water. But tonight, her appetite had abandoned her, her nerves rendering her mouth as dry as the holly branches adorning the walls.

She kept telling herself to relax, to focus on the festive air and engage in conversation, but her attention repeatedly drifted to Lord Hawthorne. Seated across the table, he played his role with dramatic flair, his handkerchief a near-constant presence as he sniffled and dabbed at his nose. Once, he sneezed so forcefully that the room fell briefly silent before polite murmurs of concern resumed.

Don't overdo it, she thought, suppressing an eye roll as the assembled guests exchanged meaningful glances.

If the marquess had not been born to privilege, Emmeline mused, he could have made an enviable career on the stage. From the moment he had descended the staircase earlier that evening, it had been glaringly obvious he was suffering from a "severe relapse." Too obvious, in fact. Mr. Moorefield, seated uncomfortably close to her, was watching Hawthorne with barely concealed suspicion.

A harper had been stationed in the corner of the dining chamber, his strumming mostly drowned out by the boisterous conversation and laughter. But at the conclusion of the feast, Sir Edmond tapped his knife against his crystal goblet, calling for silence. "Ladies and gentlemen," he announced, his voice ringing with cheer, "a final song from our young musician—an ancient ditty, familiar to our ancestors." He gestured magnanimously toward the harper, who nodded and began to sing:

Here we come a-wassailing among the leaves so green,
Here we come a-wandering, so fair to be seen.
Love and joy come to you, and to you your wassail too,
And God bless you and send you a Happy New Year.

The young tenor's voice carried through the chamber, though Emmeline's mind wandered, her smile polite but detached. After a few stanzas, followed by applause that felt more enthusiastic than deserved, the ladies excused themselves from the table, leaving the men to their port and cigars.

Back in the hall, the women gathered around the roaring fire. One young matron declared, with great authority, that the Yule log was so enormous it would surely burn until next Christmas. Emmeline smiled faintly, only half-hearing the ensuing chatter.

"Where is Miss Clara?" one of the relatives inquired, glancing around the room

"She's gone to attend the tenant's lying-in," Lady Hollybrook replied, her tone sharp with disapproval. "Entirely unsuitable at any time, let alone on Christmas Eve! I told her as much, but she would not be swayed. Admin encourages her in these whims, of course, with his old-fashioned notions."

"I only hope she doesn't catch the grippe," another observed. "Did you notice how His Lordship sneezed tonight? Quite alarming."

This sparked a lively discussion about Lord Hawthorne's constitution, during which it was speculated, with some alarm, that his blood might not be entirely blue. Emmeline found the entire conversation amusing, though she took care to hide her smile behind her hand.

The ladies were interrupted by the entrance of the gentlemen. Lord Hawthorne's absence did not go unnoticed, but Mr. Moorefield's reappearance, looking particularly sour, was enough to remind Emmeline that so far, the plan was moving along as intended. She only hoped the rest of the evening would proceed without incident.

The evening unfolded in a series of interruptions and diversions. There was dancing at first, and Emmeline gladly joined in a lively country set, hoping the exuberant movements might distract her from the invisible drama playing out somewhere beyond the manor walls. But no amount of heel-toe hops or partner changes could banish her worries. Hawthorne, Langford, Clara—each weighed heavily on her thoughts, their fates uncertain.

After the dancing, her cousin Gabriel decided to grace the company with a musical interlude, sauntering over to the mantelpiece with the studied air of a troubadour. Plucking the strings of his guitar, he launched into a French love song aimed squarely at Miss Evans. Unfortunately, Gabriel's pitch was as uneven as his French pronunciation, and Emmeline winced through the performance, silently willing it to end.

Relief finally came when Sir Edmond waved Gabriel to a halt. However, her reprieve was short-lived. It became apparent that Sir Edmond's objection had little to do with Gabriel's tuneless warbling and everything to do with his choice of song. With a fatherly nod of encouragement, Sir Edmond suggested a repertoire more in keeping with the evening's spirit. Thus redirected, Gabriel struck up a series of old English carols, to which Sir Edmond tapped his foot with evident pride, entirely oblivious to his son's continuing lack of musical talent.

Time dragged on as the reverie extended to the servants' hall. Finally, after much delay, the spiced wassail and the Christmas pudding were brought forth, marking the evening's close. One by one, the company bid each other goodnight and Merry Christmas, their voices echoing warmly in the great hall. Sir Edmond chuckled as he extinguished the last of the candles. "There's no better night in the year for sleeping," he declared jovially. "As the Bard himself wrote, 'No spirit stirs abroad... so hallowed and so gracious is the time.'"

That's what he thinks, Emmeline mused wryly, her candle in hand as she ascended the stairs. Spirits were very much stirring tonight, and she only wished she knew how they were faring. Had Hawthorne and Langford reached the Channel? Was Clara safely on her way back? Or had Mr. Moorefield caught up with them? Though Clara had claimed not to mind a scandal, Emmeline knew it would be far from pleasant for her.

Sleep, she was certain, would elude her entirely. But as she lay in bed, staring at the flickering shadows on the ceiling, the faint strains of music drifted through her window. At first, she thought it might be

A MARQUESS FOR CHRISTMAS 241

the carolers from the neighboring village come to serenade the manor. The sound lulled her, and her worries faded into the background as her eyelids grew heavy.

The next thing she knew, someone was shaking her awake, not gently but with urgent insistence.

"Miss, get up. Hurry!"

The young chambermaid stood beside her bed, clearly in a fluster. Her cap was askew, her buttons were misaligned, and her apron hung untied around her waist. Her face was flushed with excitement—or panic.

Emmeline bolted upright, her heart pounding as the maid's frantic shaking brought her out of a deep, fitful sleep. "Hawthorne!" she gasped, her voice raw with fear. "What's happened? Did something go wrong?" The maid blinked at her, momentarily taken aback. "I don't know nothing about that, miss. But Lady Hollybrook wants to see you right away!"

Even as relief trickled through her, the knot in her chest refused to loosen. What if something had gone wrong after all? What if the maid didn't know because no one knew yet? The thought sent her flying out of bed, her hands trembling as she fastened her dressing gown.

"What's going on?" Emmeline asked groggily, sitting up.

"Oh, such a to-do, you can't imagine!" the maid exclaimed, wringing her hands. "Lady Hollybrook wants to see you straight away!"

Emmeline entered the bedchamber cautiously, the unmistakable sound of Lady Hollybrook's voice rising in shrill fury guiding her to the center of the storm. Lady Hollybrook stood in the middle of the room, her face red with indignation, waving a letter in the air like a battle flag.

"You're responsible for this. I know you are!" she shrieked, her voice cracking with the force of her anger. "It's all your fault!"

Emmeline, who had at least taken the time to brush her hair and tie her dressing gown properly, blinked at the accusation. "My fault?" she managed, though her voice was calm compared to the chaos in front of her.

"Now, now, my dear," Sir Edmond interjected, his tone placating as he stepped between them. Clad in somber clothing and clearly roused from his sleep, he gave his wife a gentle shake of the head. "Let us not be hasty. I'm sure Emmeline knows as little of this affair as we do."

"Don't you believe it!" Gabriel burst out, his disheveled state doing little to dull the sharpness of his glare. His nightshirt, cap, dressing gown, and slippers robbed him of dignity but not conviction. "She and Aunt Clara became thick as thieves in no time—deuced odd, if you ask me! And if you think it was Clara carrying food to the tenants all those times, well, you're queer in the attic, sir. Besides, she and Hollingsworth were practically inseparable."

He snorted at his own unintended witticism. "Thick as thieves! That's good, that is. I'll wager my best monkey, it was her idea to go to Hollingsworth's place for mistletoe. Hawthorne would never have done such a thing on his own!"

Emmeline straightened her spine, summoning patience. "Would someone kindly explain what this is all about?" she asked, her tone remarkably composed despite the rising cacophony.

"You don't know?" Gabriel sneered, though he was swiftly silenced by a sharp look from his father.

"It seems," Sir Edmond began gravely, "that your Aunt Clara has eloped with Mr. Hollingsworth."

Emmeline's mouth fell open in genuine shock. "Has she? Truly? Oh, but I don't think—" She stopped herself abruptly, realizing any protest might lead to more questions than she was prepared to answer.

"And worst of all," Gabriel continued with rising indignation, "they helped themselves to Hawthorne's rig to do it!"

"That is hardly the worst of it," Lady Hollybrook interrupted, turning on her son with uncharacteristic vehemence. "The worst of it is that your aunt is dragging the family through the mud once more by marrying that... that... gold-digger!"

"Are you certain there's no mistake?" Emmeline asked, though the words came out more cautiously than she intended.

"You know damn well there's not," Gabriel spat. "I'm still convinced you put her up to it."

"That will do, Gabriel," Sir Edmond said firmly, his frown silencing his son before turning back to Emmeline. "There's no mistake. An ostler arrived from Dover not long ago, returning Lord Hawthorne's rig and delivering a note from Clara. It seems she and Mr. Hollingsworth are on their way to France to be married." He paused, his gaze steady. "Gabriel believes you might have been privy to their plans. Were you, Emmeline?"

"No," Emmeline replied, her tone steady and truthful. "I had no idea they were actually eloping." Then, after a pause, she added with a small, defiant smile, "But I will say, I think it's famous."

"Famous! Famous?" Lady Hollybrook's voice rose to a fever pitch. Her massive frame trembled with outrage as she pointed an accusatory finger at her niece. "My sister-in-law runs off for the second time, mind you, with a fortune-hunter criminal, and my own flesh and blood calls it famous!"

"Well, I don't happen to think him a fortune-hunter," Emmeline said bravely, lifting her chin. "Mr. Hollingsworth has a position now, you know. And I'm not sure being incarcerated for debt makes one a criminal in the truest sense. But the main thing is, I'm convinced he truly loves her."

"Great heavens!" Lady Hollybrook screeched, her voice shaking the walls. "And after all I've done for you! To think I've nursed a viper in my bosom! I want you out of my house immediately. Immediately! Do you hear me?"

"Yes, ma'am," Emmeline replied coolly, though her insides churned.

"Now, now, dear," Sir Edmond intervened once again. "Be reasonable. This is Christmas Day. She can't possibly leave now."

"Right, you know," Gabriel added with a smirk. "Coaches won't be running."

"First thing in the morning, then," Lady Hollybrook snapped, unwilling to relent. "And don't let me see you in the meantime. I intend to write to your mother immediately, Miss St. Clair. She will know I am washing my hands of her entire family. If this is the thanks I get for trying to find a husband for one of her five daughters, well, the other four need not expect any help from me!"

Emmeline remained silent, her composure unbroken even as Lady Hollybrook's tirade reached its crescendo. But inside, her resolve only hardened. *If this was the fallout of Clara's elopement, so be it.* She would endure it. For Clara's sake, for Hollingsworth's—and perhaps, just a little, for the sheer exhilaration of it all.

Chapter Twenty-Four

Emmeline spent all of Christmas Day balancing on the knife's edge of anticipation, her nerves stretched taut from the morning service to the sumptuous Christmas dinner. Even the spectacle of the boar's head, borne in on a silver platter with great fanfare, failed to elicit more than a cursory glance from her. Her attention remained fixed on the sound of every door opening, every creak of a footstep, hoping against hope for Lord Hawthorne's return.

But he did not come.

When the day finally yielded to evening, she climbed into bed with a heavy heart, only to be plagued by dreams of his small craft being tossed about in the unforgiving channel waters. In her mind's eye, the sea surged and roared, swallowing him whole, and she woke repeatedly, clutching the bedclothes as if they could anchor her to sanity.

The following morning dawned gray and misty. Tearful goodbyes marked her departure from Hollybrook Manor. She bid an especially heartfelt farewell to Polly, who had stayed behind to fully recover from her illness. The maid, flushed and teary, wrung her hands nervously before suddenly reaching into her apron pocket.

"Miss Emmeline," Polly said hesitantly, her voice trembling. "Miss Clara left this for you before she went. Said you should have it when you left." She thrust a folded piece of paper into Emmeline's hand. "I didn't want to forget it. She seemed so sure you'd understand."

Emmeline's chest tightened as she took the note, her fingers trembling. "Thank you, Polly," she murmured, tucking it into her reticule. "Take care of yourself."

Polly gave her a watery smile, dabbing at her eyes with the corner of her apron. "Safe travels, Miss."

With a determined breath and a hastily wrapped cloak, Emmeline followed a footman down the carriage drive to the gate. The coach from Dover arrived shortly, and she climbed to the top, shivering in the damp cold as the vehicle lurched forward. The misty countryside slipped by in silence, but Emmeline's thoughts were anything but quiet.

The worst part of this wretched Christmas visit, she realized with a pang, was that she might never know what had become of Hawthorne. The thought of him—whether battling the icy waters or simply gallivanting around France without a second thought for her—gnawed at her heart.

"Well," she murmured aloud to herself, her voice muffled by the wind, "of course he hasn't drowned." If calamity had struck someone as prominent as Lord Hawthorne, the London papers would already be screaming the news.

The morning light tempered her fears, but only slightly. More likely, she thought bitterly; he had stayed to sample the delights of France, heedless of the anxiety he'd left in his wake. The realization stung. But what could she have expected? The man was a marquess, not a saint.

A rueful smile played on her lips as the coach picked up speed. She tightened the strings of her bonnet, forcing herself to take comfort in the small victories. Clara's elopement, at least, had not been an unmitigated scandal. Sir Edmund had sought her out before her departure.

"I think Clara might find happiness as Mistress of Hollingsworth Hall," he had confided. "Arabella's tantrums aside, I'm sure my sister will do quite well. And don't worry about your mother, Emmeline. Family is everything, after all. We'll see to it that your sisters are well-supported."

It was a relief to hear, though the thought of being responsible for dashing her mother's hopes had weighed heavily on her. As the countryside blurred into a muted palette of winter hues, Emmeline let her mind drift.

She had warned her mother that the trip to Hollybrook Manor might prove a mistake. But even in her wildest imaginings, she had never anticipated the devastating consequences to her own well-being. She had gone to please her family, to ensure her sisters' futures, and now she was returning home with a bruised heart and memories she'd never entirely shake.

Lord Hawthorne, with his infuriating arrogance, his maddening charm, and his devastating kisses, would haunt her thoughts for the rest of her life. She was painfully aware of that. He had left a mark, indelible and utterly unfair, for she knew with absolute certainty that he had already forgotten her.

The word *fair* had no place in the world of men like Hawthorne, and yet she found herself clinging to the faint hope that someday, somehow, their paths might cross again.

When the coach reached a smoother stretch of road, Emmeline pulled the note from her reticule, her breath catching as she unfolded the paper. The words were penned in Clara's familiar hand, hurried but steady, each line brimming with emotion.

Dear Emmeline,

By the time you read this, I will be far away, chasing a happiness I once thought lost forever. I know this will cause you trouble—perhaps more trouble than I can bear to imagine—but I also know your kind heart will forgive me.

You've always been braver than you realize, my dearest niece. Clever, too. I suspect you knew before I did that I could not let Graham slip through my fingers a second time. What we had all those years ago was real, Emmeline. It's still real. And life is too short for regrets.

I've tried to live quietly, to be the woman society expects me to be, but it's a life without joy. Graham has offered me a second chance at something beautiful, and I mean to take it, no matter what obstacles lie ahead.

Please know that this decision wasn't made lightly. I've thought of the whispers, the scandal, the hurt I might cause—and yet I still believe this is right. True happiness is worth fighting for, even if the battle leaves scars.

When we're settled, I'll write again to tell you everything, and I hope you'll write back. I will need your humor, your advice, and your stories to remind me that I'm not entirely cut off from the family I love.

For now, be patient with Lady Hollybrook. Her fury will fade, as it always does. And know that I am endlessly grateful for your understanding and your friendship. You are, without question, the most extraordinary young woman I know.

With all my love,
Clara

Emmeline blinked rapidly, willing away the tears that blurred the words. Clara's love and conviction radiated from the page, filling her with a bittersweet mixture of pride and sorrow. True happiness is worth fighting for. The phrase echoed in her mind, stirring something deep within her.

If Clara found her second chance, perhaps there was hope for me too—though it wouldn't come from a marquess with a devil-may-care grin. Some women are simply meant to admire courage from afar.

The coach rumbled on, leaving Hollybrook Manor—and its ghosts—behind. Emmeline pressed her forehead against the cold glass, watching the world blur by. An ache settled in her chest—not just worry, but something deeper. She loved him. The realization was as terrifying as it was undeniable. She loved Lord Hawthorne with all his infuriating arrogance and unexpected tenderness.

Enough of this nonsense! Emmeline resolved she would not become one of those languishing heroines who wasted away for unrequited love like the hapless figures in the dreadful novels she sometimes indulged in. Determined to distract herself, she turned her attention to the winter landscape rolling by. The frost-coated hedgerows and skeletal trees had a stark beauty that, for a moment, dulled the ache in her chest. She even exchanged pleasantries with the elderly man huddled under layers of shawls behind her, grateful for the distraction.

But her fragile calm shattered at the sound of rapidly approaching hoofbeats. She twisted in her seat to look, clutching instinctively at her neighbor's sleeve as the sight of a flashy black-and-red curricle barreling toward them made her stomach drop.

"Good heavens!" she exclaimed, watching as the rig's driver, a figure clad in a jaunty beaver hat and a five-caped greatcoat, cracked his whip with a flourish. The sharp crack echoed like a pistol shot over the icy air.

"The fool's trying to pass on this narrow stretch!" the coachman bellowed, yanking the reins to steer their unwieldy vehicle to one side. Passengers shrieked as the coach wobbled dangerously, the horses snorting and stamping in protest.

Once the coach steadied, the curricle's audacious driver pulled up beside them, signaling the coach to stop.

Her breath caught at the sight of him—wind-tousled hair peeking from beneath his hat, eyes bright with that familiar mischief. "You... you... numbskull! Ninnyhammer!" Emmeline shouted over the din, her fury rising as the coachman, muttering a colorful stream of curses, begrudgingly complied.

"Well, I had to catch you, didn't I?" drawled none other than Lord Hawthorne as he vaulted down from his rig, his grin as rakish as ever. Ignoring the chaos he'd caused, he held out his arms. "Come on, jump down. I'm driving you home."

The crisp air carried the faint scent of sandalwood as he leaned closer, his gloved hand warm as it clasped hers.

"Didn't one coach satisfy your bloodlust?" she shot back, but the relief washing over her dulled the sting of her retort. His presence—alive, whole, and maddening as ever—was the balm she yearned for. She allowed him to help her down, her skirts swishing against his greatcoat as he settled her in the curricle's passenger seat.

Once they were moving, leaving the coach and its irate passengers far behind, she folded her arms and fixed him with a glare. "I suppose you've already sampled the delights of France and decided to return for the sheer pleasure of being scolded?"

"Gratitude, as always," he said, his tone mocking. "I thought you might be dying to know how your rescue scheme played out, so I hurried back to tell you. But clearly, I should have anticipated a tongue-lashing about my excellent driving skills."

He glanced over his shoulder, apparently satisfied with the growing distance between them and the coach, and slowed the horses to a more comfortable pace.

Emmeline sighed, her irritation giving way to curiosity. "I am sorry," she said grudgingly. "Tell me everything."

And so he did, launching into a detailed account of Christopher's escape, punctuated with descriptions of the lodgings he'd secured for him in Calais. "He'll stay there for a while until he decides his next move. So, as that prosy old Shakespeare said, all's well that ends well."

"Well, that's a relief," Emmeline replied, trying—and failing—to muster enthusiasm. "And I do appreciate the trouble you've taken."

"Oh, but that's not the only reason I chased you down," Hawthorne said, his voice rich with mischief.

"It's not?"

"Of course not. I promised Christopher I'd deliver a letter to your sister, and I needed someone to point me in the right direction."

"Oh, you did, did you?" she snapped. "You could have waited and taken Polly. It would've saved her the coach trip."

"Damn, so I could have." He chuckled. "Now why didn't I think of that? I suppose I simply wanted your company, Emmeline. A lowering thought, isn't it?"

Before she could respond, he added with a sly grin, "It must have been that last kiss. Quite devastating, really. I kept telling myself on the way back across the Channel that it was all due to my weakened condition—having been shot, then taken with the measles and the grippe. No wonder I found your kiss so earth-shattering. By the way, how was it for you?"

"It was... nice," she said, her voice deliberately cool.

"Nice?" He shot her a look of incredulous outrage. "You have the gall to call an experience that rocked me down to the soles of my Hessians *nice*?"

"How should I know?" she retorted, her cheeks flushing. "I haven't much basis for comparison."

"Well then, take it from me," he said, his tone turning serious. "It was a regular Waterloo of a kiss."

"Oh," she murmured, taken aback.

"And," he continued, his voice softer now, "as if you didn't know it all along, that's why I've chased you down. I have to know where you live, don't I? If I'm to come courting."

"Is that what you wish to do?" she asked, her voice barely above a whisper.

"It's what I *have* to do," he replied with a glum sigh, though a spark of humor danced in his eyes. "You have no idea how maddening it was," he confessed, his voice losing its teasing edge. "I couldn't get you out of my mind. Every mile across the Channel, every moment in France—I kept thinking of you. Wondering if I'd see you again."

"So you see, I must know where you live. Unless, of course, you'd rather we just tool on to Gretna Green this very minute?"

"Gretna Green! You know I can't elope."

"I was afraid you'd say that."

Silence fell between them, broken only by the rhythmic clatter of the horses' hooves. Emmeline's mind raced, her heart pounding as she tried to absorb his words. She stole a glance at him from beneath her lashes, noting the way his strong profile was illuminated by the pale morning light. The sight made her heart ache in ways she was only beginning to understand.

Noticing her scrutiny, he turned to her with a wicked grin. "By the way, Miss St. Clair, you do realize, don't you, that I'm a splendid catch? Far above your touch, if I may say so.

"Above my touch?" she snapped, jolted from her reverie. Her eyes narrowed as she measured the distance between their seats. "Above my touch? Oh, I think not, Lord Hawthorne."

Before he could respond, Hawthorne slowed the horses to a halt on the roadside, the curricle rocking gently as it came to rest. The frost-kissed countryside stretched before them, muted and serene. He set the brake and turned toward her, his expression softened by something far more earnest than his usual teasing.

"What's this?" Emmeline asked, her pulse quickening as she glanced around. "Why are we stopping?"

"The horses could use a rest," he said lightly, though his tone held a note of gravity. "And... there's something I need to say."

Her frown deepened, her breath catching in her chest. "What is it?"

Hawthorne shifted, his gaze searching hers as though weighing his next words. "I'm not particularly good at declarations, but I've never been more certain of anything in my life. Emmeline, I—"

He never finished. Acting on impulse, Emmeline closed the distance between them, her hands clutching the lapels of his greatcoat as she pressed her lips to his. Her kiss silenced him, a bold, undeniable answer to the question he had barely begun to ask.

For a moment, he froze in surprise. But then his hand rose to cup her face, his gloved thumb brushing her cheek as he kissed her back with a fervor that left her breathless. The cold air around them melted away, replaced by a warmth that spread through her chest, her limbs, her very soul.

The world beyond the curricle vanished. The frost-coated hedgerows, the skeletal trees, even the horses, faded into irrelevance.

All that remained was the perfect, consuming moment—the firm yet tender pressure of his lips, the faint rasp of his glove against her skin, and the intoxicating warmth that chased away the chill.

When they finally parted, Emmeline's cheeks were flushed, and her breath came in shallow gasps. Hawthorne's grin was softer now, tinged with an emotion she could barely name but instinctively understood.

"Was that your way of saying I'm not above your touch?" he murmured, his voice husky.

"Perhaps," she replied, her lips curving into a sly smile. "But let's not let it go to your head, Lord Hawthorne."

"Too late," he said, his laughter rich and unrestrained as he flicked the reins to set the curricle in motion once more. "Far, far too late."

The curricle rolled on, but Emmeline no longer cared about the frost or the cold or the miles ahead. The future stretched before her, wide open and full of possibilities, and for the first time in her life, she felt truly alive.

Epilogue

Christmas Eve, One Year Later

The warmth of Hawthorne House enveloped everyone like a cherished memory, its grand dining room glowing with the golden light of candelabras and the soft shimmer of garland threaded with holly. Snow dusted the windowsills, but inside, the air was fragrant with roasting meats, spices, and the unmistakable scent of a Yule log crackling in the hearth.

At the head of the table, Lord Hawthorne stood with a commanding presence, his dark hair gleaming in the light and his grin as rakish as ever. He raised a goblet of wine, his voice carrying effortlessly over the hum of conversation.

"To family, both old and new," he declared, his gaze lingering on his wife, who sat at the opposite end of the table. "And to the unexpected joys of the past year."

Emmeline smiled back, her cheeks pink from the warmth of the room—and perhaps from the attention. Seated in a chair slightly cushioned for her condition, her hand rested absently on the gentle swell of her belly. She returned her husband's toast with her own glass of mulled wine, careful not to spill on the embroidered gown her mother had insisted she wear.

Her mother, Charlotte St. Clair, beamed proudly from her seat midway down the table, flanked by Emmeline's three younger sisters—Isabelle, Margaret, and Louisa—who were barely containing their excitement. Louisa, the youngest, had been caught whispering just moments ago about how "splendid" Hawthorne House was and how she hoped to see more of it in the future. Charlotte had gently shushed her, though not without an indulgent smile.

"It's settled," Louisa declared as dessert was served, her eyes sparkling as she admired the garland-draped staircase. "I'm going to marry a marquess, too. Or at least a viscount."

"Let's focus on finishing your embroidery first," Margaret quipped, earning a ripple of laughter. Even Charlotte joined in, shaking her head affectionately at her youngest daughter's boundless imagination.

The table erupted in applause and cheers. Even Gabriel—stationed beside Sir Edmund—clapped a little too enthusiastically. "Hear, hear! And to Lady Hawthorne," he added, grinning at Emmeline. "For making my cousin the happiest of men, which I frankly thought was impossible."

Sir Edmund chuckled, giving his son a good-natured clap on the back. "A toast to Emmeline indeed. And to Arabella," he added with a wink toward his sister-in-law, "for predicting it all along."

Arabella, who sat ramrod straight and regal despite the revelry, nodded solemnly. "I always knew Emmeline was a remarkable young woman," she intoned, earning a pointed snort from Emmeline. "And I daresay," Arabella added with a smug tilt of her chin, "she has proven to be a splendid marchioness. A credit to the family name."

"Oh, Aunt Arabella," Emmeline said, her eyes sparkling with mischief, "I shall treasure those words forever."

As laughter rippled down the table, Gabriel leaned in toward Hawthorne, his voice carrying enough to turn heads. "I've been meaning to tell you, Cousin—I've taken the liberty of commissioning a curricle of my own, just like yours. Red and black, naturally. Only fitting since you've outgrown it and so kindly gifted me your old one." He puffed up with pride. "You know, I've had no fewer than three compliments on it in the last week alone."

Hawthorne rolled his eyes but smirked, muttering something about "poor London roads never being the same again." His teasing only delighted Gabriel further, who launched into an enthusiastic description of his latest drive.

Meanwhile, Rosalind leaned in close to Emmeline, her presence a calming contrast to the lively chaos around them.

"I've received another letter from Mr. Langford," Rosalind murmured, her voice low enough not to draw attention. She slipped the folded missive discreetly into Emmeline's hand. "He's in fine health, staying in Calais for now."

Emmeline's smile widened, relief blooming across her face. "That's wonderful news," she said softly. "Is he... well, otherwise?"

Rosalind nodded, a faint blush coloring her cheeks. "Well, enough to suggest that I might visit the Continent soon. Perhaps this spring."

Emmeline's eyes widened. "You wouldn't."

"Why not?" Rosalind countered, a playful glint in her eyes. "Surely you don't think I'll remain here forever."

Before Emmeline could respond, a loud cheer from the far end of the table redirected their attention. Gabriel was attempting to teach one of the younger St. Clair sisters a poorly accented French toast, which had set the entire table roaring with laughter.

Rosalind rose gracefully, casting her sister a knowing glance. "We'll speak more later."

Emmeline watched her go, her thoughts briefly straying to Christopher and the curious turn Rosalind's life seemed to be taking. Whatever lay ahead, she thought, it would be an adventure worthy of a story all its own.

The lively din of conversation filled the dining room as servants moved gracefully between the guests, refilling glasses and clearing dishes. Emmeline couldn't help but marvel at the scene—the clinking of crystal, the soft hum of laughter, and the occasional burst of Gabriel's exaggerated French, all weaving together into a tapestry of holiday cheer.

Hawthorne, ever the charismatic host, stood to announce the next round of festivities. "Now that we've all indulged in Sir Edmund's excellent roast goose, I suggest we retire to the drawing room for a proper toast before the Yule log is brought in."

A chorus of agreement followed, chairs scraping back as the guests began to rise. Hawthorne made his way to Emmeline's side, his hand brushing hers with casual familiarity. The small gesture sent a pleasant thrill through her, even after months of marriage.

"Are you comfortable, love?" he asked, his voice low and intimate despite the surrounding bustle.

She smiled up at him, her hand instinctively resting over the swell of her belly. "Perfectly. Though I'll admit I may need a moment to recover from all that food."

"Take your time," he murmured, bending closer. ""But don't be too long, or Gabriel might start a new tradition involving my curricle."

Her laugh was soft but genuine, and it warmed him to his core. "Go on, then," she said, giving him a playful nudge. "Preside over your guests."

Hawthorne lingered a moment longer before joining the others, who had already begun migrating to the drawing room. Sir Edmund and Arabella led the charge, with Gabriel trailing behind, regaling anyone who would listen about his curricle's superior speed.

Emmeline remained seated for a moment, savoring the brief reprieve. It wasn't long before her mother appeared at her side, her expression brimming with maternal pride.

"My dear, you've truly outdone yourself," Charlotte said, her voice filled with warmth. "This has been a most wonderful Christmas."

"I can hardly take the credit," Emmeline replied modestly. "Hawthorne has a talent for entertaining."

Charlotte smiled knowingly. "And for finding a wife who brings out the very best in him."

Before Emmeline could respond, a commotion near the door drew their attention. The butler, looking slightly harried, was announcing unexpected arrivals.

"Mr. and Mrs. Hollingsworth!" he declared, stepping aside as Clara and Graham entered, shedding their travel cloaks.

A collective gasp went through the room, followed by Edmund's booming laugh. "Clara!" he exclaimed, striding forward to embrace his sister. "You sly thing, sneaking in like this."

"I couldn't resist," Clara replied, her cheeks flushed from the cold—or perhaps from happiness. She turned to Graham, who looked equal parts dashing and delighted. "We didn't want to miss the chance to see everyone."

Arabella, who had risen from her seat with a mixture of shock and apprehension, hesitated only a moment before bustling forward. "Clara, my dear! How... unexpected."

"It's lovely to see you too, Arabella," Clara said with a faint smile, though her eyes twinkled with mischief.

Emmeline watched the reunion with quiet satisfaction, grateful for the opportunity to see Clara so happy—and for the chance to witness Arabella's grudging acceptance of the match.

As the party moved toward the drawing room, Hawthorne reappeared at Emmeline's side. He offered his arm, and she took it gladly, letting him guide her away from the hubbub.

"Did you see Clara?" she asked, glancing over her shoulder at her sister, who was now deep in conversation with Edmund.

"I did," he said, a faint smile tugging at his lips. "It seems love runs rampant in your family."

"And in yours, apparently," she teased, tilting her head to look up at him.

He stopped suddenly, turning to face her fully. The rest of the guests disappeared into the next room, leaving them alone in the quiet glow of the dining room.

"You've given me everything, Emmeline," he said softly, his hand rising to cradle her cheek. "More than I ever thought I deserved."

Her breath hitched, her heart swelling with emotion. "And you've given me more than I ever dreamed possible."

Hawthorne's lips curved into a slow, tender smile. "Merry Christmas, my love."

And with that, he kissed her. It was a kiss that held the depth of his feelings, the promises of their future, and the undeniable passion that had brought them together. Her arms slid around his neck as she melted into him, the world around them fading until only the two of them remained.

When they finally pulled apart, their foreheads touched, their breaths mingling in the stillness.

"Come," he whispered, brushing a stray curl from her face. "Our guests are waiting. Let's show them how splendid a marchioness you truly are."

Emmeline laughed softly, her heart lighter than it had been in weeks. Together, they walked hand in hand toward the drawing room, ready to celebrate the joy of Christmas—and the love they had found against all odds.

About Violet Sinclair

Violet Sinclair is your passport to a bygone era of passion and extravagance. With an insatiable love for history, she dives headfirst into the world of ballrooms, lavish gowns, and Regency England. When she's not jet-setting with her adventurous sons, you'll find her indulging in her true passion: crafting sultry tales of love and desire, all while basking beneath the Florida palm trees. Step into her world, where every word is a whispered secret and every story a tantalizing journey into romance's heart.

https://violetsinclairromance.com/

Also by Violet Sinclair

The Duchess Diaries Series

Awakening Wicked – Book 1

One year after the death of her husband, the Dowager Duchess of Devonshire gladly shed her mourning clothes. At six and twenty, Lilly is one of the richest and most influential young women of the ton. And quite possibly the most innocent of the widows. Finally free from her horrid marriage, one devoid of love, tenderness, and any kind of pleasure, the last thing Lilly longs for is the company of gentlemen.

Determined to show Lilly all the joys of being a widow, her oldest and dearest friend, Lady Anne, convinces Lilly to join her for the weekend at the Rycroft's infamous house party in Surrey. A weekend that promises to awaken a passion Lilly knows lays buried deep inside her. A desire that will put Lilly on her way to becoming one of the ton's most wicked widows.

The stage is set. The players are in place. What or whom will be next on Lilly's list of awakening?

Wicked Widows Club – Book 2

The dowager Duchess of Devonshire's return to London high society is a fabulous one indeed when she accepts an invitation from Lady Pettiford to join an exclusive club of free women. The old countess runs the secretive Lady's Side, hidden behind the walls of the famed Whitterfield's gaming hell. Here the widowed women of the ton are free to pursue every pleasure—with their money, their desires, and most importantly—their bodies.

London's season of royal splendor and hidden debauchery is beginning. The ladies and gentlemen of the ton are flooding into town eager to mingle and posture, for gossip and scandal. Debutantes prepare to preen and attract proper husbands. And the Duchess has an agenda of her own. Awakened to her sensuality and sexual cravings, Lilly boldly explores new sensations and lustful fantasies in the pursuit of fulfilling her wicked list.

Wicked Wager – Book 3

In this third tantalizing installment of the Duchess Diaries Series, the audacious Lilly, the dowager Duchess of Devonshire, and Lady Anne embark on a daring game. The stakes are as scintillating as they are shocking.

The young and innocent Lady Jane has entered the scene. Intent on saving her from the potentially harsh realities of the marriage market, Lilly and Anne devise a cunning plan. They will test the mettle of Jane's suitors in a way only they can – through seduction. Each dalliance becomes a litmus test to eliminate unsuitable candidates and protect Jane from an ill-suited match. And an opportunity for these gorgeous widows to tally more gents off their scandalous lists and fulfill their wicked wager.

The Art of Being Wicked – Book Four

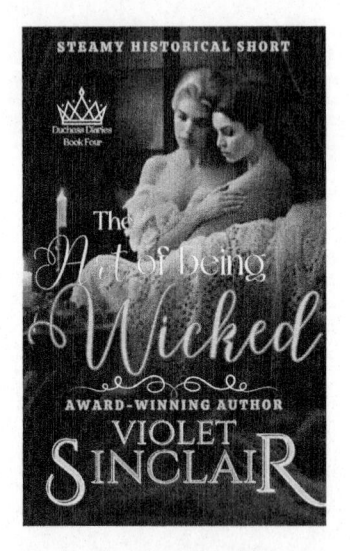

Behind the glittering façade of London high society, repressed passions smolder. When recently widowed Lilly, Dowager Duchess of Devonshire, receives a scandalous invitation, she's tempted to indulge her forbidden desires. But in this provocative world of illicit art and masked balls, embracing sensual freedom comes at a high price.

As Lilly's wanton adventures entangle her with her dearest friend and a seductive artist, she discovers that true liberation lies not only in unbridled pleasure, but in daring to be her authentic self.

A Hauntingly Wicked Eve – Book Five

When the enigmatic Marquess Blackthorn sends Lilly, the daring Duchess of Devonshire, an invitation to his notorious All Hallow's Eve masquerade ball, she cannot resist the lure of an evening cloaked in mystery and decadence. Venturing to the shadowy Ravenswood Hall with her trusted friend Lady Anne, Lilly finds herself caught up in a dizzying night of dark delights and unrestrained passion. But as ghostly whispers swirl through the manor's haunted halls, she begins to realize there are more secrets between these walls than she ever imagined.

After a passionate encounter with the Marchioness Blackthorn, Lilly becomes enthralled by a seductive masked stranger whose touch ignites her body like fire. She knows she should resist, yet cannot help surrendering to the raw, primal desire that consumes her. But is he truly flesh and blood, or something far more dangerous? Trapped in a dizzying world of illusion and sin, Lilly must navigate the tangled passions of the living and the dead if she hopes to uncover the truth.

With shocking twists that will leave you breathless, A Hauntingly Wicked Eve is an erotic story alive with thrills and temptation. Let Violet Sinclair sweep you into the haunting, decadent world of the Duchess Diaries once more.

Uncover their sordid adventures and unexpected discoveries in a world where pleasure and propriety collide. The rules of society are about to be rewritten, and every reader will want an invitation to this ball.

A Very Wicked Highland Christmas – Book Six

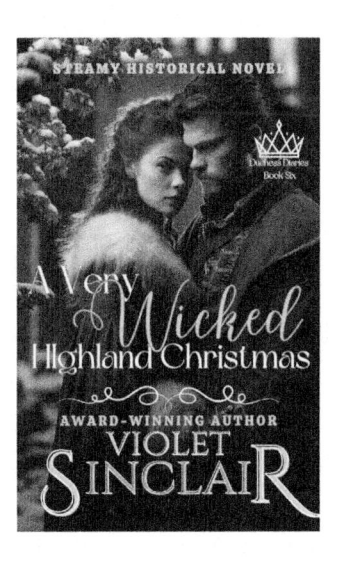

Join Lilly as she discovers love, passion, and her true self in the enchanting halls of Glenmoor Castle this holiday season.

When hearts are as wild as the Highland winds, love knows no season.

This Christmas, Lilly's return to Glenmoor Castle is about more than holiday cheer—it's about seduction, secrets, and a second chance with the earl who still haunts her dreams.

Lilly never imagined that her widowhood would be filled with such... wicked intentions. With a list of suitors from her past to tempt and tease, she arrives at the frost-kissed Glenmoor Castle for a Christmas she won't soon forget.

Graham, Earl of Crawford, is a laird bound by duty but yearning for love lost. When Lilly, the woman who once chose a title over his heart, reappears, their past passion reignites with the flicker of the Yule log.

As the Highland cold sets in, the warmth of newfound love blossoms, yet, with every stolen kiss, secrets of the past threaten to tear them apart. Can the magic of Christmas and the spirit of the Highlands heal old wounds and guide Lilly and Graham to a love that endures?

Step into the sixth installment of the Duchess Diaries, "A Very Wicked Highland Christmas," where the festivities are as intoxicating as the desire, and the spirit of the season may just bring the gift of love for those brave enough to unwrap it. Dive into the pages of this sizzling historical romance, where passion burns brighter than the Yuletide fires and love is as unpredictable as a Scottish storm.

The Lady's Side Series

Silk & Discretion – Book One

In the glittering world of Regency London, where whispers behind silk fans and closed doors can make or break a reputation, Lady Anne Hayworth finds herself at a crossroads. Widowed and longing for independence in a society that prizes male dominance, Anne's life takes a thrilling turn when she is introduced to The Lady's Side Club—a secret haven for the elite women of London.

"Silk & Discretion" is the first book in the captivating "The Lady's Side" series, where hidden desires meet daring actions. Within the walls of this exclusive club, Lady Anne discovers a world where women defy convention and embrace their desires, free from the constraints of societal expectations.

Haunted by the shadows of her abusive marriage, Anne's journey to self-discovery is anything but easy. As she navigates the treacherous waters of high society, she must also confront her own fears and desires. When she crosses paths with Arthur Crowley, a man of mystery with his own scars, Anne finds herself drawn into a passionate awakening that promises liberation and love.

But with her newfound freedom comes danger. Rumors and deceit swirl around Anne, threatening to ruin her reputation and her newfound sanctuary. Armed with her wit, the support of the fiercely loyal women of The Lady's Side Club, and the unexpected affection of Mr. Crowley, Anne takes a stand for her future.

From the opulent ballrooms of the ton to the intimate gatherings of The Lady's Side Club, Anne's story is one of courage, passion, and the quest for true independence. "Silk & Discretion" weaves a tale of sensual discovery, empowering friendships, and the unyielding strength of a woman determined to write her own story.

As alliances are forged and secrets revealed, Lady Anne Hayworth emerges as a beacon of hope and a trailblazer for women daring to challenge the status quo. Will she succeed in reclaiming her life and securing her heart's desires, or will the weight of scandal and society's expectations prove too much?

Her Viscount's Secret

In Regency-era England, Jane Seymour dreams of publishing her illustrations of rare birds, but societal expectations threaten to clip her wings. Enter Sebastian Westwood, the brooding Viscount with secrets as dark as his estate's shadowy corridors. When circumstances force them into a marriage neither expected, Jane and Sebastian must navigate a landscape of half-truths and hidden passions.

As Jane works to complete her magnum opus in the newly built aviary, she finds herself falling for the complex man behind the Viscount's mask. But Sebastian's past threatens to unravel their budding romance. With Anabelle, Sebastian's young ward, caught in the middle, Jane must decide if love is worth the risk of a broken heart.

Amidst the fluttering of rare birds and the rustle of sketch papers, can Jane and Sebastian build a love strong enough to weather any storm? Or will the secrets of Westwood Manor tear them apart?

"Her Viscount's Secret" is a sweeping Regency romance that will captivate fans of Julia Quinn and Lisa Kleypas. With its unique blend of artistic passion, family secrets, and tender romance, this novel proves that sometimes, love is the rarest bird of all.

The Black Earl and His Rose

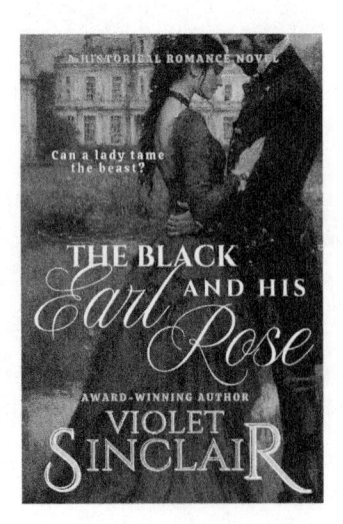

A Beauty. A Beast. A Love That Defies All Odds.

Lady Rose Sheffield has never quite fit into the mold of a perfect lady. With her sharp wit, cutting tongue, and a refusal to conform to society's expectations, she's always been an outsider in the world of ballrooms and polite conversation. When a scandal forces her from London, she finds herself in the untamed countryside, working for the brooding Earl of Ashbourne.

Henry Grayson, the Earl of Ashbourne, has earned the moniker "The Black Earl" for his reclusive and tempestuous nature. Preferring the solitude of his estate, he has little patience for society and even less for the fiery young woman who disrupts his peace. But Rose, with her fierce independence and unflinching spirit, stirs something in him he thought long dead.

As sparks fly between them, Rose and Henry must navigate a world where propriety and passion are at odds. In the wild countryside, they'll discover whether love can heal old wounds—or if their pasts will forever keep them apart.

The Black Earl and His Rose is a captivating historical romance filled with biting humor, deep emotion, and the undeniable chemistry between two souls who were never meant to fit in—but may have just found where they belong.

The Lady Who Dared

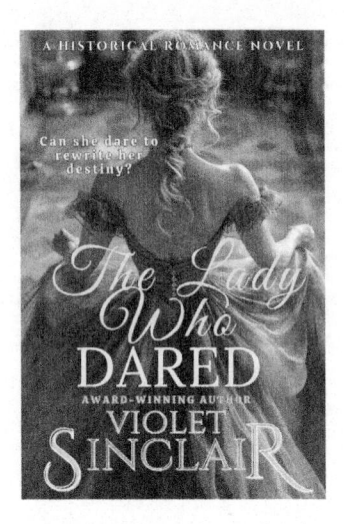

In a world of propriety and intrigue, she dared to rewrite her destiny...

Lady Juliette Harcourt has always lived by the rules of high society, until tragedy left her a widow with little more than a crumbling estate and her younger sister to protect. Now, as she steps into London's glittering social season, she has one goal: secure her sister's future at any cost.

But society is a battlefield, and Juliette must navigate it with precision. When a charming yet dangerous Earl takes a keen interest in her, and a mysterious stranger stirs long-buried desires, Juliette realizes that the stakes are higher than she ever imagined. Torn between duty, scandal, and the shadow of a dark past, Juliette must decide: will she risk everything for love, or will she safeguard her heart and her family's honor?

Full of forbidden romance, cunning schemes, and breathtaking ballroom drama, *The Lady Who Dared* is an irresistible regency romance for readers who crave passion and intrigue.

Printed in Great Britain
by Amazon